I0549116

Almost
A
Hero

STEVE PAUL

Steve Paul

NOTE: If you purchased this book without a cover you should be aware that this book is stolen property. It was reported as "unsold and destroyed" to the publisher, and neither the author nor the publisher has received any payment for this "stripped book."

This is a work of fiction. Names, characters, places and events described herein are products of the author's imagination or are used fictitiously. Any resemblance to actual events, locations, organizations, or persons, living or dead, is entirely coincidental.

Almost a Hero

Copyright © 2015 Steve Paul

All rights reserved, including the right to reproduce this book, or portions thereof, in any form.

Edited by Jake George (www.sageservices.com)

Cover artwork by Sage Words Services
www.sagewordsservices.com

A Sage Words Publishing Book

www.sagewordspublishing.com

ISBN 978-0-997092-0-0

Printed in the United States of America

Dedication

This novel is dedicated to my wife Judy, who gave me encouragement and insightful suggestions, and our pups, Callie and Barney.

I would also like to thank Jake George, owner and publisher of SageWordsPublishing for bringing *Almost A Hero* to print. This is my fourth novel published by Jake, and hopefully there will be more to come.

And last but not least, I would like to give a big shout out to Dave Napoletano and his wife Lisa, our new friends in Mesquite, Nevada. Judy and I found out how extraordinary of a real estate agent and all around great guy Dave is.

Steve Paul
September 17, 2015
Rawlins, Wyoming

Prologue

"Oh God! Keep going!" He stole a quick glance over his shoulder and screamed, "RUN!" He bumped into the side of his partner and pushed him away. *Take him!* Behind them, flickers of light from burning torches and ghostly shadows danced off the cavern walls. When the war cries came, high pitched and drawn out, both men whimpered from a primal fear they'd never experienced before. A fear they were going to lose their lives.

"I can't go much farther," the tall man panted. Images of his mother flashed through his mind. Fingernails edged in black grime dug into his palm from a death grip on the handle of a dented metal lantern he clutched as he ran. A chain around his neck holding a small copper band etched in gold bounced off his chest.

He looked behind him again. "Oh, Lord, help us. Mama," he cried, trying to get his legs to run faster, trying to outrun the certain death that chased them. He switched the lantern to his other hand. "God, I wish we hadn't come back," he whimpered. *It's so cold.*

The second man was shorter and burly, but his stubby legs churned out enough speed to keep up with his partner. "Ahhh!" he cried out, reaching behind him. "Help me!" He staggered and would have fallen if the tall man hadn't taken his arm and pulled him forward.

He gripped the shaft in his friend's back and yanked the arrow out, then towed him along still maintaining their momentum. "Keep running… it's our… only chance. We gotta… make it out," he said to the shorter man.

"This way." The tall man turned into a narrow cleft in the wall, dragging the other man with him. They stumbled over some small rocks and the lantern dropped to the ground. "Leave it," he said as the shorter man leaned over to pick it up. "I see some light." Exhaustion and hope cracked his voice. "C'mon!" *If he don't keep up, I'm leaving him.*

A shaft of white light appeared ahead. "We're gonna make it." Expectation bloated his voice as the ground dropped away. They fell six feet and landed in a narrow hole with smooth walls of rock. The fallen lantern above cast an eerie, spastic glow reflecting off the solid, impenetrable wall of granite behind them.

The shorter man groaned and sat up. "My leg's broke, you go."

"I can't, we're trapped." The tall man got to his feet and saw the shaft of sunlight shining in from a fist-sized hole beyond him. He picked up a handful of ragged, sharp-edged rocks.

They heard them approaching – a sound like the scurrying of rats.

"Why aren't you all dead?" the tall man yelled. "You're supposed to be dead." He began to sob and threw a rock. It bounced harmlessly off the side of the wall. He sat down hard and pulled his legs up next to his chest. "Go away… go away… don't…."

Chapter One
Three years ago

When the young man entered the cell, his eyes were wide and a primal fear showed out of them. His arms held a folded blanket, a hand towel, a change of prison clothes and a small box of personal items.

"Here's a new roommate for you guys," the guard said, opening the unlocked cell door and leading the man in. "To break the ice, his name is Ronnie Sanderson, number 316687."

There were two sets of two bunk beds with three bunks made up and one empty top bed. The mattress was stained and thin. The guard pointed to the empty bunk. "That's yours, unless one of these guys decides he wants it now." He turned and left.

Sanderson cleared his throat. "This one okay?" he asked, nodding to the empty bed.

"Yeah. Make it up and we'll talk some." The speaker stood up. "My name's Gavin, that's Reese, and the educated looking one is Dick." He didn't stick his hand out nor did any of the others.

No one spoke, they watched him as he began to make his bed and later, put his personal things on an open shelf. He took a small portable radio and plugged it in.

"Nice radio, let me see it." Reese said from the bottom bed he sat on. He wore a sleeveless sweatshirt and had huge biceps and wide shoulders.

Sanderson looked at each man, sweat beading on his forehead. He handed Reese the radio. "Keep it. I don't want to be hurt in here. I can pay you to keep me safe."

"Is that right? Every new fish says that," Gavin said. "You got a connection or something?"

"My father has money. He'll pay you to help me."

"How long are you in for?" Dick Millhouse asked, lying on the other top bunk.

"Eighteen to thirty-six months. But I can get out early with—"

"Yeah, yeah. Good behavior. What'd you do, steal an old lady's purse?" Reese asked. His eyes were small and looked cruel. He fiddled with the radio.

"I wish. They got me for transporting drugs with intent to sell."

"Hey guys," Gavin said. "He didn't say he was innocent or set up. So you were guilty, huh?"

Sanderson got a wild-eyed look. "No! I... I don't know what to say. I never thought I'd end up here. I'm a first offender," he stammered.

"Whoa, settle down. What did you get caught with?" Gavin asked.

"Cocaine."

"How much?"

"Eight kilos, already packaged for selling."

"Man, no wonder you got jail time. Your old man in on it?" Gavin was the only one asking the questions.

"God, no. He's third generation New York City family business, shit like that."

"No kidding. And his baby boy is in the joint doing time. Interesting. What kind of business?"

"He certifies and brokers antiquities from private holders." Sanderson looked to each man. "He has money, he'll pay you to keep me from getting hurt or..." He opened his hands. "Please, I don't know what to do."

"You don't sound like a hardcore dope runner," Millhouse said sympathetically.

"I'm not, I'm not. A friend in college asked me to help him out, drop a couple of packages off in New Jersey. I got busted when I crossed the state line."

"You're trying to shit us, Ronnie," Reese said. He stood up and loomed over Sanderson. "Nobody gets federal pen time for the first time if they don't have a rap sheet. What else?"

"Ah… the car was stolen and there was a pistol in the car."

"The friend supplied the car?" Gavin asked.

Sanderson nodded. "The gun wasn't mine either. The feds found it under the seat."

"Sounds like you were set up. Your friend get caught?"

"Yeah, but he disappeared. I haven't heard from him since."

"You stupid shit. He fed you to the wolves…and most likely his connection, too. He's probably in the witness protection now, laughing his ass off at you."

"I never thought about that," Ronnie said, his eyes still haunted. "I'm supposed to go to the work assignment officer now, can you tell me where his office is?"

Gavin took him by the arm and opened the cell door. He pointed down the walkway and put his mouth close to the kid's ear. "Down the stairs and past the showers. Be careful, there's guys here who cotton to fluff like you."

Sanderson looked wildly around. "Will you go with me?"

"Sorry, no. You gotta learn, kid." Gavin went back into the cell, leaving the door open. "You better get going before you get in trouble with the screws for being late," Gavin said.

Sanderson gripped the railing with a white knuckled hand. "God, I'm scared. Please."

"Don't act scared. That's the worst thing you can do."

Gavin watched as Sanderson trudged down the walkway and disappeared down the metal stairs. His footsteps echoed off the concrete walls.

"C'mon, we don't want him raped first thing."

7

Reese got up from his bunk and lifted the mattress. From inside an open seam, he took a shank out and stuck it in the waistband of his pants.

Millhouse licked his lips and asked, "You got something in mind?"

"I got a feeling about him. Something good is gonna come from this," Gavin replied.

The scream they heard and the guard ignored came from the shower area. A young Latino stood against the open entryway, arms folded across his chest when they came up to it.

"The line forms here, the going price is a pack of smokes." The Latino said. His hair shined and tattoos covered his arms.

"Beat it, Garcia, the kid in there is with us," Reese said, moving in close.

"Don't try no crap with me, Compton."

"Look, Taco," Reese said, pulling the shank out and pricking Garcia's neck. "We said he's with us, now scram." He lowered the shank.

Jose stared into Reese's eyes and puffed his chest out. "I don't give a rat's ass about that fish, Compton, and don't think you can pull your Aryan shit on me, man." He backed away and strutted off with his arms swinging behind him in a motion that was called, "pickin' cotton."

When they entered the shower room, Sanderson lay flat on his stomach with his pants pulled down to his ankles. A huge black man with fat layered over his belt and his shirt straining the buttons kneeled over him, an erection showing from under the flaps of his shirt. His knees pinned Sanderson's slightly spread legs to the shower floor.

"Felix, he's with us, put that nasty weapon away," Gavin said.

"What chu mean he's wiff you?' Sweat beaded on the black man's face. The erection began to slowly subside, like air being let out of a long balloon.

8

"He's our new cellmate, dude, he's like, one of us," Reese said. His fingers curled around the handle of the shank that was back in his waistband.

Felix's eyes went to the shank and back to Sanderson. He sighed and grunted as he pushed himself up. After fumbling with his pants he held his hand out to Gavin. "Y'all gots to give me some smokes for not buttin' your boy. Y'all hear me?" he said in a heavy southern accent.

Gavin shook his head. "Can't do it, man. Like I said, he's with us. But tell you what I'll do, you can have his dessert tonight. That work for you?"

"Showa, I ain't greedy." Felix bent over and pinched Sanderson's cheeks. "Yo sure is a pretty one." He nodded to Reese on his way out of the shower room.

Sanderson's body shook from racking sobs, his pants still around his feet as he lay on the floor.

"Pull your pants up and quit your bawling, goddammit," Gavin said. "The first thing to remember is act like a man. You gotta be strong, don't show any weakness."

They escorted him to the job assignment officer. Gavin went up to the desk. The man behind it wore thick glasses that rested on a long, thin, nose that sprouted hair wildly out of each nostril.

"Hey Wayne, how about assigning him to the library with us?" Gavin put his hand on the desktop. Several bills peeked out from under his palm.

With a quick grab the money disappeared from under Gavin's palm. Wayne picked up a clipboard and wrote on a paper it held. "Okay, he's in the library."

"Thanks, you're a pal," Gavin said, smiling.

On the way back to the cell, Sanderson thanked the men over and over until Reese told him to shut up.

They went inside and Gavin closed the cell door. "What did you learn today, kid?"

"I need protection while I'm here, and friends. I'm not a criminal like these animals in here," he blushed. "I don't mean you guys, you saved my ass, literally."

Gavin winked at Reese and tilted his head toward Sanderson. Reese turned away then backhanded Sanderson across the face, knocking him into the bottom bunk. Sanderson started to scream until Reese's hand covered his mouth and pulled him out of the bunk and dropped him to the floor. Two quick kicks to the ribs took the air from Sanderson's lungs. Millhouse stood at the cell door, his bulk obscuring the scene in the cell.

"I'm gonna show you something," Gavin said, kneeling down and gripping Sanderson's hair. He shoved Sanderson's face into his crotch then pulled it back. Gavin slapped him across the face, splitting his upper lip. "You're ours. We can do anything we want with you, understand?" Gavin slapped him again. Blood flew from Sanderson's nose and he started blubbering.

"Shut up! I told you, act like a man! You don't do it by bawling. This is just a small lesson on what could be. Reese, get him a towel," Gavin commanded as he took his hands off the crying, bloody, young man.

Reese yanked the hand towel from the shelf and threw it at Sanderson. It landed on the floor.

"Here," Gavin said, picking up the towel and handing it to Sanderson. "It could have been much worse. You were a knee bend from getting butt-fucked less than a half-hour ago. There are animals in here, but we aren't like them. We're going to protect you... for a fee, of course. Now clean yourself up, quit sniveling and we'll talk."

Sanderson did as he was told. After wetting the towel and wiping the blood off his face, he held it against his nose and sat on the floor, his back against the wall. His eyes still showed stark fear.

Gavin dropped a sheet of paper in his lap. "Reese here will pass the word you're to be left alone because you're with us. Everyone associates with groups and we stick with the white crowd, and Reese is an Aryan. They're a little radical, but strength in numbers, right?"

He waited for an answer, and when he didn't get one, he went on. "No one is going to make you their punk as long as you do what we say. We've got a lot of time together so you'll eventually appreciate us, Ronnie. Now that list is what we want first. Any questions?"

Sanderson scanned the paper. "Cigarettes and candy bars? That's all?"

"For now. Cigarettes are the same as money in here. We—"

"Hey, McQuery." The cell dimmed from the light being blocked by the massiveness of the man standing outside the cell door.

Gavin turned to see who called his name and held hands out. "What now, Felix?"

"I gives ya two cartons of yo favor-ite smokes fo' one poke wiff the pretty boy."

"What do you say, Ronnie?"

Sanderson's face was bright red. He pushed himself up from the ground. One trembling hand went behind his back. "Get your ass out of here, you piece of shit," he yelled.

"Showah, pretty boy, showah." Felix said. The cell became brighter from more light coming in through the cell door when he left.

"Well done, kid. You learn fast," Gavin said. He went to the door and watched Felix lumber down the walkway.

Chapter Two

Edward Sanderson spent a large sum of money trying to keep his son out of prison. After the boy was sentenced and taken to the federal penitentiary in Hoboken, New Jersey, he was overwhelmed with guilt.

"He's not a bad boy," he told his lawyer, Arthur Santine, one afternoon in his office.

"Of course not, Edward. He was the victim of circumstances."

"I'm going to bring him into the business when he gets out. Put him in charge of the acquisition department."

"Are you sure that's wise right now? Ronnie's been gone almost a year and a half, he'll need some time to adjust."

"Amazingly enough, he's learned quite a bit there. An archaeologist took him under his wing and taught him about Indian history and artifacts. It's funny, before he went to prison he didn't care one whit about the business. Now he wants to get involved."

"Perhaps I should check into the archaeologist and see what his credentials are," Santine said.

"No. Stay out of it, Arthur. For the first time since his mother died, we're talking to each other, rather than arguing. This experience has been difficult for him, yet I feel it's been beneficial, and I won't tolerate interference."

"I'm just trying to protect your interests, Edward."

Sanderson walked around the desk and patted Santine on the back. "I know, old friend, but I have faith and trust in people, where you're always suspicious. And the Lord will protect me."

Santine rose from his chair and looked sadly at Sanderson. "I hope you don't regret it."

*   *   *

"Dad, I've got some friends getting out the same time as me. They've kept me safe," Ronnie Sanderson said into the telephone. "One of them is Dick Millhouse, the archaeologist I've told you about. Can you put them up until they get on their feet?" He held his breath waiting for the response. Gavin stood next to him, his head close to the earpiece of the telephone.

"Of course, son. I'll get them rooms at the Stansbury Hotel and we'll discuss what we can do to help them." There was a pause. "When shall I pick you up?"

"I don't want you coming here and seeing me leave prison. We'll take a train and meet you at the hotel next Tuesday. Can you arrange for the rooms, three of them?"

"You'll be staying at the house, won't you?"

"Certainly, the rooms are for my roommates. You'll meet them at the hotel. You'll like them, and they *aren't* criminals. They were innocent."

"I'll take care of everything, Ronnie. The tickets and reservations will be delivered tomorrow."

"That's great, Dad. I think we've...."

"We've what?"

"Begun a new beginning... between us, I mean."

"I think we have too, son. I've been praying for this for a long time."

*   *   *

The hotel rooms were on the third floor and each had an honor bar and sitting room. Ronnie sat on a bed talking on the telephone to his father.

13

"Remember, be polite and grateful to the kid's old man," Gavin said to Reese and Millhouse. "I believe this is going to be the opportunity of a lifetime."

Ronnie hung the phone up and said, "All right! Dad will be here in an hour. He says he'll talk to you and see if he can put you to work."

"That's great, kid," Gavin said. "We're looking forward to meeting him."

Ronnie left forty-five minutes later to meet his father in the hotel lobby. He told the men the elder Sanderson wanted to meet with them and visit.

"We'll play it like we said, if the old man will buy what we tell him," Gavin said.

"What if he doesn't believe us or tells us to piss off?" Reese asked, opening the mini-bar.

"Don't drink any booze now, we want to give a good impression. Don't talk unless he asks you something, okay?" Gavin said to Reese.

"Sure, don't worry so much. So what'll we do if he doesn't give a shit about giving us anything?" Reese asked again.

"I've got an idea in case that happens," Gavin said, frowning. "Maybe hold the kid and make the old man cough up some big bucks, but that'll be a last resort."

"Okay, be on your best behavior," he said when there was a knocking on the door. He got up and opened it. "You must be Mr. Sanderson," he said, putting his hand out. "Come in, please. I'm Gavin McQuery."

Sanderson introduced himself as he shook Gavin's hand and walked into the room. He seemed to nod approvingly at the two men sitting on the couch when they rose to their feet.

"Hello, I'm Edward Sanderson. It's a pleasure to finally meet you gentlemen. Ronnie has spoken highly of you all."

Ronnie beamed and looked to Gavin as if to say, "See, I told you."

14

Reese introduced himself, saying, "Reese Compton, the pleasure's mine. Millhouse vigorously shook Sanderson's hand. "Dick Millhouse, sir."

"I'm in your debt for teaching Ronnie so much about antiquities," Sanderson said to him. "You seem to know your archaeology."

"You're welcome," Millhouse replied.

"What do you all say we sit down and see if I can help you." He motioned with his hand to the table surrounded by six chairs. "Then we can go out for dinner."

After everyone had settled in the chairs around the table, Sanderson cleared his throat and clasped his hand together and laid them on the tabletop. "I want to start off by saying I believe in the Lord and think everyone is made in his image. He forgave a murderer, as I'm sure you all know. I harbor no prejudgment on your actions in the past. This is a new beginning for you, and Jesus willing, it will be beneficial for all of us." He stopped talking and looked at each man and his face softened when his eyes met with Ronnie's.

"I'm not interested in the crimes that sent you to the penitentiary," he continued. "But tell me your skills and we'll see what we can do to use them. Why don't you start," Sanderson nodded to Gavin, "and just go around the table." He produced a small notebook and pen and put it on the table in front of him.

"I have a degree in accounting and worked for a museum in acquisitions," Gavin said. "My strong suit is contacts with buyers and sellers."

Millhouse smiled at Ronnie. "As you know, I'm an archaeologist, I've taught it and practice the profession. Early Native American artifacts. By the way, Ronnie has been an excellent student. He probably has the knowledge equal to a Bachelor of Science degree right now."

"There's no doubt I'm in your debt for helping him. Ronnie's told me he's taken a great interest in your profession.

Gentlemen, so far I'm impressed with your credentials. Reese, surprise me - what's your skill?" Sanderson asked.

"I don't have a degree, if that's what you mean. Ex-army. I've done security work and been a bodyguard. Raised in Wyoming and I ride for the brand."

"Uhh, what do you mean by that?"

"If you hire me, I work for you and your interests, no one else," Reese replied. He looked Sanderson in the eye.

"I see. Let me mull over some possibilities and I'll get back with you all in the next day or so. In the meantime, just sign for anything within reason you want from the hotel. Ronnie has told me numerous times how you kept him from harm. I want to show my gratitude, and I have some ideas on how to do it."

"We have faith in you, Mr. Sanderson," Gavin said. "Our debt to society has been paid. All we want is to be able to work our way back into the mainstream and try to be an asset. The Lord has been with us too, I might add."

Sanderson shook their hands and left with Ronnie. When the door closed, Gavin opened a drawer and brought out a bottle of whiskey and three glasses. He poured each glass half-full, handed them to Reese and Millhouse, then held his in the air. "Yessir, here's to the Lord and a profitable future." The glasses clinked and they knocked the whiskey down in one swallow.

"Let's find us some hookers," Reese said. "I need to make up for some lost time."

"Don't we all," Gavin countered. "Just don't charge them to our rooms, eh?"

"Yeah, at least for the time being," Millhouse said. He started laughing and then broke into a fit of coughing. "Goddamn cigarettes, I think I quit smoking too late."

Chapter Three
Eleven months later

Edward Sanderson's hands trembled when the archaeologist confirmed the authenticity of the pygmy Indian mummy. The two men were in the laboratory of Sanderson's company, History, Inc.

"It's a full grown adult and I've never seen anything like this before. Here, look. The skull is crushed. Probably died in a fall or battle. He has to be at least two hundred years old. Where did you get it?" Richard Millhouse asked.

"An old man sold it to me. He used to own a car lot or something in Wyoming and lost all of his money in the stock market. He had it stuffed in a box in an attic and had forgotten about it, he said. There's supposed to be a whole tribe of them that lived in a mountain."

"Did he find it?"

"No, he bought it from some gold miners, back in the forties. They discovered the mummy while they were digging a mine and brought it out. The old man even got a map from them showing where it was found." Sanderson puffed his chest out. "Now I have it and I didn't have to pay very much."

"He didn't try to find the rest of them?"

"No, he didn't think it was real at first. He was just trying to help the miners out," Sanderson said. "He's a good Christian so I know he's telling the truth."

Millhouse picked the copper headband up and held it in front of him. "This could be worth a fortune," he muttered.

"You don't sell things like these, Richard. You gather them and have a display. One where every major museum will clamor for. I'll be famous as the man who found a lost Indian tribe." His eyes seemed to glitter. "This is the Lord's direction for me. I want you to start documenting everything. Find out anything you can... I'll need a name for him, of course."

"I'll make some discreet inquires," Millhouse said. "There has to be some information about him. Nothing this unique could have gone unnoticed without a professional knowing about it. Someone should have published a paper on it."

Sanderson took the headband from the archaeologist. "I'll keep this. Tell Gavin to come to my office." He turned and left the room.

Gavin rapped on the door, opened it and stuck his head in. "You wanted to see me, Mr. Sanderson?"

"Come in and sit down, Gavin," Sanderson said, motioning to a chair in front of his desk.

McQuery entered and took the seat. "What can I do for you?"

"How long have you worked for me?"

"Nearly a year, and I can explain..."

"Explain what?" Sanderson interrupted. He held a laminated paper in front of him.

"Ah... my absence the other day. A terrible case of the flu." He coughed.

"Tell me, what do you make of this map?" Sanderson put the paper down in front of him.

He bent over it for a moment, then looked at Sanderson. "What can I say? It's a map and shows how to get to a mine."

"And this?" The headband reflected a dull glow from the wall lights.

"May I?" Gavin reached for it. He turned it around in his hand and his index finger stroked the curve. "This looks like gold etched in copper or tarnished silver."

"The map shows where this came from. I want you to see if we can find that mine. Go into the lab and have Richard show you the Indian. It was wearing the headband. There's supposed to be more of them there, in a mountain in Wyoming," Sanderson said. Excitement made his face flush.

"It shouldn't be hard to find some buyers for them." Gavin's hands tightened around the headband until his knuckles were white. "Exquisite craftsmanship."

"You sound just like Millhouse. I won't sell them; I'll *display* them. This could put me in the history books." He put his hand out and twiddled his fingers at Gavin. "Let me have it back." When he had it in his hands again he ran his palm over the headband lovingly. "I've always liked the west, you know. I could easily live out there. Maybe have a gentleman's ranch and raise horses. That would read well on my autobiography." Sanderson's excitement was still obvious. "Isn't Reese from somewhere out there?"

"I believe so. I'll ask him, if you like."

"It's not important. I want you to find out how the mummy was found. Could we legally excavate and retain our findings? This has to be kept quiet. If my competition finds out about this mummy we could lose out on finding anymore."

"Leave it to me, Mr. Sanderson. I'll get Reese and we'll see what we have to do to get the rights," Gavin said smoothly.

"Good, I can always count on you, can't I?"

"Taking care of the Sanderson family is my highest priority."

"The Lord guided you to me," Sanderson said, putting a hand on Gavin's shoulder. "I feel an adventure coming for Ronnie and me."

"I agree… this could have quite a significance in all our lives."

* * *

"Let's see what you have, Dick," Gavin said walking up to the archaeologist. He looked around and lowered his voice. "Why didn't you tell me about this mummy?"

"I've been busy researching it. You haven't been around much so don't jump my ass," Millhouse said defensively.

"Settle down, I was just asking. Sanderson wants me to check out the place it was found. Can you enlighten me on the map?" Gavin put in down on the table. "X marks the spot. Very original."

"The men who found it were miners, not surveyors. I'm—"

Gavin's hand clamped on Millhouse's throat. "Knock this crap off, Dick. You don't talk to me in that condescending tone, got it?" He squeezed hard then released his grip.

Millhouse fell back coughing. "I'm sorry. I've been under a lot of pressure from Mr. Sanderson on this." He rubbed his throat. "I wasn't trying to be condescending... really."

"So tell me about it." Gavin patted him on the back.

"What we have is apparently an old Indian tribe that's unknown to us. I've looked in all my reference books and can't find anything remotely close to them. If they really existed—"

"Really existed? There's one right here. I'd say that proves they existed." Gavin snorted. "Sometimes I wonder about you educated guys."

"Okay, if this isn't an anomaly, then there's a pygmy tribe of Indians that lived more than a hundred years ago; at least this fella tests out to about 150 years old by carbon dating.

There could be a burial chamber inside a mountain in Wyoming, at least according to the map. Your guess is as good as mine if there really is one," Millhouse said.

"And it's not a baby that had a disease or something like that?"

"No, his teeth and bone structure are those of an adult about sixty years old."

"What about the mine Sanderson mentioned?" Gavin asked

"I told him it was a mine, but it's the tomb or burial area. I was afraid he'd get religious on us if he knew it was a tomb," Millhouse replied. "I think the band is a headband, worn by royalty or the elitist of the tribe."

"Could we sell it for much?"

"Oh yeah. The artifacts I sold before the Feds got me brought in some big money, bought by people who want the rare, museum type artifacts that the general public will never see."

"What do think the headband is worth?" Gavin asked, a thoughtful look on his face.

"Conservatively, I'd say in the neighborhood of $50,000. If we could find some intact bodies, they'd go for over $125,000, perhaps significantly more. I still have some good contacts."

"And there should be more of these in the tomb, if we can find it."

"You haven't understood what I've said, have you, Gavin? If there's a tomb and pygmy Indians are buried in it, we're talking *hundreds and hundreds of thousands of dollars. Maybe millions.* Don't you get it? No one has ever seen these things, let alone own one. If there's more of them, certain people will want to have one for themselves," Millhouse said enthusiastically.

Chapter Four

Reese was raised in Casper, Wyoming, about sixty miles north of the Ferris Mountain Range. He and Gavin flew to Denver, took a twenty-seat puddle jumper prop to Casper, and rented a Chevy Tahoe to drive to Rawlins. Reese told Gavin he had an old buddy he grew up with who now lived there, working the oil rigs in the Red Desert.

"Things might have changed since I was here last, but the Ferris used to be total wilderness. No roads or trails and almost all government land. My buddy ought to know more; I called him and he was going to do some checking for me," Reese said from the passenger seat in the car on the way to Rawlins.

"This guy dependable?"

"Yeah, no sweat. The cops caught him after we robbed a liquor store. He never squealed on me. Funny thing is, his family was pissed at him, not for robbing the place, but for getting caught. There were four kids and they were all half-screwy. I even took his sister out some. One hot chick." His face lit up. "I oughta look her up. Man, what a piece of ass."

"Try to think with your brain and not the head of your dick. This guy isn't nuts enough to screw things up if we use him?" Gavin asked.

"Nahh, Ike's a good head. He'll do anything we tell him. He's bored with the working life," Reese replied. "How'd the old man get the Indian shit?"

"He was a little tight-lipped about it. An old cowboy sold the mummy and map to him for a couple thousand bucks. The guy had told him he'd bought it from a car dealer back in the fifties, in Cheyenne. The dealer showed it in some freak shows for a while then fell on hard times. The cowboy bought it and put it away when the public decided it was fake and quit paying to see it. Guess he forgot about it for fifty years until he needed some money to get in a home or something. Apparently Sanderson had a deaf ear to the Lord when he bought it." Gavin laughed, then frowned. "I hate those holier-than-thou assholes. Sanderson's the worst one I've been around."

"If this turns out to be real, you have a plan for us to make some money?" Reese asked.

"I'm working on one. It all depends on location, location, location." Gavin looked out the car window at a herd of antelope grazing in the sagebrush. "I can't believe how desolate this country is. Give me the east anytime." The highway dipped into dry valleys and sagebrush- covered hills, the two-lane blacktop stringing out in front of them like an asphalt snake. They passed two ranch entrance gates, both closed.

"There you go," Reese said, pointing to the west. "The Pedros are on the left, then the Ferris."

"Holy shit," Gavin said quietly. "How can we even try to find something up there?"

The Ferris rose from the east and loomed higher as if the gods had decided to make them into a crown of limestone cliffs, craggy outcrops and trees that hid the ground beneath them. The peaks were capped with patches of snow remaining from the winter.

Reese patted a briefcase. "If Millhouse got the coordinates off the old map transposed to that new BLM map right, we ought to be able to find the tomb with the GPS."

"You're going to be able to get us up there and back, right? I mean, we won't get lost?" Gavin felt, and his eyes showed - uncertainty - for the first time since he could remember.

"This will be a switch, won't it? Me telling you what to do," Reese said.

"Only while we're up there, so don't get too cocky," Gavin shot back. He hit the brakes and turned onto a dirt road. Gravel crunched and dust flew up when he slid to a stop. He shut the engine off and climbed out of the Tahoe. Reese joined him. Gavin stared at the Ferris range and spoke so low Reese had to strain to hear him.

"This might take us a longer than what I thought. A bit more complex." Gavin said, turning back to the Tahoe. "Let's get to town before dark."

It was early afternoon when they checked into The Lodge at the east end of Rawlins. The wind blew steady and hard, making them wrestle their luggage into the rooms.

"Get a hold of your friend and see if he can join us for dinner here," Gavin said. The connecting door between the two rooms was open and he sat on the bed. "I wonder how long the wind's going to blow this hard. Damn near knocked me down."

"This little breeze?" Reese snorted. "You haven't seen the wind blow. She can get up to gusts of over sixty miles an hour. It's from being on the high plains."

"Great. No cities and hurricanes every day." Gavin pulled the bedcover back and lay down. He poked the TV remote on. "Close the door, will you? I need to relax for an hour or so. Tell your friend to be here around seven." His attention was on the screen when the door closed. He got up and locked it.

* * *

"At least the wind's calmed down," Gavin said later. He, Reese and Ike Bodine sat around a small table in Reese's motel room, an opened bottle of bourbon in the middle. He turned to Bodine, a thin man with a pockmarked face, greasy black hair and protruding front teeth. *He looks like a rat that had smallpox.* "Reese vouches for you so there's three things you should know: one, we get caught and it's probably the needle. Two, rat us out and I guarantee you'll die hard because other people are in with me. And three, this works out and you'll have more money than you know what to do with. Think it over, this is the only time where we let you pass on it."

Gavin poured the three a drink, made a mock toast and sipped from his glass. He sat back in the chair, his eyes moving from one man to the other.

Bodine picked his glass up and downed the drink in one swallow. He slammed the glass down. "I'm in. Working my ass off twelve hours a day, seven days a week on an oil rig ain't gonna get it. Might lose some fingers and I ain't ever gonna be a driller."

"You're sure?" Gavin asked.

"Yeah. I've never been accused of being too smart. I got two brothers still in the pen and a sister went to college. And she bitches about not making enough money to live, so I guess I ain't too dumb."

"How long you been in Rawlins?" Gavin refilled their glasses.

"Around three years, not counting the four I spent in the pen. Why?"

"I thought you could tell me what kind of town it is. Like, it looks like a place getting caught up in a boom. Is there a lot of crime?"

"Not much. Last year there was a big deal on some horses getting shot. Some government dude killed some guys that were in on it, but there was some other stuff but I don't remember all of it."

"Are you shitting me?" Gavin asked, disbelief in his eyes. "A government agent kills somebody over horses and gets away with it? What was he, FBI?"

"No, not that kind of fed." Bodine's eyes lit up. "Bureau of Land Management...that was it. The dude's taking care of wild horses and a bunch got shot and killed. Lemme see... I seen the picture of him in the newspaper. He looked like a big guy, older than us. Calhoun. His name's Calhoun. He's a ranger or something and kills at least two guys who was shooting them horses. Like I told you, there was something else along with it, but damned if I remember. I just thought, whoa! I ain't screwing with no horses if you can get your ass killed. You want, I can try and find out some more about it."

"Forget it, if I get interested, I'll check the newspaper. Anything else we should be aware of?" Gavin winked at Reese.

"Don't think so... just a regular town. Like Casper, but smaller, and not as much stuff going on." Bodine slapped Reese on the back. "Me and Reese were good buddies. Hung around together all the time until he joined the army. He tried getting me to join, but I wouldn't. We're back together now, right?"

"You bet. You should have gone with me, I made some good bucks," Reese said.

"Well, I'm here now. I ain't missing out this time. Nobody can say Ike Bodine don't learn from experience." He started to laugh, and to Gavin, it sounded similar to a donkey braying.

Gavin went back to his room, locking the connecting door. Next on the agenda would be to see if they could find the tomb. One thing to say about Reese's army years, he could work a map and compass. Gavin found that out when they went white-tailed deer hunting in the New Jersey Pine Barrens. They had gone in and got out in one piece, thanks to the compass and map. Gavin hadn't any idea where they had been or where they were until they came upon their truck in the small clearing.

* * *

The memory of the Jersey deer hunt made him get a pen and paper and write a list of items to buy.

He was up and dressed by seven in the morning. Reese answered the door after the first knock and they went to breakfast in the dining room.

"Where's your buddy?" Gavin asked, looking at the menu.

"Ike left about an hour after you. Before you bitch, he's not the smartest, but we can use him and he'll keep his mouth shut."

They quit talking when the waitress came up and took their order. After she left, Gavin leaned closer to the table. "Let's just make sure he's dispensable, okay? At least until we see what happens on this thing. Hell, it could turn out to be a wild goose chase."

"I thought the Lord spoke to Sanderson," Reese said.

"It wouldn't surprise me. Hell, maybe we'll find the place."

When they finished eating, Gavin gave Reese some money and told him to get any equipment he thought they'd need for their, as he called it, expedition into the damn mountains. Gavin decided to check with some real estate agents about land for sale in the general area of the tomb, if they located it.

They met back at Reese's room at eleven. He had canteens, sleeping bags, backpacks and MRE's he'd bought from the local army surplus store.

"I've got some leads if we find anything," Gavin said, taking a backpack and filling it with supplies.

"Like what?" Reese asked. He opened his suitcase and took his GPS out and a map with the logo of the Bureau of Land Management on it.

"A small ranch for sale, between the Pedro Mountains and the Ferris. On the north side. I think I remember driving by the gate with the name on it. The Steamboat Lake Ranch." Gavin replied.

"Sounds familiar. How big?"

"Two thousand acres deeded, a house, buildings and some leased land."

"Sanderson would like that…a gentleman's ranch," Reese said, almost sneering.

"Have you found a way for us to get in the general area?"

"Yeah." Reese opened the map on top of the bed. "There's a road that takes off from Highway 287. It bears to the southeast after a couple of miles down but it looks like there's a two-track going from it up to a place called Young's Pass." His finger ran along the map. "We'll hike from there to the coordinates on the BLM map and hope the GPS will narrow it down. Simple."

"You really think we can find it, Reese?" Gavin asked. It was the first time he'd sounded uncertain.

"I think we've got a damn good chance. There's landmarks and some pretty good detail from the original map. All we need is a little luck."

"Let's hope Sanderson does have an in with God," Gavin said wryly.

They threw their packs in the back of the Chevy Tahoe and headed north out of Rawlins, with Reese driving.

At milepost 48, on U.S. 287, a gravel road took off toward the north Ferris. Reese turned on it and told Gavin, "Get the GPS out and turn it on. I want to be able to start the track back when we get off this road."

Two and a half miles down the road, a two-track veered to the west, cutting through sagebrush and toward a cleft in the mountain. They took it and churned through sand and rock for an hour until the track started climbing through a long ravine with high rock walls on each side. Reese had the

Tahoe in four-wheel drive and the tires spun and clawed their way up.

"Oh my God! Are we going to make it?" Gavin wiped sweat from his face. His safety belt was cinched as tight as it would go. The Tahoe bucked and slammed down hard, the sound of metal hitting rock rang out. Reese jammed the brakes on.

"Shit! They've cut the road out."

"Who?"

"Probably the BLM. They've blocked the road so no one can go up any farther." He nodded to the right.

A sign with an arrow on it stated: *No motor vehicles allowed. Wilderness Area. Turn around here.* The arrow pointed to a small open area cut out of the bank.

Reese backed up and pulled into the turn-around. He shut off the Tahoe and got out, walking to the cut bank. Gavin unbuckled his seatbelt and opened the door. "What is it?" he yelled.

"There's two more cuts. We hike from here. Give me the GPS." He leaned in and brought the map out, setting it on the hood. Gavin climbed out and gave him the global positioning system.

"We'll start off to the east and work our way up the mountain," Reese said, slinging his backpack over his shoulders. "It looks like three, maybe four miles to get in the general area according to the coordinates." Without waiting for Gavin to comment, he began climbing up the side of the cut, digging the toes of his boots in for traction.

At the top of the cut, thick strands of trees and brush surrounded the mountainside. Reese waited and caught his breath while Gavin made his way up the side, panting after fifty feet. His chest heaved when he finally made it to the top.

"I forgot what such a high altitude can do if you're not used to it," Reese told him. "No use pushing so hard we can't make it. We'll find us a game trail to walk. If you get too tired, holler and we'll stop and rest."

Gavin nodded and wiped sweat off his forehead. They took off through the timber, weaving a path around fallen trees and tangled brush interwoven into the deadfall. Reese found a trail they followed that probably elk and deer used to traverse the side of the mountain. When it would turn down hill, they would climb until they found another one. Every fifteen minutes to a half an hour, they stopped, rested and drank water.

The sun arched toward the west and shadows started lengthening when the white limestone formations came into view. Like huge shark's teeth, they rose high into the air; ragged and sharp, forming peaks on individual formations. Reese turned toward the backside of the first mass.

"Why don't we go below them?" Gavin asked. His face was red from exertion and he sat heavily down on a boulder. "We're going have to climb over that loose stuff to get behind it. That's if we can. They might be growing right out of the mountain."

"Rocks don't grow out of a mountain. These are left after the ground and the softer rock around them eroded," Reese replied, propping a leg on the same boulder Gavin sat on. "Why don't you wait here and I'll check it out. Catch your breath."

"Good idea, I'll do it. Just don't get hurt or lost. I couldn't get back to the truck if my life depended on it," Gavin said. "Does seem like half the time the ground was so rocky and hard we didn't leave any tracks."

"That's why the GPS," Reese said. "Every time we've turned or taken a different direction, I've marked it. I just hit track-back and it shows the way back. Hell, it'll even show if you deviate off the route. I'll have to show you how to work it sometime."

"Yeah, you do that, but later. I'm too tired to try to learn something new."

"All right. You wait here and I'll climb up and check it out." He took another swallow from his canteen and stood up. "If it looks good, I'll yell at you and you can come up."

"Yeah, yeah." Gavin got off the boulder and lay down on the ground on his back. He tilted his hat over his eyes.

Reese shook his head and looked at the tall mound of broken rock. He leaned over so his hands were on the slope and started up the side at an angle. "I'd move over a bit if I were you," he said. "This stuff could slide down and get you. Might break your head open."

Gavin scrambled to his feet and trotted down the trail until he was away from the slope where Reese climbed. He stood and watched Reese for a few minutes then sat down with his back against a tree. Small rocks tumbling down kept his interest in the progress Reese was making. He passed from Gavin's view when he circled and disappeared behind a row of boulders.

"Hey, man! You gotta see this. Unbelievable," Reese's shout came from above.

Gavin jumped to his feet and walked warily to the slope. "What is it?"

"It's like a highway. It'll be cake after this." Reese's voice bounced off slabs of granite and limestone. "I'll throw you down a rope." The stripped climbing rope uncoiled in the air as it dropped down near Gavin. "Hold on a minute, I have to tie it off." The rope moved and pulled back a few feet. "Okay, come on up…and bring your backpack," Reese yelled.

Gavin wound the rope around his wrist and forearm and began pulling himself up the slope. Since it was more direct rather than at an angle, like Reese had gone, his feet slipped more and small rocks cascaded down behind him. He stopped when he reached a flat-topped crag and flopped his butt on it.

"Can you give me a hand and pull on the rope? I'm getting pretty pooped."

"Yeah, no problem. Catch your breath first." Reese loomed over the edge above him. "I didn't realize you're so out of shape."

"That's because I've always used my brain instead of my brawn. Not necessarily like you, I might add."

"Maybe, but at least I can take care of myself," Reese said. "You've been sitting there blowing now long enough. Come on and I'll pull your dead ass up."

Gavin twisted off the crag and began to pull himself up. The rope moved, almost dragging him up the slope. "Leave it alone, I can do it," Gavin shouted. "Goddamn gorilla," he said under his breath. His muscles felt like they were going to pull out of his shoulders as he climbed higher, almost vertically, as the top of the slope came in sight.

A hand came over the top, grabbed his arm, and pulled him over the crest like a sack of flour.

"Oh my aching ass, I've strained everything in my body," Gavin moaned, lying on his back and gulping air.

"You did good. It's tougher than what most people think," Reese said. He took his canteen and handed it to Gavin. "You better drink some water or you'll get sick."

"Thanks" He uncapped the lid and took a swallow.

"Not too fast," Reese admonished.

"Yeah, I've seen the movies. This tastes better than anything I've drunk lately." Gavin spoke with water still in his mouth and it dribbled out the sides.

"It looks like this shelf of rock runs along the side for miles. You ready to go?"

"We aren't going to walk too much further, are we? I'm ready to pack it in for the night." Gavin rubbed his shoulders after he stood up.

"A half hour, then we'll set up camp," Reese said. He took the canteen back and slung it over his arm. The GPS hung from his neck and he poked a button.

The half-hour turned into an hour with Reese haranguing Gavin to go a little more. Finally they came to a clearing that opened up to the backside of the limestone formation. Reese set up two half shelters together and placed their sleeping bags in it. With a small campfire heating coffee and eating their MREs, the night covered them like pitch poured over the mountains.

Gavin produced a flask and poured some whiskey in both cups. After taking a sip, he closed his eyes. "Do you think we have a chance of finding it?" he asked, keeping his eyes closed. "It seems more like a pipe dream. I don't know what the hell I was thinking."

"Look, you're tired and worn out from doing things you've never done before. Everything always looks worse when you're at that point. Yeah, I think we'll find it. Tomorrow. According to the GPS, it's not far."

Gavin was huddled against the cold in his sleeping bag when the sun rose high enough to lighten the clearing they'd camped in. The smell of fresh coffee cooking came into the shelter and he opened one eye. "Man, it's freezing," he said, his teeth almost chattering.

"It got cold last night, there's frost on the ground," Reese said from outside the tent. "C'mon, breakfast is ready. We need to get an early start."

Chapter Five

Gavin ran into a strand of trees and came back a few minutes later blowing into his cupped hands. "Almost froze my pecker off pissing," he said with a little laugh. "Should have warmed my hands up first." He took the offered cup of coffee and plate of scrambled eggs, bacon and biscuits. "How'd you get those eggs up here without breaking them?"

"I can't believe you're serious, Gavin. I scrambled them up before we left. Don't you know anything about being in the country?"

"I do… hire what you need done."

Twenty minutes later they were walking east behind the limestone bluffs. Reese stopped after two hours and held his GPS out in front of him. "Okay, we're in the vicinity if this thing is anywhere near right. You go down between the outcrops – look for caves or talus slopes, anything where there was some digging. I'll check on this side of them."

Gavin stooped over and looked inside a small cavern made by two huge slabs of stone lying against each other. He put his flashlight inside and saw a solid wall a short distance away. "Shit." He straightened up.

"Gavin! Hey, man, I've found something!" Reese yelled, excitement making his voice carry louder. "Get up here."

Gavin jogged farther along the bottom of the slabs and saw a trail working up between the outcrops. When he got to the backside, he slipped on a slope of small rock that began from a cut in the stone. He caught his breath and noticed the rock didn't appear to have any kind of opening until he turned around a jutting edge of limestone that looked like an elephant's ear.

"Reese, you in there?" he yelled into the opening.

"Come on, you won't believe this," Reese yelled back.

* * *

The opening was the size of a door then ten feet in, opened up to a monstrous cavern with a smooth floor of stone and a current of fresh air blowing in his face. He saw a light above him and came to a ledge. His light beam showed cut out steps in the limestone. Even he could see where someone had busted parts of the walls and hauled them out. An ore cart sat below the excavation, empty. Rough openings went in several feet then abruptly stopped as if the shaft was abandoned when no gold was discovered in the short distance they'd mined. A beam of light hit him in the face.

"Look at this," Reese whispered. He shined the flashlight over a high rim to the side of one of the abandoned shafts. Gavin stretched up and saw a sight that made his heart pick up beats.

"I think those are crypts," Reese said. "Goddamn crypts," he said louder. "We found it, can you believe this? We found it!" Reese let out a whoop that echoed a hundred times.

Chapter Six

The rope was made into a ladder and thrown over the rim. Reese hauled himself up and over the rim and dropped to the ground. He secured the end of the rope ladder around a forming stalagmite. He turned in a slow circle playing the light from his flashlight over the walls. "C'mon over, you can make it." He let out a whistle. "This is something… we've hit the mother lode."

Gavin dropped down the last few feet and stood next to Reese. He shined his light over a row of rectangular stone containers set into a wall of glistening rock. "They look like they're carved into the wall," he said in a low, astounded voice, "or… out of the wall." The light illuminated hieroglyphics and pictures painted as a mural, depicting a history of a tribe; or so it seemed. It covered every wall they could see.

Reese grabbed the end of a stone box sticking partially out and shoved down with all his strength. There was the slightest movement. Gavin put his light on it. Reese picked a piece of fractured rock up and slammed it down on the box. A crack showed next to the wall and he brought the rock down again. The end of the box crumbled and an object fell out, hitting the cavern floor and shattering.

"Hold on," Gavin shouted. He knelt down with the flashlight in one hand and picked the shattered pieces up with his other hand. "Oh, shit." He held his hand up.

It looked like a broken porcelain doll head cradled in split leather, with thick hair still clinging to the pieces of skull. The jawbone clung by tissue turned into rawhide string ages ago.

"We ruined it. No more touching this stuff, we've got to get Dick up here… he'll know how to get them out without busting everything up." Gavin knelt back down and ran his hand around the crumbled rock. He raised his hand triumphantly. In it, he held a copper and gold band.

* * *

"Mr. Sanderson, I believe the Lord is watching out for you."

"You have good news for me, Gavin?"

"We think we found the site, but there's better news.'

"Tell me, now," Sanderson demanded.

"There's a ranch for sale near the mountain. It's not big, as far as Wyoming ranches go, but an available grazing lease takes in the part of the mountain where the tribe lived."

"Where are you now?"

"Casper, we contacted a realtor here who specializes in land. If we have a base, we can do our business in Rawlins and keep everything confidential," Gavin said. He was betting Sanderson was greedy enough he wouldn't go with giving the site location away to the government. "This will make you famous, but maybe I should contact the Bureau of Land Management and tell them about the discovery. They have rules on this."

There was a pause and he could hear Sanderson breathing into the phone. "Have you actually found anything, or is this speculation?" Sanderson asked.

Here goes nothing, Gavin thought. "We have found something. A tomb...and there's stone crypts we think were used for burials. I'll tell you, Mr. Sanderson, I think the Lord guided us to it. *He* has a plan, I feel. For you." He almost laughed out loud.

"I... I've felt the same thing, Gavin. Especially since Ronnie is with me now and leading a clean, god-fearing life. I have you to thank... you and the Lord."

"Well, I think the Lord wants you to release these people from the mountain and allow others to benefit from their presence. Something that won't happen if the government is involved."

"Praise the Lord, I think you're right."

* * *

"What'd he say? You've got a crap-eating grin all over your face," Reese said after Gavin hung up the telephone. They were in a motel room in Casper, an unopened bottle of Wild Turkey whiskey sitting on the table, with two glasses next to it.

"What'd he say, you ask? Tomorrow..." he opened the whiskey bottle and poured both glasses full, "he told me to check out the ranch and make a deal. He'll wire me the money to close. And get this, I can go up to $750,000."

"Let's take the money and skip. Screw those pygmy Indians,' Reese said.

"Don't be a fool. There's more than twice that much worth of artifacts in the cave. People will pay a fortune to own one, especially one that no museum has. The other thing is the money for the ranch won't be in cash. It'll be a wire to the owner's bank account from Sanderson's bank." Gavin raised his glass in a toast. "Like the song says, *We're in the money.*"

Chapter Seven

"Mr. Sanderson, Mr. Murray, nice to see you again so soon," the realtor had said. He was middle aged and wore an expensive looking suit. He smiled a lot. The ranch gate was standing open and his Cadillac Escalade sat in the middle of the road.

"My pleasure, Mr. Greer. Let's hope this will be a beneficial trip for both of us," Gavin replied.

"Please," Greer said, smiling. "Call me Henry."

Gavin and Reese followed the agent down the road to the ranch. After being shown the outbuildings and main house, they sat at the dining room table and went over the available leases. They made an offer and waited as the realtor left the house and called on his cell phone.

"Congratulations, your offer has been accepted. If the owner didn't have cancer, the price would have been quite a bit higher. He just wants to tie up his affairs," the realtor said, smiling. "Illness is tragic to some and a benefit to others."

"Tell me where to have the money wired and I'll contact my bank when we get to Rawlins," Gavin said, signing the offer papers.

"This is really your lucky day, Mr. Sanderson. I have the power of attorney to handle all the financial matters. We can wrap this up as soon as the money arrives." Greer handed Gavin a sheet of paper. "Here's the legal description and wire transfer bank number. This should be everything you need."

"Why don't we plan on meeting you at your office day after tomorrow," Gavin said. "I would like to get in as soon as possible."

"Of course. If you're ready to go, I'll get back and start getting everything ready for your signature Wednesday. Simple as that."

On the way back to Rawlins, Reese slumped in the car seat. "Man, you're good. Hell, I know who you are but for a little bit I even thought you were Sanderson."

"Thank you. I will be Sanderson in a week or two. Start calling me Ed from now on. You've got to get used to it. Gavin McQuery is going on a hiatus."

They spent their last night at the motel before moving to the ranch and preparing for the Sandersons to come out. Gavin told Bodine to drive to Billings, Montana and purchase a list of items. "One thing we absolutely can't do is have a gun around. We get caught with one it's back to the joint and the whole scheme is blown to hell. Everyone will go down, believe me. I want both of your words. No firearms."

"We need something," Reese said. He seemed determined to change Gavin's mind. "There's places to hide a gun where no one will find it."

"No chances. Here's what we're going to do." Gavin showed the list to Reese. "You know more about it than me, I'm sure. Have him get what you want."

Reese scanned the paper then chuckled. "This is good. You're a sly fox, Gavin. Crossbows and crossbow pistols. No registration, no laws against an ex-con having one. Perfect. But why have Ike go all the way to Billings?"

"Yeah," Bodine chimed in. "That's gonna take me a couple of days. Why can't I just go to Cheyenne or Casper?"

"Because if we need to use them, I wouldn't think the cops would check out of state to see who bought some bows and arrows." He patted Bodine on the back. "After you get back, shave your beard off... and wear a cowboy hat when you buy the stuff."

"You gonna pay for gas and chow?"

"Of course. But here's the final question," Gavin looked to Reese who moved to stand in front of the door. "Are you in with us all the way? This is going to make us rich, but there might be some things you have to do that'll be the ultimate crime. You understand what I'm saying?"

Bodine nodded his head and drew his finger across his throat. "Yeah, I understand what you're saying. I ain't ever gonna get much money working hard for it. I'm in all the way."

Reese came away from the door and gripped his shoulder. "Hey, man, I'm glad you're with us. I said we could count on you, didn't I, Gavin?"

"You did my man, I never had a doubt."

Gavin gave Bodine an envelope of cash and gave his instructions again. "Buy the cross-bows and arrows in Billings and wear a hat. The less anyone can notice about you the safer for us in the long run." He opened the connecting door to his room. "I'll talk to you later," he said to Reese. "Drive careful and we'll see you day after tomorrow," he told Bodine.

Forty-five minutes later, there was a knock on his door and Reese came in.

"He's not the sharpest guy I've ever met, but as long as he'll follow orders and not get too many dumb spells, we can use him," Gavin said, lying on the bed.

"I'm not worried. He used to do about anything I wanted him to do. I wasn't here when he got busted, but it probably helped him being in the joint for a couple years."

"I hope you're right. Tomorrow we'll meet the realtor and I'll sign the papers."

* * *

They decided to meet for breakfast in the motel restaurant at seven in the morning and leave for the ranch around eight. The realtor had left his home number with Gavin and had agreed to meet them when Gavin called him after leaving Bodine and Reese earlier.

Gavin crawled into bed and had a hard time not smiling. *I got me a golden goose for a while,* he thought, pushing the remote to turn the TV on. He didn't think he'd get much sleep because of his excitement.

* * *

Bodine left early in the morning toward Casper. The best route to Billings would be north from Casper to Sheridan then Billings. All four-lane. He couldn't see why he had to drive all that way. Sure, the safer the better, especially if you buy something that might be used in a big gig. But hell, nobody knew him in Cheyenne. And it was two hundred miles closer. He could go there instead, buy the bows and stuff and then party for a while. No one needed to know. Yeah, Cheyenne sounded better and it was only an hour and a half east from Casper.

Two hours later he parked at the sporting goods store next to Sears in the mall. *Ahhh, forgot the cowboy hat,* he thought, rummaging through the storage area behind the seat of his pickup. *So what? Crap, no one's gonna remember me, and I got a hat.* He pulled the bill down on the hat he had on. It was blue with the logo, Pax's Enterprises, in a white square sign that covered the cap front.

After buying what was on the list, his packages contained three crossbows, three crossbow hand-helds, and two dozen arrow bolts with semi-target tips. The receipt for cash was tapped to one of the bows. Bodine found his way downtown and checked into a decaying motel that advertised kitchenettes rented monthly for two hundred and fifty dollars. A few cars were parked in front of rooms and after getting a room for the night, he walked five blocks down the street to a bar that looked like a place he could pick up a woman. The trip was working out just fine. He had a nice little chunk of Gavin's money left over that would pay for his partying. He'd even give back some change... if he were asked for it.

The booth gave him a view of the front door. When a good-looking woman walked in alone, he'd come up and ask if he could buy her a drink. The three he'd hit up in the first half-hour gave him a cold stare and turned their backs to him. After his fourth drink and no luck on getting a honey, he decided the hell with it and he'd just get drunk. Hell, why not, he was gonna be in the money pretty soon.

At closing time, Bodine was still there, six sheets to the wind, telling the bartender just how he was going to be rolling in the bucks.

"Yeah, sounds interesting. You're going have to leave now, time to close," the bartender said. Bodine followed him to the door and heard it lock as it closed behind him.

"You'll see. You'll all see," he mumbled, staggering down the sidewalk toward the motel. "Ike Bodine's gonna be stinkin' rich one of these days. Then we'll see if you bitches still turn your backs on me."

Chapter Eight

The paperwork was completed on the ranch and three weeks later, the real Edward Sanderson and his son Ronnie were picked up at the Denver airport by Gavin. After the luggage was loaded into the van Gavin rented; they left Denver, taking I-25 to Cheyenne, then I-80 through Laramie to Rawlins.

Trees leaned into the hard wind that blew when they came into town. Gavin took them to a new restaurant that had recently opened for dinner. He hadn't been in town since they took possession of the ranch. They bought supplies in Casper until the time came when Gavin took over Sanderson's identity.

"Is it always this windy?" Sanderson asked. He watched out the dining room window at a door shaking in an old theater across the street.

"Not always, but quite a bit. It should die down after the sun sets.

As they ate, Gavin asked if Sanderson would like to stay overnight in town or go on to the ranch.

"How long will it take to get there?"

"A little over an hour. I just don't want you to be too exhausted. It takes a little time to adjust to the altitude. How're you doing, Ronnie?"

"Great. I think I'm going to love it out here," Ronnie replied. He looked around the room. "Is Dick doing any excavating?"

"He's been setting the site up. You can't go too fast or some of the artifacts might be damaged, and we don't want

44

that. He wanted you to be there before he started the actual work."

Millhouse had flown out two weeks ago and was taken to the site by Reese. The two of them and Bodine spent most of the days making a passable trail without it being obvious. Reese's last question when Gavin was preparing to leave to pick the Sandersons up was, "When are we gonna do them?"

Gavin had been contemplating that. Should he let the father and son enjoy the ranch they bought for a short period of time? Maybe forget the whole plan and just steal the artifacts and sneak away? "Tomorrow. The four of us so everyone is involved. No one less guilty."

Reese smiled and nodded his approval. "I agree. We don't want to take any chances on someone else meeting them. That'd blow the whole thing or add another one to whack."

Gavin's drive to Denver to pick up the Sandersons had him questioning himself if he was inherently evil or nuts. He should keep going south and break away from everybody. He hadn't killed anyone yet, so there was still time. There was money available to him from Sanderson's business account he had access to. Maybe that's what the kicker was. Sanderson had treated them all well. A little too religious, but he had taken the three of them and brought them into his business out of gratitude for taking care of his son.

I could make a good living with Sanderson. I can call off Reese and we can live on the ranch and let Dick work the site. We'll skim some of the artifacts and make a nice bonus. I'm going to do that. Cancel the plan. Reese will be pissed, but too bad.

* * *

Sanderson cleared his throat. He rode in the front passenger seat as they headed north toward the ranch. "A good meal. I'm afraid I have some bad news, Gavin."

Gavin's guts tightened up and he narrowed his eyes. "What's that?"

"I feel the Lord has given me direction. My attorney is in the process of selling the business. I'm going to notify the proper government department about the site so they can arrange to have it protected or made into a tourist site, like the cliff dwellings at Mesa Verde, in Colorado."

"That's very noble, what's the bad news," Gavin asked.

"Well, Dick being an archaeologist and Reese's background warrant keeping them, but I won't have a position for you. I will, however, see if I can find something for you with one of my business acquaintances. There will be a generous severance package too, of course."

"No thanks," Gavin said quietly. He turned to face Sanderson. "Why don't you see what we've done, then decide then what you'll do? I think you'll be in for a pleasant surprise." He turned to Ronnie, who rode in the back seat. "How about you, Ronnie?"

"I'm sorry, Gavin, I have to agree with my father." He turned away and looked out the side window.

"That's fine. I've been getting antsy anyway. It's too wide-open here for me. What if I leave at the end of the week? I'd still like to show both of you what we've done there."

"Certainly, we'd like you to show us what you've accomplished. We have two months before I have to return home. Ronnie and I have things to see so I've left orders not to be disturbed."

"I believe this will work out just fine for me, Mr. Sanderson. To tell you the truth. I hadn't been certain of a direction to go concerning my career, and now, thanks to you, a weight has been lifted off my shoulders," Gavin said.

"I told you the Lord has given direction. For both of us." Sanderson beamed.

* * *

The ranch house had all the lights on. The tour of the buildings and main house ended as the last bloody rays of light colored the sky.

"It is a magnificent sunset," Sanderson said. "Gentlemen, we're tired and ready for bed. Tomorrow we have to have a discussion. Gavin is already aware, but he's not going to talk about it until after we meet. So... goodnight." Sanderson and Ronnie went to separate bedrooms, ones that Reese and Gavin had abandoned the night before.

"What's going on?" Reese demanded in a harsh whisper. They sat in the kitchen. Gavin nodded his head and they walked to the bunkhouse. Millhouse and Bodine lay on bunks.

"Let's have a drink." Gavin took a bottle out of a cupboard and poured four glasses full. "Sanderson and Ronnie are trying to throw a wrench in our deal, but it's too late. We do them tomorrow. Hell, before their meeting so we don't have to listen to his religious crap."

Reese and Millhouse exchanged glances. "What's he figuring on doing?" Reese asked.

"He's planning on giving the site to the feds." Gavin sneered. "The Lord told him to. Like I've said, you can't trust these religious fanatics."

"Are you kidding me? Is this gonna screw us up?" Millhouse asked. He adjusted his glasses and lit a cigarette.

"I thought you quit smoking," Gavin said.

"For a while. Stress, man. I'll quit after this is over." He blew the smoke out of his lungs and coughed.

"No, this doesn't change anything. He hasn't contacted anyone yet. We just might have to go a little faster on the excavation. Give us three to four months max to clean it out."

"How do you want to do them? I'm figuring Ronnie goes with the old man," Reese said. His eyes had a look of anticipation.

"Carefully, I can't emphasize how careful we have to be on every move we make from now on. No mistakes and no going off half-cocked. Now, here's what we do."

Chapter Nine

Edward and Ronnie Sanderson woke up to the smell of fresh brewed coffee. Edward walked into the kitchen dressed in a robe. "This mountain air gives a man an appetite. And look at this breakfast! Ronnie, come and eat," he shouted, sitting down at the table. "This looks wonderful."

Gavin added a stack of pancakes to the platter of bacon, sausage, hash brown potatoes and scrambled eggs on the table. "I thought I'd cook you up my famous hungry man breakfast. This always gets the guys going."

Sanderson took a sample from each pile of food. Ronnie joined him, filled his plate without looking at Gavin, and then both men bowed their heads.

"Thank you Lord for the bounty we're about to receive. With your guidance and love, our lives will be rich in devotion. Amen."

"Amen," Ronnie muttered and began eating.

"This is excellent," Sanderson said between bites. "Perhaps I should rethink my personnel plans."

"Sorry, Mr. Sanderson, I've already got some job interviews back east, thanks to the Internet."

"Good, let me know if I can help you in anyway." Sanderson put his fork down. "You know this isn't personal, don't you? You've been an asset to the company...your talent lies in numbers and management, but when the business is gone, I've no place for you. The ranch needs someone with ranching experience, wouldn't you agree?"

"Absolutely, and you did say the Lord is directing you, right?"

"Ummm, yes. With visions while I sleep. I know the path I'm going to follow," Sanderson said. "I have left orders not to bothered by my attorney until I return, which could be as much as two to three months. So Ronnie and I can learn about the land and possibly see the mummies' tomb without being questioned or interrupted by my office."

"I wonder..." Gavin smiled. "After you dress, I'll show you the site if you like. My last contribution."

"Perfect. Your attitude is why you'll be receiving an enviable severance package. More than the others, I might add."

"Dad, maybe you shouldn't discuss that right now," Ronnie said. He pushed his plate away from him and stood up. "Maybe you and I can visit later," he said to Gavin.

"Sure... and no hard feelings." Gavin stuck his hand out.

Ronnie looked at the hand then at Gavin. A smile broke across his face. He grabbed Gavin's hand and pumped it hard. "Thank God. I didn't want you to be angry with me or Dad. I can hardly wait to see the site." He left the kitchen.

"You are a gentleman," Sanderson said stretching his hand out and shaking Gavin's. "Ronnie had been worried. He was afraid there might be a confrontation."

"His fears were ungrounded now, weren't they?" Gavin released himself from Sanderson's grip and picked up the platter. "When you're ready, we'll get on our way."

* * *

Reese and Bodine rode four-wheelers in front of the Kawasaki Mule, a small pickup looking four-wheeler that held two people in the front seat and two in the rear seat. Gavin drove with Sanderson in the front; Ronnie and Millhouse rode in the back. Millhouse continued to wipe his forehead as they drove over the prairie toward the base of the Ferris Mountains.

"What's the matter, you sick?" Ronnie asked Millhouse.

Millhouse nodded his head and ran a hand over his face. "A touch of the flu. I'll be okay."

Ronnie leaned close and put his hand next to Millhouse's ear. "You're going to stay with us and run the site excavation. Just don't say anything to anybody right now," he whispered.

Millhouse pulled away and vomited over the side of the Mule. He waved Ronnie off.

They came to the ruins of a dilapidated sawmill dug into a ridge with its log walls crumbling and the roof caved in. Gavin stopped and shut the engine off. Bodine and Reese pulled alongside and killed their engines.

"There's some artifacts inside I thought you'd like to see. Not as old as the mummies, but unusual nevertheless." Millhouse stayed in the outfit while Sanderson and Ronnie climbed out and followed Gavin to the building. "Right at the bottom of the wall, by the corner, there's a rock with some pictures carved on it." He moved to the side and away from the Sandersons.

Sanderson bent over and raised back up turning in the direction of Gavin. "There's nothing—" the nineteen inch arrow from the crossbow hit him in the middle of the chest, flinging him back into the wall. His eyes squeezed shut from the pain and his face had a look of bewilderment. "What…" His legs collapsed but he stayed upright. "Lord—" Another bolt hit him in the upper chest and blood bubbled out around the shaft.

Ronnie froze when the first arrow hit his father. He put a hand out to him when the second arrow made a meaty thunk and Sanderson's eyes rolled back in his head. Ronnie turned at the same time an arrow hit the wall next to him. He bolted down the ridge, zig-zagging.

"Don't let him get away, dammit," Gavin yelled. He reached into the duffel bag in the box of the Mule and pulled a crossbow pistol out. "C'mon, Dick. Get your ass out of there."

"I can't," Millhouse said. He had his hand to his mouth. "I can't do it."

"Wait," Reese said, holding a hand up. "I'll get him." He put a belt across his chest that held eight arrows.

"Are you sure?" Gavin demanded. He stood on his tiptoes watching the fleeing figure of Ronnie.

"Oh, yeah. I'm good at this." Reese took off at a lope, not looking back.

Chapter Ten

Ronnie didn't know or care where he was running as long as it was downhill and away from those murderers. A portion of the ridge's top layer was made up of pieces of dried, ancient wood chips and small gravel sized bits of rock - making the footing treacherous and unstable.

Dad, oh God, Dad. Tears blurred his eyes. He wanted to get to a large grove of aspen and pine trees at the bottom of the slope and to the east. If he could get into the trees, he might be able to hide and then work his way to the highway and flag down a car or something.

His foot shot out from under him and he did a slow summersault landing on his back. *Nothing hurt, nothing hurt. RUN!* Ronnie scrambled to his feet and charged downhill. He thought he saw a dark shadow high up the ridge behind him coming his way. His chest heaved and he gulped the thin air trying to oxygenate his burning lungs.

"Keep going, man. Don't give up!" Reese's voice carried down to him.

Like being dosed by ice cold water, fear shriveled his testicles. *Not Reese. He's crazy.* Ronnie got his second wind and raced down the last fifty feet and into the timber.

He dodged around and jumped over fallen trees. A thick canopy of overhead branches blocked most of the sunlight. His running footsteps, the snapping of dead wood splintering and breaking when he stepped on them, and gasping breath was all he heard. Almost falling from exhaustion, Ronnie stopped and leaned against the trunk of a towering pine. He looked wildly around and tried willing his heart to quit beating so hard against his breastbone. He was sure the sound echoed out of the forest like a bass drum beating to a march.

Tears slipped out from the corner of his eyes and dribbled down his cheeks. He muffled a sob of fear, pity and sorrow.

A soft brush of clothing against a pine bough made him jerk his head in the direction of the sound. He couldn't see anyone, maybe his imagination.

WHACK! The arrow lodged in the tree trunk grazing his left ear. Ronnie fell to his side and on hands and knees scrabbled out from under the limbs then getting to his feet and running as hard as he could toward what he hoped would be the highway and safety.

Sharp pine needles cut and scraped his face as he blindly ran through a second growth of pine trees. The terrain began to rise and he saw the forest open into a high clearing surrounded by huge monolithic boulders that seemed to be strewn on the edge of the clearing. Ronnie staggered to a cleft and saw below him in the distance... the highway. Several semi-trucks and cars moved down the blacktop, probably on their way to Rawlins and Casper.

He felt a surge of energy. *I've made it. I'm gonna beat them.* His legs protested with a deep ache when he began to climb over a shelf of rock.

There wasn't any pain at first. One minute he was on his way to freedom and the next he was flat on his stomach still on the shelf. Ronnie shoved himself over with one of his hands. When he rolled on the arrow sticking out of his back, he screamed out from agony and frustration.

His hair was grabbed and pulled his head up, exposing his neck. He couldn't defend himself. "Please, don't kill me," he begged. Quick thoughts flooded his mind: finally a relationship with his father; sitting around drinking with his friends, laughing and talking about their future. His mother.

"Don't." Goddammit, his life wasn't going to end this way, snuffed out for some Indians that had been dead for hundreds of years. No way, by God.

The knife's blade reflected the glint of the sun in his eyes. Warm, moist liquid splashed off his chin with each beat of his heart and pooled under him. Ronnie's eyes blurred from tears of hate. His last thought was, *God, no!*

* * *

Reese was hot and sweaty as he pulled the arrow from Ronnie's back and wiped the blood off the knife blade on the dead man's pants. It had been a long run, but exhilarating. There was a scraping sound as he dragged the body off the shelf and shoved it between two slabs of rock leaning against each other. He'd come back later with the four-wheeler and retrieve the body. The brush was hard to cut, but he got enough to cover the opening of the gap. *Thanks kid, it's been fun.* Reese turned away and headed back to the mountain.

* * *

"Let's just hide him in the sawmill," Bodine said. He looked to Millhouse for support.

"Use your head. How many people explore old buildings like this? We'll take him down and bury both of them in the breaks over there." Gavin pointed to an area where the sagebrush and prairie began at the mountain's edge. "Who's going to notice some digging in the middle of nowhere?"

"You gonna help?"

"Dick is. Get your sorry ass over here and help Ike load Sanderson into the back of the Mule," Gavin ordered the archaeologist. His eyes narrowed and he walked over to Millhouse, grabbing his shirtfront. "Just because you didn't help kill him, don't think you're safe. If we're caught, we all get the needle." He pulled Millhouse to his feet. "Now suck it in and help Ike."

"Look, I want out. I... I didn't realize what was going to happen. Give me my share of what we have now and I'll disappear. I swear, you'll never hear from me again." Millhouse said.

"You'll stay until we're finished. No negotiating, no quitting. Understand?"

"Yeah, I understand. Let me go." Millhouse slapped at Gavin's hand.

"Dick, I like you. Don't push me," Gavin said. He released the shirtfront and stepped back. When he felt sure Millhouse wasn't going to try and attack him, he reached in the back of the Mule and took a rolled tarp out and dropped it on the ground.

Millhouse trudged over to the sawmill building and lifted Sanderson's legs off the ground. Bodine had the dead man's shoulders. Together they carried the body to the Mule and dropped it into the vehicle's bed.

"I'll wait for Reese. Dig a grave big enough for two bodies. Come on back up when you're finished," Gavin said, shading his eyes and looking toward the north. "I'm going to give him another hour then I better go look for him."

The sun hadn't reached high noon when Gavin heard a yell from below him.

"Gavin, bring a four-wheeler and come down." Reese had his hands to the side of his mouth. He stood outside the grove of trees.

The Honda locked its brakes and fishtailed as Gavin rode it down the slope. Reese climbed on the back. "Let's get the other one. I have to bring the kid back on it; he took me on a little more of run than I figured he could. Too damn far to carry him."

On the way back up to the sawmill, Reese asked Gavin what they were going to do with the bodies.

"Ike and Dick are digging a grave over there." He nodded at the two men off in the distance, partially obscured by the Mule. "They aren't going to be found. I've got a tarp here if you need it." Gavin stopped by the other Honda and pointed to the rolled tarp on the ground. "You need me to go with you?" he asked, while Reese tied the tarp to the Honda's back rack.

"Nah, I can do it. Just have his final resting place ready when I get back with him." Reese gave a wolfish grin and started the four-wheeler. "A chase like that makes a man feel alive." He revved the engine and took off down the mountain, gravel flying up behind the tires.

Millhouse and Bodine had dug into the side of the hill under a scrub oak. After shoveling for an hour, a cavern large enough for two bodies had been dug. They deposited their body behind a swarm of roots that protruded down like tentacles from the scrub oak. The roots now looked like a living curtain. After packing dirt over the late Edward Sanderson, whose final resting place lay at the end of the hole, Bodine and Millhouse crawled out from under the roots and squatted by the opening. Millhouse lit a cigarette.

"I thought you were nuts when you started digging under the oak, but it turned out good," Millhouse said, blowing smoke out his mouth. He took a handkerchief and wiped sweat off his forehead.

"Yeah, I'm not as dumb as everyone thinks," Bodine countered. "I like to sit back and see how things go." He shook his head when Millhouse offered him a smoke.

"So... how do you think it's going with two murders now?" Millhouse asked.

"I can live with it. Remember, it had to be done or we wouldn't get nothing," Bodine said. "Money's everything. You can buy booze, cars and most of all, women. Good looking ones, not dogs."

"That's pretty important all right. I mean, to get good-looking women instead of bowsers. Me, it's history through artifacts. Don't get me wrong, I need money to indulge my pleasure, I guess the killing shocked me. Easy to talk about but when it comes time to actually kill someone, it's a different story. At least with me... and I'm not a goody two shoes."

"After the first time, it's easier to do again. You pissed Gavin off, my man. You better get your head out of your ass and make amends," Bodine said. "You're smart, Dick, you'll come around."

Millhouse seemed to mull it over in his mind. "Once again, you've surprised me with your astute observations. Point taken. Thanks."

Their conversation was interrupted when the sound of a four-wheeler coming up from below had them scrambling to their feet. Reese stood on the foot pegs and manhandled the Honda over tall clumps of sagebrush. On the back, a blue covered bundle rocked from the violent thrashing of the machine.

"Here's one more for you," Reese said, pulling up next to them. He leaned over and looked into the hole. "Sanderson already in there?"

Millhouse nodded.

Reese untied the tarp from the four-wheeler's rack and dumped it to the ground. It landed with a heavy thud.

"You want the tarp back?" Bodine asked.

"Leave it. The inside's too bloody. Me and Gavin are going to head back. Make her look like nothings been dug here, Ike."

"No problem. Me and Dick will take care of it."

They watched Reese ride to the top of the ridge and stop at the sawmill. A moment later, both Gavin and Reese were riding the Hondas down the slope toward the ranch.

"See, just answer yassir, and do what they want. Gimme a hand." Bodine kneeled by the tarp and began dragging it to the hole. "Must be a lot of blood," he said, looking at a growing stain at one end.

Millhouse put his hand over his eyes to shade them from the sun and watched the other two men disappear down the mountain. "Let's shove him in lengthwise, then turn him."

"See, I said you was smart." Bodine grinned, showing teeth with dark brown stains.

* * *

Reese and Gavin sat at the desk in the office of the ranch house sipping whiskey when they heard the Mule coming.

"Dick is starting to worry me a little," Gavin said. "I'm beginning to wonder if we can trust him to keep his mouth shut and do his job. He told me he wanted out. Give him his share of what we have."

"He'll be okay. He's not quite the bad boy he tries to be." Reese emptied his glass with one swallow and poured another inch into his glass. "I'll keep an eye on him, but we need him for now, don't you think?"

"Yeah... for now."

Chapter Eleven
Present

The dust devil drew sand and dirt high into its funnel as it danced down the prairie. It stopped on the edge of a sand dune for a moment then broke up and disappeared, leaving only the wind. Bailey Calhoun watched it through squinted eyes and a pounding headache. A hell of a day to have to count cows grazing on leased land. Too many beers the night before and he'd forgotten his damned sunglasses.

He'd been standing outside the pickup, his armpits wet, shirt stained dark from sweat, looking through binoculars at a distant cattle herd. The hood of the truck burned his skin when he'd tried resting his elbows on it to hold the binoculars steady. It always seemed like it was hotter on the south side of the Ferris Mountains.

Oh, man, why'd I do it? He put a hand on the side of his head and rubbed. *I wonder if I puked it'd help?* He took a deep breath. *Suck it up, Calhoun, another hour and you can get back to town and chug down an ice-cold one.* He made one last sweep with the binoculars when he saw a boot where the dust devil had finished its life out. Not only a boot, but also it seemed to have a leg connected to it, sticking out of the eastern edge of a sand dune. His fingers touched the holstered .40 Glock and he looked behind him out of sudden uneasiness.

Adrenaline surged through his veins and blood hammered in his temples so hard from the hangover it nearly blinded him. He was a Bureau of Land Management law enforcement ranger, not a cop anymore. He hadn't been a cop for over twenty years. When it came time to nab somebody trying to rip off some artifacts or antiquities– fine. Riding a four-wheeler where

60

you shouldn't –you'll get busted. Overgraze *our* land and you might have some explaining to do. Mess with what might be a body– not my job.

He laid the binoculars on the truck seat and trudged toward the sand dune. *This is a possible crime scene. Don't trample any evidence that might be here. Just take a look and see if it is a body. Man, I hope it's just trash.*

He tried to remember some procedures from years ago and not keel over from the effects of so much booze the night before. Maybe it'll be a pile of rags and an abandoned boot, or if it is a body, some old bum who took the last walk of his life before he died naturally. But he knew instinctively it would be more than that. Bums and derelicts didn't wander the desert out in the middle of nowhere.

Bailey cursed silently. The two-way radio in his truck had uttered its last static gasp a couple of days ago and had been shipped to Cheyenne to be fixed - which meant he'd have to drive almost ten miles over two-track dirt roads to the Stone Gulch Ranch to use the telephone so he could call the sheriff's office. He looked up and saw several turkey buzzards circling overhead. Never too far away for a tasty treat.

He spit and walked upwind in the direction of the boot. The desert sucked away the moisture from his saliva.

No signs of tire tracks from trucks or ATVs, only sand blown against the sagebrush like dirty whitecaps on a lake.

It was a body. A man, he thought, lying face down in a shallow grave with sand over part of his back and shoulders, the rest of the corpse exposed from the course of the dust devil. He wanted to maintain his distance so there wouldn't be any evidence he might stomp on and obliterate with his size thirteen boots.

Bailey squatted down and tried to see a wound. The hair on the back of the dead man's head was matted and dirty. He could see what looked like a spray of dried blood on the shirt collar, but no hole. *Don't do it, you know better.* He stood up and watching the sand in front of him, walked closer to the body. He knelt down again and could see the bullet hole this time, a smooth hole, not ragged— the entrance — and he was shot close enough to burn the hair away. The way the guy looked was different than some of his buddies who took a small arms round in the head in the last hurried days of Viet Nam. No mass destruction, just a hole, like a finger pushed through the skin of a rotten apple. It didn't stink too bad and no bloating he could determine, so he'd probably only been there a day or so.

The clothes didn't look old or threadbare; Bailey couldn't tell the age of the person other than what little of the hair was visible and not bloodied, gray and waving in the wind. He could see one hand lying out to the side, its fist clinched. There was a sparkle of something hidden by the flesh of the palm, but he knew better than to try and open the hand to see what was in it. Bailey would like to have seen how much rigor mortis the body had, if any, but he wasn't going to find out. He remembered it took somewhere around twelve hours to set in and the rigor came and then left. He couldn't recall if a body got rigor again after the first time. Touching the body would be a bad move, disturb the body of a possible murder scene and he'd end up getting busted.

A glint of sunlight forward of the corpse caught his eye. The crack from his knees and an unintended grunt when he stood up reminded him of his passing years. Bailey called it middle age, which it was, if he lived to be a hundred.

A pair of gold-colored wire frame glasses lay on the sand with one of the lens intact and pieces of the other still clinging to an empty lens frame. *They most likely blew off when the guy was shot,* Bailey thought, so the bullet probably came out the front of the guy's face or the force of the bullet hitting his head was enough to send them flying.

Bailey went back to his truck, got in, and took off down the road toward the nearest telephone.

A green Ford pickup, with the insignia of an antelope's head on the side door, rumbled down a bluff. A game warden. Bailey flashed his lights, honked his horn and accelerated. The Ford's brake lights came on and the truck pulled to the side of the road. Bailey parked behind it and saw the warden getting out of the truck was Catlyn Ropper.

"What's up, Bailey?" She walked back toward his pickup with a nice stride.

"There's a body back up the road, can you radio the sheriff's office for me? Mine's out." Bailey pointed over his shoulder with his thumb. "Guy's been murdered."

"Murdered? Wow! Hold on." Catlyn went back to her truck and a moment later motioned for Bailey as she held the microphone up in her hand. "You tell them the info, it'll save me being the third baseman."

He gave the dispatcher the location, told them he'd go back and wait, and yeah, don't worry, he wouldn't approach the scene.

"I've got to go back and wait for them. They said they'd like you there, too."

"I don't know why, I haven't seen him. But, what the hell, no problem. You want me to have the dispatcher call your office and fill them in?" Cat picked the microphone up and waited for his answer.

"Sure, I appreciate it."

"How'd the guy get killed, do you know?" she asked.

"Looks like he got shot in the back of the head. I didn't move him so who knows what else they'll find? I'll meet you down there." Bailey got in his truck and turned around. As he drove back down the road, he took a bottle of Pepto Bismal out from his console and chugged a third down. When he stopped at the area, he threw four Certs into his mouth and got out as Cat pulled up and parked behind him.

"This isn't a good day for me, Cat. Not even counting finding the body, I feel like I oughta be dead," he said, rubbing the back of his neck.

"Too much partying?"

"No, it's not booze, probably the twenty-four hour flu." He wondered if she believed his bullshit. Probably not, Cat was a smart woman. "It's lucky I was out here and found him now," he said, changing the subject.

"Why's that?" she asked.

"He's buried on the east side of the sand dune." Bailey pointed in the direction of the dune. "If the dust devil wouldn't have uncovered him, the wind would have eventually moved the dune over him. Hell, after a week or two, he might not have been found for fifty or sixty years, if at all."

"Really."

"Yup. And me deciding to check some cows on leased land today. Guess this is somebody's lucky day."

"Just because of a mini-tornado and some cows. Imagine that," Cat said, looking in the direction he pointed.

"I'm going to sit in the truck and rest my eyes until the deputies get here. You can join me if you let me doze a bit."

"You go ahead, I've got some paper work to do and this will be a good time to finish it," she said and then frowned. "I was out around here yesterday and didn't see anything. No outfits, no nothing." Cat shook her head and climbed in her truck.

Bailey appreciated her tight-fitting pants. *Are those department issue?*

* * *

A little over an hour later, a sheriff's Bronco and a black, four-wheel drive Suburban the county coroner used to pick up corpses, came into sight. Bailey woke up with a start when Cat banged on his pickup's hood.

"Here they come, make yourself presentable, sweetheart," she quipped. "You look like crap, if I may so rudely say." Her hand slid in the window and on his arm. She squeezed it hard. She waved at the vehicles as they came nearer.

He looked in the rear view mirror and saw bloodshot eyes and a ragged face lined with troubles looking back at him. *I do look bad,* he thought. *I gotta ease off on the booze a bit. Maybe hold myself to a six pack at a time.*

The corner walked with the deputies as they took their equipment out of their vehicle and began to video the scene from the road. He was waiting for them to finish so he could begin his own check of the body. A statement was taken from Bailey, and later, Cat.

"You didn't approach the body?" Undersheriff Jordan asked Bailey, while looking at the footprints in the sand. He had close-set eyes and a gut-roll covered his belt buckle.

"I had to make sure it wasn't a pile of rags, but I didn't touch anything," Bailey said defensively. "I know the drill."

"Since you seem to be half drunk, I need to know," Jordan said.

"Piss off, Jordan. I'm sober and left things like I found them. You got a problem with me, call my supervisor." Bailey saw Jordan staring at his bloodshot eyes. He turned his head and slowly shook it.

"Don't get upset, Calhoun. I'm just making an observation." Jordan smirked and walked away. After the sheriff had suffered a heart attack, Jordan reveled in being the big gun running the office while the sheriff recouped.

A deputy holding the video camera filmed the grave, body and surrounding area. He put the video down and with a small hand camera, took digital pictures of the scene.

Finally the body was completely uncovered and put into a body bag, carried to the coroner's suburban, and loaded into the back by the coroner and two deputies. Jordan told the third deputy to get in the Bronco.

"Oh, by the way." he stopped. "If you think of anything more, Calhoun, call us, okay? Cat, you're looking good, hon, talk to you later."

She nodded, her arms crossed. "Shove off," she said to his retreating back. "What a fat, worthless piece of shit."

The coroner's wagon had already left with the body, dust from the road still riding the wind from the receding Suburban. The Bronco spun its tires as it started toward town, spraying Bailey and his truck with sand and gravel.

"Son-of-a-bitchin' Jordan," he said to Cat, harshly. "What a piece of work."

He thought he saw her eyes fill with sympathy. "Don't say anything. I know I seem like I'm pissing my life away, but I'm not." He patted her shoulder as he walked past her to his truck. "Thanks for your help. I'll talk to you later." As he pulled away, the image of her standing in the road was in his rearview mirror.

Chapter Twelve

On the drive back to Rawlins, Bailey felt the humiliation of Jordan's words.

Amazing how a guy can fall from the fraternity so quick, he thought.

From hero to drunk in less than twelve months. From comradeship to avoidance, to finally tolerance as long as I don't go over the line too much. Who needs them?

After the wild horse incident and until the big C grabbed Dana, he had been riding pretty high. It seemed like everyone knew him and wanted to say hello. Even though he was a little on the introverted side, he had to admit he enjoyed the attention. Now, the only attention he got were questioning looks and poor job appraisals.

When the front door closed behind him at the BLM office, Peter Wales, the District Supervisor, waited for him and motioned Bailey into his office. The hallway seemed longer than usual.

"The sheriff's office called and advised me of the body you found. Hell of a note. You okay?" Wales asked.

"Yeah, I'm fine. A bit of a shock, you know. Guess it was luck I was there at the right place and the right time. Of course, that's only if you consider finding some guy with a bullet in his head, luck." Bailey rolled his neck. "I've had a bit of the flu so feeling a little queasy didn't help either."

"We need to talk about your *flu.*" Wales stood up and closed his office door, then sat back down and pulled his chair around the side of the desk, nearer to Bailey. "You're sweating booze. I can smell it emanating from you. If I thought you were drunk now, I'd be forced to suspend you. I ought to have you take a chromatograph test."

"I—"

Wales held his hand up. "No tales or excuses... please. I want to do all I can to help you. There's a psychiatrist the department uses in Cheyenne; you have an appointment with him next Friday."

Bailey shook his head. "I don't need a shrink. Look, I appreciate your concern, but I'm not as bad as you seem to think. What little problems I have, I'm them working out." He put a hand over his eyes. "I might be overindulging a little at night, but it hasn't affected my work."

"Undersheriff Jordan spoke with me before you got here." Wales said, leaning closer to Bailey. "He said you were 'three sheets to the wind.'"

"You can see I'm not," Bailey said defensively. "Jordan's been after my ass for the last couple of months."

"You don't think threatening to beat the hell out of him would be considered a reason?"

"There's a little more to it than what meets the eye. He—"

"I know. I know the whole story and it's water under the bridge. Seemed to me you were a little too officious, but what the hell, he didn't have a tag on his four-wheeler. Everyone knows you don't like each other."

"I didn't know liking someone had anything to do with enforcing the law," Bailey replied.

Wales sighed and handed him a piece of paper. "It doesn't, but we know you turn a blind eye to things you don't think are too bad." He scooted back behind his desk. "No more argument – next Monday, Dr. Radcliffe's in Cheyenne. Make sure you show up, Bailey."

Bailey took the paper. "Can I use my work truck?"

"Of course. This is government business. Other than lunch and gas there shouldn't be any more expenses." Wales tried to grin, but it came off weak.

Bailey sighed and stood up. "Anything else for me, Peter?"

"There's a new owner of the Steamboat Lake Ranch. He's called about securing a new lease, maybe you can take care of it tomorrow." Wales stood up also. "We're just trying to help you, nothing more or less. Everyone said you used to be a good ranger. Since I've been here, the opinion could be debatable. But I like you. Don't make me regret giving you a last chance."

"I suppose the entire office knows about the shrink appointment."

"No, only you, Dr. Radcliffe and me. If anyone hears about it, it'll be from you."

Bailey left the office tight-lipped. *Last Chance? God damn, was everything going to hell right now?*

On his way home, he stopped at the local McDonald's and picked up some burgers and fries. Across the highway at the grocery's liquor store, Bailey started to buy a twelve pack of Bud Light. *Nope. Not tonight. Did he say, last chance?* "Never mind," he said to the man behind the counter as he turned and walked out the store empty-handed.

Callie, his half Great Pyrenees - half cattle dog, greeted him with her tail wagging at the back door. She reared up and sniffed the sack of food in his hand.

"Hold on girl, dammit." Two burgers went into the dog's dish and the other two he put on a paper towel. "Time to smarten up, girl. Dana wouldn't be too proud of me right now, would she?" He downed the first burger in four bites and the last one he ate half and gave the rest to the dog. Cutting the booze out might be a little harder than he thought. His mind said no, his body said one or two wouldn't hurt. *I'm not a goddamn alky, I like the taste. Is that a crime? Hell no. I can do without it. No problem.* He opened the refrigerator and took out a wine bottle with an inch of liquid in the bottom. It went down his throat in a short gulp. *Good for my heart.*

The trash can was full, dirty dishes were stacked in the sink and clothes, both clean and dirty, were scattered around the living room. Bailey lifted the front of his shirt to his nose and sniffed. "Whoa!" He coughed.

The bedroom was dark and oppressive, the blinds pulled and the bed unmade. A smell similar to sweat and dirty socks assaulted him like a sucker punch. He gathered some clothes and took his uniform off, putting them all in the clothes washer. His reflection in the bathroom mirror made him wonder how he could have drifted so low without noticing. Maybe he did and just didn't give a shit anymore. A face puffy from lack of sleep and too much booze, beer belly hanging over the waistband of his shorts and hollow eyes with a touch of fear and realization in them. The vomit spewed from his mouth as he lunged toward the toilet. *Dammit, Dana. Why'd you ask me?*

Peter Wales came into the BLM office at 7:45 A.M. and couldn't hide his look of surprise. There was Bailey, working at his desk in a clean, pressed uniform. He walked over and asked, "You'll get out to the Steamboat Lake Ranch today for the leases?"

"I was, but the owner called and said he'd be gone until Monday, so I'll go out first thing Monday morning," Bailey replied. He made sure Wales could smell his breath and see his eyes. Clear as a reformed whore. "I want you to know I appreciate what you're doing for me, and I'm going to work on the problem." Said with the honesty of a lying whore. It still pissed him off having to go see a psychiatrist.

Wales gripped Bailey's arm. "Anything I can do, let me know. We're behind you all the way, Bailey." He went to his office with a smile on his face while Bailey watched him with a somber, tired look.

"Carbon County Sheriff's Office, Deputy Kelly speaking."

"Larry, this is Bailey Calhoun. How are you doing?'

"Fine," he said, suspicion in his voice. "What can I do for you?"

Kelly had been a pallbearer for Dana. Like most of his friends, Bailey had nearly alienated him like he had the others.

"Do you have a name yet on the dead man?"

"No, we're running the prints through NCIC. If they're on record we should know something later today," Kelly answered.

"He had something in his hand, what was it?"

"Ahhh, I don't know if I should be telling you any of this since there's an ongoing investigation."

"C'mon, Larry. You know I'm not going to blab anything. Give me a break."

Bailey heard the sigh over the telephone. "It was like a bracelet, but we think it's made from gold. There's some kind of a diagram or something on it, too."

"Can you let me see it?"

"Hell no, you pissed Jordan off again. You're *non-gratis* around here now," Kelly said.

"I might be, but artifacts and antiquities fall into my jurisdiction, whether Jordan likes it or not."

"I don't know why you have to keep screwing with him."

Bailey sighed. "I'm not. He's the one who accused me of being drunk yesterday."

"Maybe, but I'm not going to get in the middle of it. Jordan's my boss. I think a murder investigation takes precedence over artifacts, don't you?" There was a long pause. "No promises, but I'll try and take a couple of pictures and get them to you later. That's the best I can do, Bailey. Take it or leave it."

"Beggars can't be choosers. Call me when you have them, okay?"

"Why don't you meet me at the shooting range tomorrow? About ten," Kelly said. "You're off on Saturdays, aren't you?"

"Yeah. Ten, tomorrow. I'll see you there. Thanks, man."

"Keep this quiet."

"I will. I can't piss off my last buddy now, can I?"

"No, you can't," Kelly said frankly.

"You'll include a copy of the autopsy report, too, right?"

"Hell, why not? I can only get fired once." Kelly sighed again. "Don't screw me, Bailey. If you do, I'll get even."

"Don't worry, wild horses won't drag anything out of me."

When he left the courthouse, Bailey saw Cat drive by on the street in her game warden pickup. He waved, but didn't see any acknowledgement from her. *She's a fine looking woman. I wonder if she'd go out with me.* He smiled. *I can't believe I'm thinking about asking her out.* He felt a stirring that had been absent for quite a while.

Bridger Pass didn't really fall into his area, but with a couple of hours left until he could knock off from work, he thought a ride out south of Rawlins would give him some peace. He saw Cat's truck with the red lights blinking as he dropped down from the pass and onto a flat. A burly man with a full beard and collar length hair stood outside his truck hammering on the hood and appeared to be shouting. Cat stood toe to toe, in his face.

Bailey pulled behind her pickup and climbed out. "What's the problem?" he asked, ambling up to her side.

He thought she looked relieved. "Mr. Gregory here thinks it's okay to shoot at antelope with his twenty-two. He—"

"It ain't none of your business," Gregory said to Bailey, interrupting. "This doesn't have nothin' to do with the BLM, so why don't you beat it." He turned back to Cat. "You fuckin' game wardens—"

Bailey grabbed him around his throat and shoved him back onto his truck's hood. "You don't talk that way in front of women." Bailey squeezed with his thumb and fingers. "Understand, sport?"

Gregory tried ineffectively to yank Bailey's hand off. He gagged and nodded his head. "I'm gonna sue your ass," he said when Bailey released him.

"Go ahead," Cat said. "I'll charge you with wanton destruction and have your license for five years. Plus a month in jail. Your choice."

"He didn't have no cause to choke me." Gregory rubbed his throat.

"You need to watch your mouth," Bailey said.

"What's it going to be, Mr. Gregory? I think it'd be best if we forget this whole incident, don't you?" Cat opened her citation book. "I can handcuff and haul you to jail right now."

"I don't sue, you don't charge me?"

"Yeah, no charges." Cat's eyes bored into his. "But remember, there's no statute of limitations on game violations. I hear one word about this and you'll be sitting in a cell counting bars." She paused, then said, "Got it?"

"I got it. For now."

"Keep this in mind also, it's our word against yours. Two law enforcement officers against a game violator. Make it easy on yourself."

Gregory gave Cat and Bailey a dark look as he climbed into his truck.

"Jeeze, Bailey," she said, watching Gregory's truck moving down the road. "You could have gotten in big trouble. I appreciate your helping me out, but, damn, man…you're wired."

"You're welcome. Sorry if I compromised you. It felt good, though." He grinned at her and tipped his hat. "I'll see you later. Thanks for making a deal with him," he said, getting in his pickup. *I probably blew it to hell on her going out. Damn, what a nice looking body.*

He waved out the window after he made a u-turn and accelerated toward town.

* * *

The wind blew hard out of the west when Bailey showed up at the outdoor shooting range at 9:30 A.M. For some reason, the idea of actually doing a little target practice appealed to him, even if he had to aim twenty yards to the left of the target.

He didn't think the gunfire would make his headache any worse and thanks to finding a bottle of Visine in his medicine chest, his bloodshot eyes magically disappeared. *Not a drop last night and I feel like I've been on a binge.*

It took four clips of .40 caliber bullets fired at the target until he started hitting the number two ring on the chest of the silhouette. If he had to shoot anyone, they were going to have to stand still until he got sighted in. Kelly drove up in his personal pickup while Bailey was reloading the clips.

"I hope if anyone ever shoots at me, it's you," Kelly said, looking at the target thirty yards away.

"Yeah, no shit. What do you have for me?"

Kelly handed Bailey a manila envelope. He hadn't gotten out of the truck or shut it off. "The dead guy is Richard Millhouse. Guess what his profession is? Or was, I should say."

Bailey had the envelope open but closed the flap when the wind almost took it out of his hand. "Oil field roustabout? Cook? Old BLM guy?"

"An archaeologist. He's got a rap sheet with one entry listed. Grand Larceny. The dude stole and sold artifacts. He spent a couple years in a federal pen."

"I'll be damned. This makes me more involved if artifacts come into play. Now, why was he there? Did somebody kill him somewhere else and bury him by the dune or kill him where I found him and cover him up?" Bailey's face lit up. "Jordan's gonna like having to share some information with me."

"Hold on, you can't say anything to him or it'll be my ass. He'll know who gave you the information since I'm the only one who still talks to you." Kelly thumped his hand on the steering wheel. "Don't screw me, Bailey," he pleaded and warned at the same time.

"Don't worry. Like you said, you're the only one who still talks to me. You got me some pictures, didn't you?"

"Yeah, different angles, with a ruler for size comparison. I'm going to go." Kelly put the truck in reverse. "Remember, don't say anything or it's my ass." This time it was a warning.

"I won't, and thanks." Bailey took his pistol and can of bullets and clips and sat in his truck, the manila envelope clinched in his teeth. He took the color pictures out and laid them in his lap. The item was a small circular band of possibly copper, and appeared to be inlaid with gold that formed some kind of hieroglyphics. The ruler next to it showed its diameter to be about four inches. *Must be a bracelet of some sorts*, though Bailey had never seen an artifact with a similar design. God, he'd love to have it in his hand so he could check it out with the experts. If nothing could be determined by the picture, somehow, he would have to shake Jordan loose from it without screwing Kelly.

Chapter Thirteen

The sun had an hour to go before setting and Bailey could feel the urge beginning in the bottom of his gut. *Go until dark, only a couple more hours, no big deal, right? Sure.* He licked his lips and brushed a hand over his face. *No problem.*

Bloody fingers from the sunset caressed the clouds. After the third look out of the window he figured it was late enough. Cocktail hour. The first one went down smooth and took the edge off. He sat in the recliner with the open folder Kelly had given him, looking at the pictures of the bracelet again.

By the time he'd finished the eighth beer and a large glass of white merlot wine, to, he always liked the term, cleanse his palate, the folder was on the floor next to the gun cleaning kit and he had the .40 Glock in his hand. Its dull black frame reflected the light dully from the lamp and the heft felt good in his hand. *What would it feel like?* The feel of the trigger sent a morbid thrill through him and when he stuck the barrel inside his mouth, his eyes closed. His tongue slipped around the end of the barrel, tasting the gun oil. *So easy. Just pull the trigger. No more worries, no more thinking about Dana.*

"Jesus Christ!" He took the pistol out from his mouth and eased his finger off the trigger. *Is this from drinking wine with the beer?* Or did he have a death wish scratching the surface for some closure. Permanent closure if he'd have pulled the trigger. Maybe he'd cut the wine out of his drinking menu, except it gave a quick shot toward the welcoming buzz.

He took the phone and poked some numbers in. After a wrong number, he went to the desk and got the address book. No answer, the ringing tone keep going until an electronic voice told him, "Sorry, we can't come to the phone right now, leave a message and we'll get back to you." He put another set of numbers in and it was answered on the second ring.

"Knight." The voice sounded heavy with sleep.

"Hey, Travis. What's going on?" Bailey thought he might have detected a bit of a slur when he spoke.

"Bailey? You okay? It's two in the morning."

"Uh, yeah, everything's hunky dory. I wanted to talk to you about something, but it'll wait until Monday. Sorry I woke you up, I didn't realize it was so late."

"We can talk, what do you have?" Travis asked in a tired voice.

Did he hear a sigh?

"It'll keep. Like I said, I didn't know it was so late."

Bailey hung the phone up thinking he'd probably screwed himself again if Travis squealed to Wales. He'd find out Monday if he was in deep shit.

One more call. Too bad he had to be loaded to make it.

"Ropper," she said, sounding alert.

"Cat, how're you doing?"

"Bailey? What's the matter?"

"Nothing. I had an urge to talk to you, without it being work related. Look, I don't bullshit over the phone very well. Any chance you might like to go out one of these days?" *There, it was asked. Hopefully she'll turn me down gently.*

Her voice grew husky. "I've been hoping you'd ask me sometime. You've interested me for a while now, ever since the seminar you gave about the refuge last spring."

"Maybe I'll call you later this week and see what you're doing."

"Do that," she said through a yawn. "I'll be expecting to hear from you."

His clothes left a trail to the bedroom. The sweat made for soggy dreams.

Bailey, now. If you love me.

I know I'm a cold-hearted prick, but what you're asking me...

Help me go.

He shot up in bed. The sheets were soaked from sweat running down his sides and off his back. In his mind's eye he saw her lying in bed, a monitor hooked up showing her respiration and heart rate. One slim plastic tube ran down to the needle inserted into her arm, a morphine drip to try and ease the pain. It was all they could do. The insurance allowed a home health care nurse to come by once a day. Since the chicken-shit HMO wouldn't let her go to anyone except those in their system, which meant only Wyoming doctors, he'd spent his savings and re-mortgaged their house so she could go to John Hopkins Hospital. John Hopkins had the leading technology and research for pancreatic cancer, but they couldn't do anything either.

"Take her home and make her comfortable," the doctor had said.

"How long does she have?" Bailey couldn't believe it, not Dana.

"Two to three months," we can't be more accurate. She could even go six, but I doubt it."

"Will she be in a lot of pain?" Tears welled in his eyes.

"There's drugs to help. I'm sorry. I wish I could give you some hope, but I can't." The tears he must have seen form in Bailey's eyes didn't appear to embarrass him, he had to be used to giving death sentences.

Again, like so many nights, he lay back down and stared out the window until he fell asleep. It usually took several hours and this night wasn't any different.

* * *

Sunday didn't repeat the night before. Bailey went dry. He decided during the work week, and especially before meeting the shrink Friday, discretion would be prudent. He did use the Visine again before leaving for work Monday morning. A wonderful over the counter medication.

He peeked in the field archaeologist's office and saw it empty. "Hey, Dora. Where's Marc?" he hollered down the hall.

"Not in yet, obviously," she replied.

"He should be though, right? I mean, he's not out of town or on vacation?"

"Hold on to your horses, it's not even eight yet."

Travis knocked on Bailey's open office door and poked his head in the doorway. "Did you want to talk about something?"

"Not right now," Bailey replied. "I need to look into a few things then we'll get together. Sorry about the call."

"No problem. I've felt the same way sometimes. I've wanted to talk some things over and didn't realize how late or early it was. It's cool." He leaned against the door jam.

It is cool. He won't say anything, at least this time.

"What are you doing today?" Travis asked.

"Why?" Bailey steeled himself for some good Samaritan talk.

"I'm gonna be out at the refuge later, you want to have lunch at Grandma's? Just eat, nothing else," Travis jingled keys in his front pants pocket.

"Yeah. How about around noon or so. I've got to go over to the Wood's place first."

"See you there."

"Travis?"

"Yeah."

"I don't know if I've told you, but you're doing a good job. I'm proud of you," Bailey said. "How many more hours you need to qualify for the enforcement ranger title?"

"One more semester and the on-the-job with you." Travis looked at Bailey with a puzzled look. "Why?"

"Maybe I can start working with you pretty soon. After I get some stuff settled."

"I'd appreciate it, Bailey. Enough so I'll buy lunch if it's not too much." He smiled and left.

He's not a bad kid. One you can ride the river with.

His phone rang; it was Marc asking what he wanted.

The archaeologist's desk overflowed with books, maps and stacks of paper.

"Your desk looks worse than mine," Bailey said, coming into the office and tossing the pictures on top of the desk blotter.

"We do more work, therefore more desk clutter. What's this?" Marc picked the pictures up and scrutinized them. "Interesting, what is it?"

"I hoped you could tell me. A dead man had it in his hand. The guy was murdered."

"Holy smoke." Marc put the pictures down and took a thick book off a shelf. He leafed through it then picked another book and thumbed through it also. "I hate to admit it, but I don't know. There's nothing in the reference books, nothing I've seen before, but it's definitely older Indian. I'd say a couple hundred years or better." He looked at the pictures again. "I don't recognize the hieroglyphics. Want me to send them to the HAC at district?

"What the hell is HAC?" Bailey asked, reaching for the pictures.

"Honcho Archaeologist in Charge. Gifford Chandler. A bit on the arrogant side but knows his artifacts," Marc said, releasing his hold on the picture.

"No thanks, I'll be there Friday, do me good to mingle with the upper echelon of the BLM."

"Let me know what you find out, will you?"

"Sure. Thanks for your help," Bailey said.

* * *

The road to the Stone Gulch Ranch made its way through gullies and sagebrush heading in the direction of the south side of the Ferris Mountains, with its ragged limestone outcroppings and a dozen peaks. The range stretched for better than eighteen miles from the west to the east. After the tree line ended, towering peaks of naked rocks laced with fissures and black ravines reached high into the clouds that were settled over the mountain top. A rugged, untamed wilderness where few people went because of the absence of trails and every slope so steep a herd of mountain sheep had been transplanted there.

A two-track dirt road, sometimes impassable after the wind blew hard and covered the road with deep drifts of sand, worked in and out of arroyos and gullies and over ridges and hills. The ranch used to be a stage stop back in the late 1880's and a corner of the jail still stood at the ranch entrance. This was the eastern edge of the high plains Red Desert. A person could drive the back roads all day and never see anyone. In the late fifties and sixties, modern man had searched for oil and gas and left his equipment rusting away and scattered over the prairie. One never knew when he'd come upon an empty oil tank, an abandoned well pump, the remnants of a forgotten pumping station or a running gas compressor still chugging and backfiring as it pumped natural gas to a buried pipeline. A perfect place to kill someone and hide the body until the coyotes dug it up and feasted, unless a dust devil uncovered the grave and someone happened to find it.

The ranch house was built into a hill and couldn't be seen until you drove through the gate and past the barn. The ranch lay in a large gulch shadowed by the Ferris Mountains. Bailey saw Albert and Jean Wood unloading hay bales from a trailer and the hay stack they were making inside the barn. They waved when they saw him and kept unloading the bales. Their dog ran up and jumped up, pawing the side of the truck door.

"Barney, get the hell off." Albert yelled.

Bailey parked his truck, and with a perfunctory greeting, climbed up on the trailer and started heaving the bales off.

"Albert, you and Jean are too old for this, why don't you get some help?" Bailey panted after picking up and throwing a dozen bales to the ground. Jean grabbed the wire holding the bales together and dragged them to the stack.

"We do when we have some hard work, but this is easy," Albert chided, trying to keep from grinning. "You aren't getting tired already are you, Bailey?"

"Nope, I can do this all day if I don't have a heart attack." He grunted and threw another bale of hay from the trailer. "If I die here today, bury me overlooking the prairie, okay?"

After the trailer was empty, Albert, driving a tractor with a bale fork on the front, lifted the bales and settled them on higher tiers of the stack. When the last bale was set and the tractor shut off, they went into the ranch house where Jean brought over glasses of lemonade to the kitchen table.

Bailey had a folder with him and laid it on the table. "Time to renew the north section lease." He pushed the form over to Albert and handed him a pen. "Don't ask me why you got to fill the whole thing out every time. Guess it's good they're only due every two years."

"I'll get it done this week and mail it to you. How about something to eat?" Albert asked, sliding the pen back.

"I'd like to, but I'm meeting Travis for lunch in Lamont. I can just make it if I hurry."

"How's the young man doing?" Jean asked.

"Pretty good. He's the BLM wildlife ranger now, so the refuge is part of his job. He got a quick lesson last year, you know."

"Land's sake, I'd forgotten, the poor boy. But it doesn't surprise me he's doing well, he's always been bright." Jean gazed out the window, a thoughtful look on her face. "I had him as a student in some of my classes. He should fit in with the refuge; I remember he seemed sensitive to wildlife."

"I could never figure out why you like those wild horses so much, pain in the butt for us." Albert said, sipping from the glass. "But, you don't ranch, so what the hell would you know, huh?"

"Don't start with him, Albert," Jean admonished. "We appreciate all your help Bailey, and Albert doesn't mean anything. He's just getting ornery and nasty in his old age."

"I'm used to it. Just a cantankerous old fart, right Albert?" Bailey said.

"I've got lunch to fix, thanks again for your help, Bailey," Jean patted his arm and began to walk back to the kitchen. Music from the radio drifted out moments later.

"She looks fit, I hope you aren't working her to death," Bailey said.

"I'll go long before her, you can bet your last dollar on that." Albert snapped his fingers. "Hey, before I forget, let me show you something I found on the mountain the other day," Albert said. "It's a hell of an artifact."

"Goddammit, you know you aren't supposed to keep stuff if you found it on government land," Bailey said, exasperated. "The law says you turn them in to us, your federal land guardians." The sarcasm went unnoticed by Albert.

"Oh, right. I forgot you're the arrowhead police. Excuse me. This is damn interesting, really different. I've never seen nothing like it."

"No. I don't want to see it, not when I'm working. I'll come out some time and you can show me after we've had some beers."

"I'm not giving it to the government, they'll keep it," Albert said. A crafty look crossed his face. "I never said I found it on government land."

"You said the mountain, and it's all BLM. Nice try though. You know I'm not gonna confiscate it, but knock it off, will you?"

"Is that a promise?"

"Are you serious?"

"Yeah, I want your word."

"Okay. I won't take it. My word." Bailey couldn't decide if Albert was screwing with him or not. *Your word...is he serious?* "You can show me next time I'm here. I'll come out and pick up the lease papers Saturday."

"Okay, but I'll bet you never seen nothing like it." Albert's face darkened. "Dammit, Bailey, take a quick look."

"All right, all right, but snap it up. I told you I have to meet Travis."

On the mantle over the fireplace, bison skulls sat like guards. Arrowheads circled stone war-clubs and tomahawks displayed on the walls. Albert went through a hallway and came back a minute later.

"Here it is," Albert said, handing Bailey a small cracked leather bundle wrapped with untied rawhide strings. It fit in the palm of his hand.

"Have you opened it?"

"Yeah, damn hard to do without breaking the rawhide." He took the bundle from Bailey and set it on a lamp table. Albert slowly unwrapped the rawhide and opened the leather.

"Are you kidding me?"

"Told you it was something different."

A small mummified head the size of a large softball stared back at them. All the facial features were preserved. Long, braided black hair still looked soft and was held by a ring of copper, laced with an intricate gold design. The lips were pulled back in a dry grimace, revealing long cracked teeth with streaks of brown rot. The top of the skull was crushed.

"Where'd you find this?" Bailey couldn't take his eyes off the head.

"Up around the old plane wreck. Under a rock shelf."

"What were you doing up there?"

"Looking for arrowheads and stuff."

"Goddammit, Albert. I can't leave this. It's something the archaeologists need to see, or anthropologists. I'm not sure which one right now. Probably both." Excitement made him talk louder.

"You gave me your word, Bailey. You aren't going back on your word, are you? You promised."

Bailey closed his eyes for a minute. "Here's what I'll do, like it or not. You take me up and if we can find something like it, you can keep this for a while. If we don't find anything, then I'm taking it. I might have to anyway." Bailey bent over the table until his face was a foot from the head. He let out a deep breath and his shoulders slumped.

"I can't let you keep this. I'm sorry, if I'd known what it was, I'd never have promised."

"You're pretty low, Bailey," Albert said. He picked the head up and rewrapped the leather. "Yup, pretty chicken shit when a man goes back on his word."

"Albert! Enough complaining," Jean said, coming into the room. "You all but forced him to see it. What did you think he'd do? My lands."

"Listen, take some pictures, look at it, hold it – whatever. I'll pick it up next week. I can't offer you anything better."

Albert clutched the bundle to his chest. "All right. I shouldn't have said nothing. Next week, unless you change your mind and lie to me again."

"I won't. Still friends?" Bailey asked. He held his hand out.

"Albert?" Jean frowned at him.

His hand went out and shook Bailey's. "Yeah, still friends."

"Why don't you plan on dinner with us when you do come out." Jean said, a brief smile flashed.

"I'd like to, thanks, Jean."

"Yeah, you can stay for dinner. See you then." Albert smiled and gave a mock salute.

Bailey went to his truck and drove out of the ranch, heading for Lamont. *Now I can add being a lying son-of-a-bitch to the reputation of Bailey Calhoun.* The two-track he turned on to would lead him to an old oil field road where he'd end up just a mile south of the cafe.

Bailey seated himself at a table near the back wall at Grandma's Cafe. Travis hadn't shown yet and he wondered if he could slam a beer down before the younger man arrived. Probably not and he doubted if Minnie- patron owner/operator/mother hen to most males - would serve him anyway since he was working.

A moment later, a tall man with blond hair to his collar and wearing a BLM uniform came in, saw Bailey and waved, then leaned over the counter top and said something to Minnie. She put her hands over her mouth and giggled.

"Travis, I'm gonna adopt you someday. You're such a dear." A blush rushed to her face.

Behind Travis, Catlyn Ropper said hello to Minnie and walked over to Bailey's table. "Travis invited me to have lunch with you guys, okay with you?" Without waiting for an answer, she tossed her Wyoming Game and Fish hat on the table and dropped into a chair.

"Goddamn, a stiff drink would go good now," she said, looking Bailey in the eye. "Too bad we're working, huh?" Her fingers curled around his water glass. She picked the glass up and took a long swallow. "Our paths just seem to keep crossing, don't they? Think it's a sign?"

"Might be. Where'd you run into Travis?" Bailey asked, taking the water glass from her. He slurped some ice out of the glass and handed it back to her.

"On top of Wild Horse Lookout. Got visiting and he said he was meeting you for lunch. Took me a little bit to finagle an invite out of him. Sometimes Travis takes a minute to get the drift." She cocked her head at Bailey. "You okay? You're acting a little stressed. Worried about calling me last night? Afraid I might hold you to asking me out?"

"I'm fine, a couple things on my mind is all. No, not worried. In fact, I was wondering when to ask you out." Bailey grinned at her and admired for the one-hundredth time since he'd known her, the way she fit in the game warden outfit. A nice round fanny and the short sleeve shirt seemed like the buttons strained to break free. The pageboy haircut made her look several years younger than she probably was. Crow's feet around cold, but bright, slate-colored eyes and sun-wrinkled skin made Bailey bet her age was in her late thirties to early-mid forties. Sometime he'd ask her. In the year and a half Cat had been in Rawlins, she and Bailey got along well, and she could hand the cutting comments back as fast as she got it. His pulse always picked up speed when he saw her.

"Hey, let's do the date tonight. We can go out to dinner." Her elbows were on the table and her hands formed a cradle her chin rested in. "We'll go to the new steak house."

Bailey didn't know exactly what to say. "You mean you're asking me out on a date first?" He tried sounding funny but figured he blew it.

"Since you haven't yet, yeah. Have you been with a woman since Dana died?" she asked softly. "I'm not asking for a pity date, I like you and I think you like me. I'm tired of waiting to see if you'll ask me out. What do you say?"

Travis sat down at the table and looked from one to the other. "Am I interrupting something?"

"Maybe, maybe not," Cat said staring at Bailey. "Well?"

"Yeah... but how about tomorrow night instead. Around eight. I've got to run over to the Pathfinder and the Steamboat Lake Ranch so I probably won't get back until late tonight."

"I'll make us reservations at the Blake House for eight then. Tomorrow night." She smiled and turned to Travis. "Sorry, kid. You're out - Bailey's in."

"Jeez, I can't believe I talk to Minnie for two minutes and you've stolen my woman." Travis picked a menu up. "But, I'm hungry, and no use crying over spilt milk. Let's eat."

An hour later as Bailey was heading toward the Steamboat Lake Ranch; he laughed at how Cat had roped him into going out for dinner. It wouldn't be a date, an old term kids used. Hell, he was an adult. Adults didn't say, *date*. There was no doubt a year of mourning should be enough, though he didn't know if he'd be able to do it or not. One small knot in his gut loosened its grip; the craving tightened some more.

* * *

He drove past the Ferris Mountains, Devil's Gate and Independence Rock, where pioneers chiseled their names on the side of it on their way to Oregon. The road stayed on top of a high plain ridge until after ten miles the blacktop dropped down off the ridge to Steamboat Lake and the turnoff to the ranch. A closed gate blocked his way.

Bailey opened the gate and drove down a gravel road that wove around the eastern perimeter of the lake. Sagebrush dotted the prairie with buffalo grass and then shared the ground with stunted scrub oak trees as the road began to climb up a narrow valley. A fast running creek tumbled and cascaded down the rocks toward the lake. Twin peaks of the Pedro Mountains formed a high barrier to the east. He drove over the top of the valley and descended down a steep grade to an open meadow where the ranch house and outbuildings stood at the far end. A pond lay to the side of the house and it gave the appearance of a guest ranch rather than a cattle ranch. There was another closed gate at the bottom of the ridge. A sign read, "NO TRESPASSING-VIOLATERS WILL BE PROSECUTED." Bailey let himself through and parked in front of the ranch house. Two men were standing on the porch facing him. From the looks they were giving him, he didn't think they were going to give him a big hearty welcome.

"How are you doing?" Bailey asked as he got out of his pickup. "I'm looking for a Mr. Sanderson."

"Can't you read the signs, Buddy? No Trespassing." The speaker was a man dressed in a light denim jacket with the sleeves cut off to show his huge biceps. He pointed his finger in Bailey's direction, using the motion so the muscles flexed.

"Yeah, I can read. Can you hear? I said I'm looking for a Mr. Sanderson," Bailey said, feeling his temper rise. He hated these kinds of assholes who tried to intimidate guys by showing the beef. "Unless you're him, slick."

The screen door opened and a man dressed in dude ranch clothes came out. He put a hand out in front of the muscle man. "Back off, Reese. I'm Ed Sanderson. What can I do for you?"

"I'm Bailey Calhoun with the Bureau of Land Management. I'm the guy who does the lease applications and renewals. Apparently you don't want any, am I right?"

"Hold on now. Let's settle down. Why would you think I don't want a lease? I contacted your office," Sanderson said.

"Because you and your pit bulls should have seen the decal on the truck. Maybe been a little decent rather than smart ass right off."

"You're right. We started off on the wrong foot. We've had some vandalism recently and I guess we're a little on the edgy side." Sanderson stepped off the porch and put his hand out. "I'm sorry. Like I said, Ed Sanderson and my pit bulls are Reese, who you've already talked to, and Ike. Really, I'm sorry." Ike Bodine nodded at Bailey; Reese stood and stared at him.

Bailey took Sanderson's offered handshake. "Yeah, me too. Must be the heat."

"Why don't you boys work on the equipment while I talk to…" he looked at Bailey's name tag on his shirt, "Ranger Calhoun."

The men nodded to Bailey again and stepped off the porch, walking in the direction of the barn past the back of house.

"Come on in and we'll go to my office," Sanderson said. He climbed back on the porch and held the screen door open.

Bailey reached in the truck and brought his briefcase out. He climbed up on the porch and when Sanderson held the door open, he went inside the house. Bailey followed him down a hallway with polished wood floors and into a room he knew from appearance would be an office. It had dark paneled walls, marble fireplace, hardwood floors and a large oak desk near open French doors leading to another covered porch. Arrowhead displays, bison skulls and other archaeological treasures sat on shelves inside three glass door bookcases built into the walls. The two armchairs in front of the desk and the desk chair were upholstered in rich, soft leather, a deep burgundy color.

Bailey had seen expensively decorated offices before at the ranches of the wealthy, *gentlemen ranchers,* but this one welcomed a man. Very masculine in the décor, but lavish.

"Nice collection," Bailey said, looking in the bookcase. "I don't know if I'd want these sitting in a glass bookcase, though. You might get them ripped off. Artifacts are getting to be popular with the crooks."

Sanderson picked a metal box up from his desk and threw it at a bookcase door. It hit and bounced off, falling to the floor. There weren't any marks or cracks where it had slammed against the glass.

"You scared the hell out of me," Bailey said, staring at the cabinet. He brushed his hand over the glass. "Plexiglas?"

"Kind of. Reinforced jetliner plastic. Similar to what Boeing uses in their 757s. Someone wants my collection they'll have to use dynamite to get it." The statement wasn't made as a boast - it was a statement of fact. "Now," Sanderson said, sitting down behind the desk, "about those leases." He waved Bailey to a chair in front of him.

Bailey sat down and opened his briefcase. He brought a dozen papers out and laid them on the desk in front of Sanderson. "I understand you want a new lease on the four sections of land in the upper northeast side of the Ferris and you want to renew the two sections leased by the previous owners. Is that correct?"

"Yes it is. I want to be able to keep people off my property. The cattle I'm bringing in are rare and quite valuable."

"Uhh, Mr. Sanderson, you can't block access to leased government land, unless it's checkerboard where someone has to drive over your owned property. Even so, it's being fought in the courts now. No locked gates, and you can't have any 'no trespassing' signs either. I thought you'd know the policy."

"No, I guess I didn't. Dammit, I came out here from Massachusetts. I got the impression from the Stewards I had control of all the land I leased. Westerners don't lie so I didn't have my attorney check." Sanderson blushed and stood up. "Guess I should have had it researched better."

Bailey felt some sympathy for the man. Wealthy as he seemed, he acted pretty decent, at least to Bailey. "I don't think you'll have much to worry about. The Ferris doesn't have any hiking or RV trails. It's rough as hell and almost all wilderness area. The hunters don't even like it up there, too hard to haul an animal out carrying it over their shoulders."

"You seem pretty certain," Sanderson said. "In your opinion I don't need to worry then?"

"No sir. Be tough to get in there. Even for your cattle." Bailey tapped the papers with his finger. "If you'll sign these I'll get them processed. Now, you can fence the land and have gates, they just can't be locked."

Sanderson picked a pen up and signed with a looping signature on the papers. When he finished he opened a hidden cabinet door revealing a fully stocked bar with a small refrigerator. "You must be off work now, join me in a drink?"

Bailey felt the craving in his stomach. He shouldn't…it wouldn't look good or be professional. "Do you have a beer?"

Sanderson laughed and gave Bailey a choice of imports. He chose a Moosehead.

"Here's to a continuing relationship with the government," Sanderson said, lifting a glass of whiskey in a toast. Out of the corner of his eye he watched Bailey drink a quarter bottle of the beer in one long pull. After tossing his drink down, he held another Moosehead up. "One for the road, Mr. Calhoun?"

"Sure, why not. Mind if I take it with me? I've got to get back to town tonight." Bailey finished the beer in his hand and took the other bottle.

"No, not at all. I'd like to get together sometime, Mr. Calhoun, visit about the land."

"Call me Bailey. Yeah, I'd like to visit. It's great country."

* * *

Reese came into the office after Bailey left, poured a drink then dropped into a chair. "I don't like the guy," he said. "Thinks he's tough. I should have whipped his ass."

"Settle down. Why do you always think you need to whip somebody's ass?" Sanderson didn't wait for an answer. "You know who I think he is?"

Reese shook his head.

"Remember Ike telling us about those wild horses getting slaughtered last year, and the BLM guy who killed two men involved in it?"

"Yeah, vaguely."

"I think it was Calhoun," Sanderson said. He seemed lost in his thoughts for a moment. "We need to be careful with him. He could be sharper than he looks."

"Maybe I need to run into him someday when he's not working and kick his ass, slow him down, if you know what I mean."

"No, don't screw with him, you hear me? The last thing we need is for a BLM ranger to be snooping around the mountain. A month or two more and we're out of here."

Sanderson didn't like the sly look in Reese's eyes. *You better keep your macho crap under control 'cause I don't want to have to worry about what you're gonna do.*

"So why bother getting the leases? I don't know why we need them?"

"I *thought* we'd be able to keep people off from where we're working. When he told me we can't—"

"What you mean we can't?" Reese interrupted. "The whole idea was to keep it so no one could come up there."

"Let me finish. Apparently you can't keep anyone from coming on leased land, so if I'd told him never mind, he might have got suspicious we were doing something illegal. I don't want to call any attention to us. Understand?"

Chapter Fourteen

On the way back to the highway, trying to sip the beer rather than guzzle it down, Bailey thought he probably screwed up royally having a drink with Sanderson. Although he was technically still on duty, he couldn't help himself when he saw the ice-cold bottle with rivulets of condensation dribbling down its sides. *The drinking might be getting out of hand*, he thought, *but nothing a little self-control couldn't take care of. Yeah, a little more self control.*

He turned east rather than west on the highway and drove to a small bar and grill fifteen miles down the road where he could buy packaged liquors. Alcova Reservoir stretched out and disappeared in the red rock canyons across the highway from the bar. The sun going down reflected light into his eyes off the water as he pulled into the parking lot. A few trucks pulling boats sat in the lot. Music drifted out from the open windows beckoning him.

I shouldn't be doing this. The truck seemed to go behind the bar on its own accord. He shut the engine off. *What the hell you doing? You can't go in a bar decked out in your work clothes. It'd take all of two minutes before someone calls the office and squeals then three more minutes to run my ass off.*

He took his shirt off leaving him with a gray tee shirt on. His gun belt went under the seat. Bailey whistled with the music, anxious to have a quick one and buy a six-pack for the ride home.

The two-lane highway stretched out in front of him like a strip of black electrical tape. Instead of air conditioning, Bailey had the window down and his elbow stuck out. There was nothing like the feel of a hot wind on his face, blowing his hair straight back and rumbling loud enough he couldn't have heard the radio if it had been turned on. A beer bottle sat between his legs. The day had been long and he was looking forward to getting back to Rawlins so he could eat and climb in the rack. The beers were taking care of the craving in his gut and letting him enjoy the ride. He wasn't drunk, just a pleasant buzz to keep the depression at arm's length.

Red ribbons left over from a setting sun an hour before were on the western horizon. The north side of the Ferris Mountains was dark and lonely and when he caught the glimpse of a light near Young's Pass, a historical joke named for a slight split of sheer granite in the mountain no one or thing could go through. He came within a heartbeat of dismissing it and continuing home, but it was one of those times when he thought he needed a little action or effort to prove to himself he earned his paycheck.

Now just what the hell am I seeing? Maybe the low life's who've been poaching Bighorn sheep over on the Seminoles, or the spooks vandalizing Sanderson's place. His hand went to where the microphone clip on the dash still held nothing. *Goddamn repairmen.* If he had a cell phone a quick call is all it would take. The government didn't furnish one so out of principal, Bailey didn't have one. *I'm not buying something they should pay for.* Checking his rearview mirror, he pulled over to the side of the road and turned his headlights off. Without looking directly at the spot, he looked slowly from the left to the right, then back again. *There! Two lights. Four wheelers or motorcycles coming down from above the pass. Goddammit, they're riding in a wilderness area. Gotta be one or the other.*

If he'd had his radio, the call would have gone to Cat. The Bureau of Land Management didn't really screw with poachers, but he could sure as hell get them for riding in a wilderness area. There weren't any cars coming on the highway so he made a U-turn and put the gas pedal to the floor. A mile down he turned onto a dirt road heading south to the Young's Pass access trail. He drank the last swallow of beer and tucked the bottle under the seat between some rags.

Excitement he hadn't felt for quite a while made his heart beat faster. *And it's not from the beer*, he told himself. This was different from the dead body he found and he could feel the adrenaline hit him like a stiff shot of whiskey. Murder didn't fall under his jurisdiction, but this did. Every few minutes there'd be a quick flash of a light on the side of the mountain. Whoever it was seemed to be riding down through the timber toward the end of the dirt road. *Yeah, some action, just what the doctor ordered.*

A deer stood to the side staring into the headlights and Bailey slammed on the brakes the same time the deer bolted across the road in front of him. He couldn't believe how pissed he got from having to stop, wasting precious minutes before accosting hardened criminals probably having a wild ride down the mountain side. His dry, wry humor failed to shake the excitement.

The access trail was rocky and mired with deep sandy washouts. He pulled the truck into four-wheel drive and low gear. It was slow going as the tires slipped over ragged rocks then spun through deep troughs of soft sand. He stopped once, shutting the lights and engine off, and stuck his head out the window trying to hear the interlopers on their way down. As far as he knew, the trail was the only way out. Steep cliffs of limestone and dense growths of pine and aspen trees covered the slopes, making it nearly impassible even on horses. A frown spread over his face when all he heard was the ticking of the pickup's hot engine cooling off in the night. *There! I hear it. Still above me. At least I think I hear it.* A breeze started blowing from the west – soft, like a baby's whisper. *At least from here on out they've got to come by me to get down the mountain.* He smiled at the thought of trapping them on the road and turning on his red and blue rotating light sitting on the dash. When they saw the lettering on the side of the truck, Bureau of Land Management Law Enforcement, he'd nab 'em.

Fifteen minutes later, Bailey looked in amazement at the deserted turn-around. No truck, no motorcycles, no four wheelers. They sure as hell didn't go by him. The last half-mile cut through a timber blow-down area where broken trees and stumps had rotten for years. No way anyone could have gone over that stuff. He took his flashlight and walked around, shining the beam on the ground, looking for tracks. None. The barricade on the trail-end stood undisturbed and the sign warning of no motorized vehicles- Wilderness Area- Hiking or Horseback Only- was still anchored to the middle of the metal barricade. The two deep cutouts would have prevented even four-wheelers from plowing through and trying to ride up the mountainside. *Nope, nobody went up the mountain from here. Maybe you're finally starting to hallucinate.*

No sounds were in the air and the breeze turned into a wind. There wasn't a moon out, and where the flashlight and his pickup's headlights didn't shine, pitch black shadows and forms were undistinguishable.

His eyes strained to see into the darkness when the sound came, riding the wind. The headlights of two four-wheelers appeared, one behind the other, from a rock cleft above the barricade. They bore down on him and as he dropped to the ground they flew over the barricade missing his truck by mere inches when they touched the ground, tires churning. Bailey rolled onto his feet and ran after them. There weren't any taillights showing from the back of the ATVs and their exhaust made a noise similar to a long, drawn-out release of air from a balloon. After twenty-five feet Bailey stopped running, his breath coming in painful gasps. A curtain of dust hung in the air and he couldn't hear anything mechanical. *What the hell were those?* he thought, trying to trot back to his truck. He got in, started it and spun around, the backend fishtailing as he tromped on the gas pedal, his temper making the blood throb in his temples.

The first deep hole in the trail threw him up into the roof. When he came back down in the seat he slammed on the brakes the same time the truck's nose bounced off the cut bank, throwing it sideways into the road where it stalled. Bailey put his forehead on the steering wheel wondering what he was doing. *A death wish, maybe?* Shaky fingers turned the key and the engine started. After several small movements backward and forward, he kept the truck in low gear and drove down the trail, looking for a glimpse of the two four-wheelers or maybe an outfit with a trailer. The breaks where the trees started growing up the mountain side and left the prairie and sagebrush behind, started at a sandstone ridge. Bailey stopped the truck, got out and climbed up on a shelf of rock and scanned the country, trying to see the lights. Nothing.

He thought he might come back out during the daylight and have a good look around. When he got off the trail and onto the dirt road, he saw the lights of a vehicle down by the highway. Again the adrenaline spiked his system and he gave the truck more gas.

Red and blue lights came on when he neared the pavement. A Highway Patrol car sat on the side of the road facing him, its spotlight beam hitting him in the face.

"Goddammit," he bellowed out the window, stopping the truck. "Get the light out of my eyes."

The door opened on the patrol car and a huge man climbed out of the driver's side. The patrolman's hand touched the pistol at his side and he pulled his hat low as he walked up to Bailey's truck.

He bent down to look in the window. "Calhoun, you jack-bastard! What're you doing out here this late?" A hand the size of an Easter ham came in the window and gripped Bailey's arm.

"Been chasing some four-wheelers, or at least I think they were. They outran me coming down the road. You see them?"

"Don't think I've seen anyone but you, and I haven't seen you for a coon's age," the patrolman said. Then softly, "I was sorry to hear about Dana, I really liked her."

Bailey felt his excitement leave like the air out of a punctured balloon. Tired sorrow gripped his chest fast - like a knife between the ribs. "Thanks, it was sudden." For some reason it embarrassed him to talk about her death. Maybe guilt, who knew? The one person in Rawlins he would have talked to about it moved to an Indian Reservation in South Dakota to counsel the Indian kids. A few months later he was lying dead in a ditch after his car had rolled off a road during a rainstorm, throwing him out and breaking his neck.

Frank "Bear" Ricconi slapped Bailey on the back, rocking him on his toes. Bailey was six foot three and Ricconi had him by several inches and twenty-five pounds.

"C'mon and get in, we'll have us a cup of coffee."

They sat in the front seat of the patrol car; sipping coffee Ricconi had poured them. "I got transferred to Jeffrey City after pissing off the Chief. I've been there about two months now. The prick extended my area to include all the way to Steamboat Lake."

"What'd you do? It had to have been something big. Hell, they haven't had a highway copper stationed in Jeffrey City for twenty years." Bailey saw a grin start to form on the big man's face.

"After I left Rawlins and transferred to Cheyenne, I got caught porkin' the man's wife." Ricconi paused for effect. "By the man himself."

"You telling me you were messing around with Sumner's wife? The head of the patrol, Colonel Sumner? Jesus, Frank."

Ricconi sighed, "If I wouldn't have been friends with the governor, Sumner would have canned my ass on the spot. The Chief got even though, he told Becky and she up and divorced me. She took more than half my stuff, including some of my retirement funds. I didn't realize the girl was so vindictive."

"And Becky was number…?"

"She was my fourth," he said solemnly. "Nice woman before the divorce, I miss her."

"You ever see any lights up there?" Bailey asked, pointing up the mountain.

"Yeah, once in a while. Almost seems like a reflection because it's just a quick glance, then nothing."

"You're positive nobody came down the road where you could spotlight them like you did me?" He had a tight grin and rubbed his stomach.

"Yup, and contrary to popular opinion about cops, I still have two eyes." Ricconi finished his coffee and put his cup in a lined knapsack. "I gotta head out, Bailey. Let's get together some time. We'll have a couple of beers and tell some tales."

Bailey handed him his cup and opened the door. "I'd like that, Frank. Looks like we better make it while you can still get in a car." He cocked his head and said, "You've grown quite a bit since I saw you last year."

Ricconi's laugh rumbled through the patrol car. "You jack-bastard, you don't look so hot yourself. I'll call you."

Bailey watched the car leave and head west, then looked up to the side of the mountain where he'd seen the lights and where the seemingly impassable terrain lay. *Call me stupid, or maybe hopeful,* he thought, *but I got a feeling there's a little more to this than a couple of guys joy riding on four-wheelers.*

He climbed into his truck, fired it up turned onto the highway and headed for town with one more glance up the mountain.

Chapter Fifteen

Bailey pulled into his driveway around ten. The moon peaked over an eastern ridge and the wind blew steady. He parked in front of the garage and let himself in the front door carrying the empty beer bottles. He'd finished the rest of the six pack on his way to town. A big white dog met him, tail wagging.

"Hey girl, missed me?" he asked, throwing the bottles in the trash and walking to the refrigerator. The dog answered by grabbing a stuffed, squeaker toy dog and shaking it side to side as she raced toward Bailey. She dropped it at his feet and waited, legs spread and head down. His foot kicked the toy into the living room. A sound of scrabbling toenails on slippery vinyl came as the dog took out after the toy. Opening the fridge door to get something to eat, he frowned when he saw the only things beside the beer taking up space were a loaf of moldy bread, a pizza carton, and a large package of hot dogs. The dog got some hot dogs and Bailey heated the remaining pieces of cold pizza.

Dana's picture on the desk seemed to beckon him. He flopped into the recliner where he could see the picture.

"I didn't think it would eat me alive like it's doing. You used to tell me I could be the most cold - hearted bastard you'd ever known. So why can't I get my life going after a year?" He stared hollow-eyed at the picture.

Bailey, please. It hurts so bad.

Do you know what you're asking me to do?

God forgive me… yes. But I need you to help me.

The folder still lay on the floor. Maybe reading it again would get Dana's pleadings out of his mind. He picked it up and stared at the picture. "God damn!" The hieroglyphics on the ring in the picture seemed to be the same as the copper band holding the hair of the mummy. He couldn't be positive without comparing the two sides by side, but he knew it was. It came from the pit of his stomach, the feeling or intuition. Call it whatever. Why didn't he take the head when Albert showed it to him? Or at least snap a picture? Somehow, and he wasn't exactly sure yet, there was a connection between the dead archaeologist and the mummy head Albert had found, because it was too coincidental, and he didn't believe in coincidences when it came to dead bodies.

First thing in the morning he would be at the ranch pissing Albert off by taking the head. Maybe this is what he needed to come back to the land of the living. So, now he'd get a good night's sleep then jump in with both feet. *Look before you leap? Nahhh. Too boring.*

The dog followed him into the bedroom and took her place on the side of the bed Bailey hadn't laid on in over a year.

The next morning, he dialed the telephone number of the Wood's ranch and listened while it rang ten times without an answer. *Seven in the morning and they're out working already? Probably knows I'm calling and he isn't going to answer the phone. The cagey old fart.*

Two hours later, disappointment covered his face when he drove into the ranch yard and saw the Wood's pickup gone. The front door was unlocked but Bailey wouldn't go in with the house empty. He'd pulled some low-life shit before, however, entering the house like a thief didn't cut it. Putting his hands up on the glass he looked in but couldn't see anything except the living room, neat and tidy.

The dirt road in front of the ranch had a turn off ten miles down that worked its way to the dune where he'd found the body. Stakes with yellow crime scene tape tied to them still marked the spot where the body had lain.

Bailey was bending down inside the quadrant brushing the fresh sand to the side a half-hour after leaving the ranch. He wanted to find something – anything Jordan and the boys might have missed. Since the bullet hadn't come out the front of the man's head, the investigators probably didn't dig up any of the sand under the body. The autopsy said the gun had been fired from a close range and left some gunshot burns and residue on the entry wound. He shoved several more handfuls to the side until blood colored sand started showing. His hands burrowed deeper and came out with a quarter clutched between his fingers. 1986, Washington's head on the front. Nothing extraordinary except it was beneath the sand where a body had been found. *I ought to take it to the sheriff's office and give it to Jordan. Might help me get along better.* Bailey looked at the front and the back of the coin and stuck it inside his pants pocket. *Screw Jordan.*

* * *

Wales spoke cordially with Bailey when he saw him in the office. "How are you doing today, Bailey? Everything going okay?"

It was the kind of do-gooder conversation Bailey hated. The old, "See, I'm showing I'm interested in you," type of crap.

After Bailey muttered thanks, he was fine, Wales slapped him on the shoulder and told Dora he had meetings the rest of the day with some environmental engineers.

Bailey didn't mingle with the other employees, he just stayed tucked away in his office with the shades pulled. A call to the Highway Patrol got the dispatcher to contact Ricconi, and no, he hadn't seen anything after visiting with Bailey. He debated calling Cat and reneging on the dinner. He wasn't ready for a… hell, *date*. The telephone seemed to magically appear in his hand. *Relax…remember how she looked? The only thing you'll probably do after dinner is shake her hand, nothing more. Put the phone down.* The handle dropped in the cradle and he wiped a bead of sweat off his face.

When he got home the first thing he did was drink two glasses of wine to slow him down. Were his palms wet? He admonished himself for acting like a kid on his first date. In a sense, it was. And yeah, he admitted, he was excited. Excited and nervous. He showered, changed clothes and drove his truck to her house.

She answered the door dressed in a soft looking, beige jumpsuit. A zipper ran from her bust line to her waist. He followed her into the house that also served as the game warden's office and over to a portable bar.

"Beer or something stronger?"

"What are you having?"

"Bourbon on the rocks," she replied, putting two glasses on the bar counter, scooping ice out of a bucket and dropping it in the glasses. She licked the water off her palm with lazy circles of her tongue. One glass was filled almost to the top with the bourbon. She looked at him quizzically, the bottleneck poised over the empty glass.

"What the hell, I'll have the same."

The glass, filled halfway with amber liquid and ice cubes clinking, appeared in front of him. He put the glass to his lips and took a swallow.

"Goddamn, Bailey. You sip whiskey, not swallow half of it in one gulp. We need to work with you some on drinking properly, don't we?"

"I expect so. Tastes pretty good even though it's burning a furrow going down my throat." He held the glass and looked self-consciously at the amount left in the glass.

Cat poured some more into his glass and hers. "Let's sit down and visit for a minute before we go."

Bailey felt his lips going numb when he finished the drink. "Mind if I do a refill?"

"Be my guest," she held her glass out. "Hit mine one more time."

She pulled her feet up underneath her in the corner of the couch. "Nervous?"

He gave her the glass and sat next to her. "Yeah, a little. It's been awhile since I've been with a woman," he said. "I didn't mean it the way it sounded. What I meant was with such a pretty woman."

Cat gently put her hand on his shoulder and ran it down his shoulder to his hand. "Thanks, you've got a good line."

He sipped the liquid and found there were only ice cubes left. "Whoa, this sneaks up on you." The glass glittered when he turned it in his hand. "May I?"

"Make it two."

Are we both slurring our words? I believe I'm smoked already.

Cat got up and turned a lamp in the corner of the room on a dim setting. "Looks like a storm coming in," she said, closing a vinyl blind covering the picture window in the room. "Let's not go out. I'll fix us something to eat here, okay?"

The relief of not going out in public with a woman surprised him. "Sure, I rather be here with you than at a restaurant any day."

Bailey thought he could hear the wind pick up and maybe some distant thunder in his peripheral hearing, but the more important thought right then was how to make a move on her. Dana always told him he didn't know when he was being hit on. *Quit it! Don't think of her. Look at that ass and those boobs. Cat's here, alive. Get your head out of your fanny.*

They were both back sitting on the couch. "What's the favorite part of your job?" she asked.

Her zipper is down a couple of inches more than a minute ago. "Artifacts. There's so much history from them. I should have been an archaeologist." Another swallow, less burning, now his lips were numb, and damn did he feel great. "You know Albert Wood?" She nodded. "He's found the most unique artifact I've ever seen." His glass was full again. *Where was the zipper now?* "A mummified Indian head."

"What's so unique about it?" Her elbow leaned on the back of the couch and she faced Bailey, her eyes not as ice-cold gray as usual.

"Because it's the size of a softball, well preserved and had been wrapped in a leather hide."

"A child. Some poor woman's child."

"No, the face was old. The lips were pulled back and his teeth looked like an adult's. You know, long and worn down. And he had a band around his hair. Looked like it was made from copper and inlaid with gold. The top of his head was crushed, too. Goddamnest thing I've ever seen."

"Show it to me... later."

"I will. I'm going to pick it up next weekend. I let him keep it for a while."

"You let him keep it? Why?"

Bailey didn't know how many glasses of bourbon he'd drank, but no doubt, he was totally shit-faced. He thought she was too. If she stroked his leg one more time, he knew he'd drag her to the floor and screw her. Not make love. No, nothing emotional, just the pure physical act of being on top of a woman again and balling.

"Before Albert showed me, he gave me some crap about being the arrowhead police and taking what he'd found. I told him I've never taken anything from him before and I wouldn't then, but after seeing it, there's no way I couldn't confiscate it. So I said he could keep it a week- to take pictures, hold it, whatever - then I'd pick it up. I've got an appointment in Cheyenne, Friday. I probably won't get out there until Saturday."

"You don't enforce the laws to the letter, huh? Me either. I turn my head on some things, let others slide. Does a little discriminatory enforcement make us bad at doing our job?" Cat leaned over to him and kissed him deep.

Bailey picked her up and carried her where she pointed. The king-sized bed bounced when they fell onto it. He pulled her clothes off and buried himself in her arms and kisses. Her fingernails scratched deeply into his back drawing blood when he was inside her. Time seemed motionless. He was overwhelmed with desire and emotion. One minute he was screwing Cat and the next he was making love to Dana.

"Wait!" he gasped, pulling out and falling to his back.

"What's the matter?" Her breath came hard and fast.

"I'm having a hard time breathing. Just a minute. God, I'm so damn drunk I can't see straight. I'm not finished with you, kid." He sat up and put his hands around his face. A low groan came out of him. "How the hell am I going to go to work tomorrow? I can't remember when I've been so drunk on my ass."

"Do you always worry about your job when you're having sex?"

"Of course not, but I'm close to being run off because of my drinking. I know Wales is going to check up on me. Goddamn!"

"Let's call in sick, you can stay here and we'll have a good time."

"I've run out of sick time. Too many days I couldn't make it in. Shit!" His voice raised from desperation.

She got out of bed and went into the bathroom, just outside the bedroom. Her naked body reflected the sweat when she came back a minute later and lay down beside him, pushing him down on his back. She crawled on top of him and put her lips on his. Her tongue shoved a small pill in his mouth. "Here, swallow, you won't have a hangover with this."

Nothing to lose, right? The pill was so tiny and coated with a smooth substance; it easily went down without water.

"The DEA won't bust in, will they?" He asked, trying to see her face.

"Trust me." Cat started kissing the top of his forehead and eased down his body.

Bailey got his breath back and felt renewed energy. A kaleidoscope of lights and sounds passed through him and muddied all sense of time. Visions of Cat's mouth, her legs open and her strength holding him to her overrode his other senses. There was a pounding of drums in his head, drums being beaten by little shriveled Indians with sightless eyes, crushed skulls and faces marked with violence. The thundering drumbeats made him feel like his head might explode, but he didn't care, he was on one hell of a ride.

Chapter Sixteen

When Bailey woke up he couldn't believe he wasn't dead. In fact, he was very much alive… and feeling reasonably well. Whatever the hell Cat gave him worked. No headache, no feeling of wanting to puke, clear-headed. His watch showed it was a quarter after six. The sun was up and he had better than an hour to clean up and get to work. A quick foreboding caressed his mind. *What if the District picks this day to give me a drug test? I gotta find out how much I have to worry.*

"Hey Cat," he yelled. No response. Bailey located his shorts and put them on. He stuck his head out the bedroom door. "Cat. You here?" A clock ticked somewhere down the hallway. He vaguely remembered seeing a clock hanging on the living room wall, the kind with a pendulum. His socks were still on and the pants went on next, then the shirt. There was a note taped on the inside of the front door.

I had a good time. I'll be home tonight-call me. Cat.

The tape made a sucking sound when he pulled the note off the door and put it on the counter. He found a pen and wrote underneath her message, *Not as good as me. I'll call. Bailey.*

After driving back to his house, he took a long, hot shower and afterwards ate a light breakfast. He put a fresh uniform on and was in his office before eight.

* * *

"Dora," he said into the phone. "Call me when you see Marc come in, will you? Thanks." A few minutes later the phone rang. Bailey answered it and put it down, then got up and walked down to the field archaeologist's office.

"You ever seen an adult Indian head the size of a big softball? Mummified?" Bailey asked, sitting down on the edge of Marc's desk.

"No, but I'd like to. Why?"

"I might have one to show you next week."

"What do you have going on, Bailey?" Marc asked. A puzzled expression crossed his face. "It sounds like you might have discovered something and you're teasing me with it. You pulling my leg here?"

"Wait until I have it. Hell, it might be a baby or some kind of an animal and I'm just screwed up," Bailey said.

"Let me see it first, okay?" There was pleading and hope in the man's eyes.

"Sure, Marc." *If I don't, you'll be added to the list of people I've been lying to.* "I'll talk to you later." He got off the desk and walked out to the reception area. The bookcase behind the counter held the official government telephone book. He took it and headed back to his office with Dora's warning in his ears. "Don't forget to bring the phonebook back."

The regional BLM archaeologist, Dr. Gifford Barlow, had bold lettering with his name and office phone number offset from the rest of the pack listed in the book. *Kind of like saying, 'Hey, look at me, I'm the best, Bailey* thought. Barlow's secretary answered the phone when he called, and made an appointment for him on Friday, at one in the afternoon. Bailey didn't think he'd be in the shrink's office more than an hour, so he had some leeway if the doc thought he might be a little whacko and wanted to talk to him some more.

No one answered at the Wood's ranch. *I'll just see them Saturday. I'll bet Albert tries hiding the thing and tells me it disappeared.* He smiled. *That'd be just like the old coot.*

Bailey keep busy most of the day with paper work and even dozed for a little while with his office door closed. Wales acted friendly toward him when he saw him, and Travis was fortunately busy with his own duties. He watched the clock, waiting for the day to end without the call to meet the official contracted drug tester. *You got the short straw today, Bailey. He'll meet you in the restroom.*

The awakened stirrings of interest in another woman surprised him. The feeling of excitement in wanting to call or what the hell, maybe see Cat again so soon surprised him.

Four o'clock finally came--the official end of Bailey's workday. The liquor store he stopped at was at the far end of town. No sense in shoving it in Wales's face. The Jack Daniel's bottle looked like what she'd had last night. He bought a liter and had the clerk put it in a brown paper sack.

A little before six he called her. "Cat, hey, thanks for last night. I had a great time."

"You're welcome," she said, her voice almost a purr. "No hangover, right?"

"None at all, but I'm spooked something will show up if they piss test me."

"Don't worry. It's not dope, per se. The only thing shows up in your blood is an increase in Immunoglobulins."

"That sounds bad too."

"Nah. It's just an infection fighting protein or enzyme. We all have them. I've been tested after I've taken it and breezed through it. It's not illegal either, at least until the state finds out about it. Then they'll pass a law and we'll be screwed, figuratively speaking, of course," she said, pausing.

"The story of my life when it comes to luck. They probably have a new test and it's a felony for using the stuff you gave me."

"Bit of a pessimist, aren't you?" she asked.

"Possibly, it's hard to tell when things are so crappy." He smiled at his attempt of humor, and wondered if he sounded as desperate to her as he did to himself when he asked, "Would you like to come over for a drink?"

"We didn't eat last night. What if I bring some dinner for us?" Cat asked.

"Sounds good."

"What time?"

This is where he wanted to keep his voice neutral. Not too anxious, not too needy. *Hell, last night could have been a fluke.* "How about seven?"

"I'll be there," she said. "You be there too." She laughed and hung up.

Bailey looked forward to having a home cooked meal besides his own poor attempts. He jumped into the shower and when he got out, wiped the condensation off the mirror and looked at his reflection.

Now, Bailey. God, I can't take it anymore.

Don't, please, Dana. Let me have this night without thinking about you.

He turned away and hoped Cat wouldn't see the anguish and pain in his eyes when she got there. *I've got to move ahead,* he thought. *If I don't, I'm going to die.*

Appreciation of promptness made him smile when the doorbell rang at seven on the nose. The smile dropped a tad in one corner of his mouth as the pizza carton was shoved into his hand.

Hope you like sausage," she said. "Oh, damn, did you think I was going to cook something? I can't cook much more than hotdogs for the main course. I always thought my ex-husband left me because I couldn't cook, the bum."

"Was he from around here?"

"No, up north. I met him in college. Enough talk of our past, is the pizza okay?"

"This is great, exactly what I wanted." He led her to the kitchen and set the carton on the table. "Drink first?"

She saw the bottle of Jack Daniels. "Good memory for being muddled."

Later, after the pizza was eaten, they sat on the couch.

Cat finished her drink and took one of Bailey's hands in hers. "I like you...very much. But I've got to leave and can't ravish you like I did last night."

"Why not?"

"A supervisor is riding with me tomorrow so I can't be whiskey saturated or smelling of satisfied sex. I'll make it up to you tomorrow night." She licked his palm with the tip of her tongue. A long stroke down his lifeline.

"You're killing me. I've got to be in Cheyenne early Friday morning. Same thing, serious supervisor stuff so I can't even hint at having been drinking. Magic pill or not. Friday night?" *She licks my hand one more time I'll be throwing the dishes off the table to give me some room.*

"Yeah, Friday night's great. My place. Be there around seven and we'll have us a time." Her lips covered his and she kissed him deep. She broke it off and stood up. "Goddamn ride-a-longs anyway. I'll see you Friday."

Bailey watched her close the door behind her. *Did she hear him panting? Must have unless she's deaf.* He was keyed up, and since she didn't leave the little magic pills, he didn't think drinking more would be prudent to his cause of showing the Man he didn't have a drinking problem.

In the medicine chest, near the back, stood several bottles of Dana's pills. The bottle with the sleeping pills in it still had several rolling around the bottom when he shook it. One went down chased with the remaining whiskey in his glass. A guy never knew when he might need something for pain or sleep. The prescription drugs had never been tossed after Dana didn't need them anymore. He shut the medicine chest door and again stared into the mirror. *Oh, man, how far down are you going?*

Thursday was a no brainer, work wise. Nothing came up that took a lot of thought or action. Undersheriff Jordan told him they had identified the body but wouldn't tell him until the next of kin had been notified. Sheriff's business, not his. For once, he didn't lose his temper, just hung up on the fat pig and wondered how he could bring up about the artifact without screwing Kelly. It'd take some thinking. Wales let him leave early since he was going to Cheyenne the next morning. A quick call to Cat later in the evening and no booze left him feeling edgy and nervous. Callie seemed to sense his apprehension and stayed close beside him, nuzzling his hand every time he petted her. "You always stick with me, don't you, Girl?" He wished she could talk, but if she could, he'd probably go nuts being told how ignorant he had been acting. When Bailey called the neighbors to see if they'd watch the dog in case he didn't make it back the next night, they told him not to worry, they always checked to be sure Callie had food and water. "I always leave her bowls full," he said, protest in his voice.

"Sure, Bailey. No problem, we'll watch her," the neighbors replied, not quite rolling their eyes.

He felt relieved to be on his way to Cheyenne the next morning. Not to see the shrink, but to get out of town. Leave the surly bonds of home, or something like that. Sleep hadn't come easy the night before, and Bailey was up and dressed before the alarm went off at six.

Instead of the Interstate, the highway over the Snowy Range Mountains appealed to him. Give him a thinking environment. Thirteen miles out of the resort town of Saratoga, he turned east on the blacktop to go over the Range. Mountains rose high with a fire lookout post on the highest peak of Kennedy Mountain, able to be seen from the road. The highway climbed and dropped through valleys and mountain meadows. Lake Marie already had cars in the parking lot. Beautiful country, but the high plains and desert north of Rawlins was his kind of country. Windswept, barren and lonesome. Not an attraction for the tourists like the mountains had where an asphalt highway ran over them to Laramie. Tents and camp trailers dotted the terrain when he could see through the fence of trees.

Yup, gimme the Ferris anytime. No one around, no highways or roads going over them. Just some dead bodies shot in the head and left half-buried in the sand dunes. Thinking of bodies, Monday, he'd tell Wales the BLM should be involved in the case because the dead man had an artifact in his hand. Somehow, Bailey would have to protect Kelly, and not mention the information came to him from the sheriff's office about the dead man and the artifact. They'll keep him out of the murder investigation, but with the ring, he sure as hell could do some nosing around. Jordan will have to give him the information on the dead guy, it goes with his case, Bailey thought. A smile stole across his face as he visualized the undersheriff rant and rave until finally, the law on Bailey's side, Jordan would throw him the folder filled with important facts and revealing pictures of the corpse. *Yeah, in a pig's ass.* Just how coincidental was it - Albert finding the Indian head and a dead archaeologist with an artifact in his hand ten miles away? In the Red Desert and plains, ten miles meant nothing. He rolled his hip over in the seat and pulled out the quarter. *Just a regular twenty-five cent piece. Not too new, not too old. What the hell was it doing in the murdered man's grave?*

*   *   *

Bailey only got lost once in Cheyenne, taking a left instead of a right on Central Avenue. A cashier at a gas station straightened him out. The older three story brick building looked typical. Parking in the rear and a hallway with an elevator and directory in the lobby.

Marlow Radcliffe, Suite 327. *Good, nice and subtle.* He was five minutes early and didn't know if he should go up or wait until the exact time. *I don't want anybody seeing me in his waiting room. Probably be full of whackos.* Bailey took the stairs and when he reached the third floor, gave a small prayer of thanks the building and office weren't any higher. It pissed him off to be out of breath. He stood outside the third floor stairway door until his breathing slowed down and his heart quit pounding.

An older woman sat at a reception desk. No one else was in the room. After giving her his name, she had him fill out a form and told him to sit down. *Doctor will see you in a few minutes.*

It always irritated him to hear the term, *Doctor,* used as a name, rather than a title. No idea why, but it just pissed him off. *Marlow Radcliffe, or, hi, I'm Doctor. Probably has the goatee, herringbone jacket with leather elbow patches and smokes a pipe.*

"Mr. Calhoun, Doctor will see you now," she said, pointing to an entryway to her right.

Bailey couldn't help the sigh slipping through his lips when he stood up. "This way to Doctor's office?" he asked, motioning.

The receptionist gave him a puzzled look and nodded.

The entryway led to a short hallway with an open door at the end. He could see a large window, a table, and two chairs against the office wall. Walking inside, he saw a man sitting at a plain wooden desk writing in a file. No herringbone, goatee, and no pipe.

The man put his pen down and stood up, sticking his hand out. "Hi, I'm Dr. Radcliffe. You must be Mr. Calhoun. Please, sit down." Radcliffe pointed to a soft-looking leather chair. Bailey sat down on the edge of the chair. After making a few more notes, Radcliffe closed the file and leaned across the desk. "I understand you might have a bit of a drinking problem."

Bailey felt the blood rush to his face in embarrassment. "Not really, just overindulging a couple of times. I'm working things out."

"Mr. Calhoun... can I call you Bailey? Good. Bailey, I work a little differently than most psychiatrists. I don't coddle people when they try to minimize their problems to me. I'm not going to ask if you loved your mother or what kind of a tree would you like to be. Looking over your file you've had several episodes of *overindulging* this past year. It appears you pulled yourself out of the dung pile for a while, then fell back in. Comments?"

Bailey's jaw clinched. "Not yet. What else you think?"

"It appears you started drinking heavily last summer shortly before your wife died from cancer. Am I correct?"

Bailey's eyes narrowed. This wasn't going like he thought. Where was the beating around the bush? This guy went for the throat right off. He must have a busy schedule.

"So what's your point?" He felt his teeth clinch and his chin move. Dana used to tell him he'd stick his chin out just before he'd get into an argument. Kind of a … *I'm not budging* stance.

"You were a Marine, hurt in Vietnam, received the Bronze Star; a police officer for five years and then the BLM. It seems you were involved in some deaths last year and hailed as a hero in the same breath."

"Yeah, I know all about me," Bailey said. "So again, what's your point?"

"Not to sound callous, but your reaction to her death doesn't sound like something you would do considering your past. What's going on, Bailey?" Radcliffe asked in a softer voice.

"Look, sport." Bailey stood up, knocked the chair back and pointed a finger at Radcliffe. "Don't tell me what kind of person I am, goddammit. You don't know me and you sure as hell can't analyze me in ten minutes. And before you start, I'm not suffering from post-traumatic syndrome, either."

Radcliffe pushed back from the desk, hands out in front of him, palms warding Bailey off. "Whoa, settle down. I might have come on too strong, but you seem to be the type who wants to cut to the chase. Please, sit back down. I apologize."

Bailey glared at the doctor for another moment then pulled the chair back to the desk and sat down. He rubbed a hand over his face. "We were getting our lives together. She had the hell beat out her by a psycho trying to get to me, and someone we trusted almost killed her. We overcame some other issues, and for a while… we were really good for each other. We got to be best friends, you know what I mean?"

"I do, not many people experience friendship with their spouses. Then she was diagnosed with cancer?" Radcliffe asked gently.

"Yeah, and then we went downhill fast. I mortgaged everything we owned so I could take her to John Hopkins Hospital. Took my savings plan from work and after it was all over she died in the same time frame the local doctor had given her."

"Are you resenting her for taking your financial security?"

"Are you serious? Of course not. Look, Dana died. I loved her, couldn't help her get cured, probably had guilt for a while being healthy while she was dying and drank myself into oblivion sometimes because of self-pity." Bailey closed his eyes and leaned his head back. "It was a tough break, but that's life, right? So now I'm working it out with a slip every now and then." He kept his eyes shut and waited for the shrink to respond.

After a few minutes of silence, Bailey opened one eye and saw the doctor staring at him with his hands clasped together behind his neck. "Well?" Bailey asked, opening both eyes. "Let me have your words of wisdom."

Radcliffe put his hands down on the desk and leaned forward. "I think we're finished for today. I'll see you next week, same time."

"C'mon, not on a Friday."

"Here's my card. If you want to talk, call me. Not to rant and rave or drunk on your ass and calling to tell me I'm a bum." He slid it across the desk.

Bailey picked it up and stuck it in his shirt pocket while he stood up. He wouldn't admit it out loud, but he kind of liked the little guy. No bullshit, at least none he could see. "All right, next week. Uh… thanks."

118

Chapter Seventeen

The archaeology department of the District BLM took up all the basement of the federal building. Bailey pushed a set of double glass doors open and saw a pleasant looking, older woman behind a reception desk.

"May I help you?" she asked, taking her glasses off.

"I'm here to see Dr. Barlow." Bailey handed her his BLM identification. In his other hand he held a file folder.

She glanced at the badge and I.D. then opened a book, turning some pages. "I don't see you down for an appointment, Mr. Calhoun."

"I made one over the telephone. One o'clock today because I happened to be in Cheyenne on another appointment. It's about a case I'm working on."

The woman gave a conspiratorial look and said, "Maybe I can sneak you in for a minute." She talked on the phone and hung up. "Go down the hallway into the lab, Dr. Barlow is waiting."

"Thanks…" He looked at the name plate, "Mrs. Emerson. I appreciate it."

"You're welcome. A small warning, Dr. Barlow is a bit brusque."

The only man in the lab wore a three-piece suit and patent leather shoes. He talked into a microphone while holding a sheet of paper. When he saw Bailey come in, he put the paper on a table and pushed his glasses up on his nose with his index finger. "I only have a few minutes, I'm giving a speech at a luncheon. You should have made an appointment," he said. He spoke with an eastern accent.

"I did, there must have been a mix-up or something. Anyway, this shouldn't take long."

"Well, what do you want? I'm giving you…" He looked at his wristwatch. "Five minutes, then I have to leave."

Bailey took the photo of the ring from the folder and handed it to Barlow. "This was found in the hand of a dead man. What kind of artifact is it?"

Barlow took the picture and studied it, turning the picture sideways and upside down. "Hmmm."

"I also saw a mummified head of an old Indian, but it was the size of a softball. There was a small copper band with similar designs around his hair."

"His? You know it was a man?"

"No, just assuming for no real reason."

"We archaeologists have such a difficult time because of lay people like yourself who make all kind of assumptions, usually wrong. You have a picture of the head?"

"No, I'm picking it up next week. It's a long story," Bailey said.

"I haven't time for a long story. It's probably a baby. There's no adult Indians with heads the size of a ball, unless it was deformed."

Bailey shook his head. "The teeth were long, and his face wrinkled. There wasn't an abnormal cranium or anything to make it look like a deformed child's head. I'm sure it was an old adult."

"Preposterous." Barlow handed the picture back. "I don't recognize the design nor the hieroglyphics. I hate to challenge your expert opinion, but I think it's a poorly manufactured hoax. Sorry, I have to go." He nodded to Bailey and strode out of the lab.

"You arrogant son-of-a-bitch," he said quietly, hearing Barlow's footsteps grow faint.

"Thanks, Mrs. Emerson," Bailey said walking past the woman.

"I get the feeling he didn't help you," she said.

"A little too busy and a little too brilliant, I'd say. He looked at the picture and told me it was fake. I just think he didn't know and didn't want to admit it."

"It's too bad Dr. Chandler retired." She sighed. "Talk about brilliant. He had a doctorate in anthropology and archaeology. I worked for him for thirty years over at the state." Mrs. Emerson leaned over the desk. "They're as different as night and day. Dr. Barlow doesn't know half what Dr. Chandler knows. He was an amazing man in his field."

"Does he live here in town?"

"No, in a nursing home in Ft. Collins. He's been there for several years. My goodness, he must be around ninety years old."

"Maybe I'll run down and see him. Is he able to have conversations?" Bailey asked. Nervousness got his thumb twitching against his pants leg.

"The last I knew he could. I used to visit him every month until he told me not to come anymore. His memory would drift a little and he feared he had the beginnings of Alzheimer's. I honored his wishes but I call and talk to the nurses once in a while and he's still aware most of the time." Her eyes glistened. "Such a dear man."

Bailey wrote down the address she gave him for the nursing home. He left Cheyenne heading toward Ft. Collins, Colorado, fifty miles away; thinking the day might not be a complete bust.

Chapter Eighteen

The LaCache Nursing Home sat between a steak house and a vacant lot just off Harmony and LeMay Streets. Towering oak trees surrounded the sprawling building, giving it the appearance of dignity and grace. Bailey parked in the visitor's parking lot and entered the front door. The first thing he saw were chairs occupied by elderly men and women in different stages of living death. Some drooled and hung their heads down while others talked animatedly to no one. *God, I hope he isn't one of these.*

"May I help you?" a female voice asked.

He turned and looked down on a small, middle-aged woman dressed in a nurse's uniform. Starched and clean. "I'm looking for a Dr. Chandler, I believe he's a resident here."

"Are you family?"

"No, government business. I want to see if he can give me any information about some artifacts." He pulled his identification out of his pocket and showed it to her. "I work for the Bureau of Land Management. I've heard he was the best, back in his day."

She glanced at it and smiled. "He'd like to hear that. Let me see if he's awake." The nurse walked down the hallway with short, quick steps. Her rubber soles on her shoes squeaked intermittently.

Bailey watched her disappear into a room then come out a moment later and motioned him to come down.

"Don't wear him out," the nurse said, going into the room ahead of Bailey. "Dr. Chandler, you have a visitor." Chubby fingers went around Bailey's wrist and pulled him around her and into the room.

The first person he saw was an attractive dark haired woman sitting in a chair near the bed. She stood up and closed the book. The pants suit she wore was stylish and accentuated her trim figure. "Hi, my name is Ann, I'm Dr. Chandler's daughter." She looked him in the eye when she shook his hand with a firm grip. He could see a measure of self-confidence in the way she carried herself.

This is a bonus. He almost blushed at the thought. There was something mesmerizing about her. *What a complexion, talk about peaches and cream. I've known her all of six seconds and I want to take her out. Settle down, boy.*

Chandler had sparse white hair combed straight back and a deep wrinkled face with a dull, ruddy complexion. One thin arm lay on the outside of a white sheet drawn up to his neck. Bailey thought the old man was asleep until his eyes opened and looked at Bailey with a mixture of intelligence and vacuity.

"Dad," Ann said softly, "you have a visitor."

His eyes turned to Bailey.

"Dr. Chandler?"

"Yes...hello," he said, and smacked his lips.

"Do you want some water, Dad?" she asked.

"No thanks, honey. Now, who are you?"

"My name's Bailey Calhoun. I'm with the Bureau of Land Management and I'd like to see if you recognize an artifact I have a picture of."

The old man pushed himself up to a sitting position. "Would you get me my reading glasses in the drawer there?" he asked his daughter.

After she put them in his liver-spotted hand, Chandler slid them on. "You should be warned, I tend to lapse into a state of semi-consciousness without warning. Dementia is a terrible thing." He took the folder from Bailey's outstretched hand and opened it.

Bailey found himself holding his breath. He exhaled slowly when the old man lifted his head and smiled.

"Amazing. It's been over sixty years since I've since anything like this. Where's the headband now?" Both of his hands held the picture in an almost death grip.

"Headband? Damn, with the ruler next to it no one thought of it being a headband. We've all thought it's a bracelet or something because it's so small." Bailey took the photo and looked hard at it. He handed it back to Chandler. "The sheriff's office in Rawlins has it. Evidence in a murder."

Excitement made the old man's voice tremble. "Mr. Calhoun, this is from the Nimerigar tribe. God, I began to doubt myself they ever existed after Meggert and Davison disappeared."

"Who disappeared?" Bailey asked.

"The men who found Onatah, a Nimerigar seer.

"Doctor, last week I saw a mummified Indian head with a smaller band like this wrapped around his braided hair. This picture was taken of an object found in a murdered man's hand."

"My, oh my, oh my... " Chandler stared at the wall then lowered his head without saying a word. The picture still clutched in his hands.

Bailey gently shook his shoulder. "Dr. Chandler? Are you all right?" *Wouldn't you know it, he's down for the count.*

Ann came over from where she had been standing by the door and took Chandler's hand. "I think he's all right but will you call the nurse?" she asked.

He stuck his head out the door and saw the nurse who had brought him to the room. "Ma'am, could you check him? He faded out."

The sheet outlined the eroding lower body of the doctor as he lay in the bed; his upper half propped up with pillows. He still sat reclined but his head hung down. The nurse moved by Ann, put a hand on his forehead and looked into his face. "Dr. Chandler has these spells. He's going into them more often and it takes longer for him to come back." Her fingers opened his hand and removed the picture.

"Yours, I assume?" She handed it to Bailey.

Bailey smelled the odors in the room. Antiseptic cleaners, food and the same smell grandparents have in their old houses. He figured it was aging, or dying. The room seemed oppressively warm though a light breeze rocked the curtains hanging over the open widow. "When do you think he'll come out of it?" He unbuttoned the top two buttons of his shirt.

"It's hard to say. Five to twenty minutes is the usual time for him. Can I get you something cold to drink? You look a little flushed."

"Please, ice water will be fine." *An ice-cold beer would be ten times better.* "Will it be okay if I sit here and wait to see if he comes around?"

The nurse said of course as she left the room, warning Bailey he might want to go outside and get some air.

C'mon," Ann said, taking his arm. "I'll go with you."

He met the nurse down the hallway and gratefully took the glass, draining it in two swallows. Outside, the oak trees blocked the direct heat from the sun. Ft. Collins had more humidity than he was used to. His shirt turned dark from sweat stains.

Bailey took several deep breaths. "I don't know what's going on. I just got hot and needed some air."

"It happens. You feel like you're smothering because it gets so stuffy feeling inside. They keep the temperature higher than normal, too. Because of the thin blood, I think."

He walked back and forth across the lawn. The nurse came out and told them Dr. Chandler had reawakened and wanted to visit while he could.

"Thanks for coming out with me, I appreciate it," he told Ann on the way back into the home.

"You're welcome. I can tell he's excited to talk to you. And don't mind me, I'll be like a mouse in the corner."

125

"Ah, I was afraid you'd left," Chandler said as the two walked in.

He didn't speak of the place where Bailey thought he must have gone. His little trip to the depths of his mind he had taken twenty minutes ago. Or maybe from his mind.

"Let me see the photograph again if you will."

Bailey gave it to him.

"Did I hear you say you *saw* a headband on the Indian mummy?" Chandler asked.

"No, the picture of it is what you said is a headband. I saw a head, it's about the size of a softball and wrapped in a leather hide," Bailey said. "It had a small band around its braids. Remember? I told you a little bit ago."

"You did? I wonder where the body is. Do you realize this is lost history, Mr. Calhoun?"

"No, tell me about it."

"In late 1938, I was the state director of anthropology and archaeology. Two men named Meggert and Davison brought me something they'd found while gold mining in the Ferris Mountains. It was the mummified remains of a pygmy-like Indian. I found out later that his tribe was called the Nimerigar. They also had some artifacts they found with the body. The Arapaho and Shoshone Indians told about them but they were only thought of as an ancient legend. Do you know what it's like to hold a legend in your hands? An anomaly only spoken about in tribal whispers? A tribe who disappeared hundreds of years ago?"

Chandler's eyes widened and a thin, vein lined arm waved in the air. "Old tribes feared them because the Nimerigar were vicious, blood-thirsty killers! They ate children, I think." Puzzlement showed on his face momentarily. "Strange, I can't remember what else they did. Meggert and Davison left the artifacts and the mummy with me for nearly a month. Uh... uh... uh."

"How do you know so much about them if they were only known as a legend?"

"I learned about them, Mr. Calhoun, from a manifest written on an animal hide and was Onatah's death shroud. He wrote his peoples' history on it."

Bailey saw the old man gasp for breath and his hands tremble. "Are you all right?" he asked, hoping the old man wouldn't die on him right then.

Ann put her book down and watched her father, her face showing the strain.

"I'm getting older, almost ready for my shroud."

"What happened to the mummy, and the two miners?" Bailey asked.

"Disappeared. They came back and got him and all the artifacts. I believe early 1933. This was before any laws governed antiquities, you understand. I never saw or heard from them again. I did hear it was displayed in a carnival freak show before the war." He lay back on the bed and closed his eyes.

"How come nobody seems to have heard about these... Nimerigar?" Bailey asked.

"I couldn't publish a paper on it when the evidence disappeared, now could I?" Chandler shot back. He sounded angry, almost defiant. "It's written... my oh my oh my. 1935. I showed my paper to a colleague and he laughed in my face when I didn't have the proof; even though I swore to him everything I had written about them was the truth. I was younger and foolish then."

"Where're the papers now?"

Chandler asked Bailey for some water. "In my file cabinet over at my daughter's house. She'll be coming here tomorrow to visit. I'll ask her where she has it."

Bailey looked to Ann, a puzzled look on his face.

She shook her head and had a tired smile.

The old man took the paper cup of water Bailey had poured for him and drank it all like a man dying of thirst in the desert. "Would you come back and visit me? Please."

"Next week... Friday. Would that be okay?"

"I'll... I'll look forward to seeing you then. Uh, Mr. Calhoun. Meggert wore a chain around his neck with a smaller, similar version of the headband on it. It was a gold etched silver band used to hold braids in place, I believe. It was the size of a small ring."

"The mummy head I saw had one on it --holding his hair --just like you're describing." *Just like I told you before.*

"Perhaps only the elders or royalty wore them. I'm not sure now." Chandler said, closing his eyes. "I'm sorry, I'm tired." His voice was faint.

The old man's chest rose and fell in shallow movements. *I'll be surprised if he lives until next week.*

"I think we better go," Ann whispered in his ear.

Outside, next to her car, she hugged herself. "As you can see, he can be lucent and cognizant of his surroundings and other times not recognize me or even acknowledge my presence in the room." Tears welled in her eyes. She wiped them with the back of her hand. "I'm sorry, sometimes it gets to me."

Bailey wanted to draw her into his chest, comfort her. "I know it's tough. I've gone through the same thing." He looked down at the ground, not sure what to do or say. "Can I see you when I come down next week? Maybe we could talk."

Ann hesitated for a moment, then said, "I'd like to visit with you. I haven't been here long enough to have made any friends. I moved back from Los Angles to be with him." She opened her purse and brought out a pen and small notebook. She wrote her number down, tore the page out, handed it to him, and asked for his phone number. "Let me know what time you'll be here and I'll meet you."

Bailey watched her drive away and thought his pulse was beating a bit quicker. He went back into the home and left his phone number with the desk, in case Chandler would happen to ask for him. He told the nurse he could come down anytime.

One or two pegs were falling into the right holes, though he wasn't sure what the right holes were yet.

Chapter Nineteen

The sun still had an hour before setting when Bailey drove into Rawlins. He'd eaten in Laramie and had a bone for the dog and a six pack for him. No conflict tonight, he thought. *I'm gonna drink some beers, get a nice buzz and watch the sun go down while I sit on the patio.* He'd called Cat and she was coming over to join him.

"Hey cowboy," she said peeking over the fence gate a half-hour later. "Wait for me, you're way ahead." Cat came through the gate carrying a grocery sack and a cooler. She promptly opened the top taking two cans of beer out, and handing one to Bailey. Her foot snaked behind the frame of a lounge chair and pulled it closer. "Oh man," she said. "I need this. One hell of a day."

"How come?" Bailey thought she smelled like fresh lilacs.

"I saw some poachers out south by Sage Creek. They killed an eight-point buck deer. I chased them thirty freaking miles and lost them down by the Little Sandstone. Goddamn, I hate poachers." Cat emptied the can and got another. "Things go all right with you in Cheyenne?"

"Yeah, I guess okay. You ever hear of the Nimerigar?"

"Hmm, no. Can't say as I have 'cept it sounds like something you'd smoke. What is it?" The grocery bag rustled as she took a can of nuts out and pulled the lid off. She grabbed a fist full and threw some in her mouth. "Well?" Cat returned Bailey's stare.

"An old Indian tribe… an extinct tribe," Bailey answered.

"What about them? They unextinct now?" She chortled.

The buzz he felt was welcomed. The wind blew as a breeze, hard enough to keep the mosquitoes away but not so much as to keep the two of them from enjoying the beginning sunset. Bloated clouds, reflecting the vanishing rays of the sun, moved in from the west, a sign of another storm on the way. "Not as far as I know. I heard about them today for the first time. Lived in the Ferris's a long time ago. You wanna stay with me tonight?" His grin felt a little sloppy.

"I thought you'd never ask," she said, holding her arms out. "Come here."

Bailey woke up before dawn and heard the rhythm of raindrops beating off his bedroom window.

"Why are you up so early?" The pillow covered half her head. The sheet came up to her ribs and one breast peeked over the seam.

"I've got to go out to the Wood's place. You want to go?" Bailey buttoned his shirt and pulled his pants on.

"No. Take your pants off and come back to bed."

"Why don't you stay here and I will when I get back." He sat on the bed and stuck his feet into his boots. "C'mon and go."

"Sorry. I've got to check bird licenses today." She got out of bed and stretched, giving Bailey a wicked look. "Call me when you get back, okay?"

"Yeah, if I don't crash my truck thinking about you standing there naked. I have to go while I'm able. I'll call you." He kissed her on his way out of the bedroom.

*   *   *

All evidence of the rainstorm had disappeared by the time he left the house. The sun burned the humidity off and Bailey knew it would turn into a scorcher. A hot wind blew out of the west before he reached the bottom of Willow Hill and waves of heat danced off the pavement.

When he turned onto the Stone Gulch road, dust outraced him and covered his truck in a thick coating. Even though the

Wood's truck was parked in front of the ranch house, he got the feeling the place was deserted. Barney didn't run up and drag his claws down the door of his pickup, and the milk cows bellowed from the barn below, like they hadn't been milked. He got out and jerked back when he heard the slam of a door. Man, he was getting spooked for no reason, he thought. Jean or Albert had to be there, going in or coming out of the house. The door slammed again, then several more times.

Bailey walked around the pickup and saw the front screen door banging in the wind. The hair on the back of his neck stood up. His thumb kissed the thumb-break on the holster, freeing the strap holding the Glock.

Be careful, maybe you're just keyed up. Yeah, keyed up. He hunched over a little and moved toward the house, keeping his hand on the pistol butt and his eyes moving. *Always be aware of your surroundings, the instructors used to say. Okay, I'm looking, but I'm not seeing anything wrong, just feeling it. Does that count?*

He climbed the porch as quietly as he could. His hand caught the screen door before it crashed into the jam again. The latch was busted off. The solid oak front door stood shut. The Glock appeared in his hand as he twisted the doorknob and shoved. It swung open.

The living room looked as if a hurricane had blown through. Furniture was turned over, books were lying in piles on the floor, and Jean's proudly displayed heirloom dishes in the hutch cabinet were on the floor in pieces no bigger than a silver dollar. There was an empty place on the wall where the picture frames of arrowheads should have been hanging. The other Indian artifacts and the bison skulls guarding them on the mantle were gone. At least he didn't see them anywhere.

Bailey crept toward the kitchen, his left hand holding the pistol out in front of him. He eased through the door. "Goddammit, no!" Albert's hands were bound behind him and he lay face down on the kitchen floor in a dark pool of blood.

"Jean!" he yelled, not caring if the murderer was still in the house and heard him. In fact, he hoped the killer was there, because he'd kill the son-of-a-bitch.

Bailey pushed the kitchen door open with one hand and half-stepped back into the living room. Sweat ran down his face as he went down the short hallway to the bedroom. A lingering look inside told him all he needed to know. Jean's hands were tied to the bedposts and there was a bullet hole in the middle of her forehead. The open eyes stared toward Bailey, as if pleading for help.

Bailey checked behind the bedroom door and next, the closet. He didn't expect anyone to be hiding in the room, he knew both had been dead for a while because the blood from both bodies looked like thick coats of paint. He lowered the pistol to the side of his leg and stood at the foot of the bed taking in the scene.

Powder burns spread around the bullet hole and darkened the surrounding tissue. Whoever killed her had put a gun barrel against Jean's forehead and pulled the trigger. The pillow was soaked with blood and semi-solid pieces of matter spread out over the back wall. The bullet probably blew out the back of her skull.

He felt his eyes grow moist. "Goddammit. Somebody's going to die for this," he promised her. Bailey wanted this to be a nightmare, like after being on a hard drunk; but the wind rattled the windows and wailed so loud he knew he was in the cold, hard, reality of the real world - where men killed for pleasure or greed.

Apparently the killer didn't worry about anybody calling the cops because the telephone still worked. He called the Sheriff's Office and reported finding the two murder victims.

"Are you kidding me, Calhoun?" the dispatcher asked. "This is the 911 number…"

"Listen to me, Crawford. Albert and Jean Wood have been murdered at their ranch. Tell Jordan to get his fat ass out here.

I'll be waiting." He slammed the phone down. It would be at least forty-five minutes to an hour before they showed up. Enough time to drive down the road aways.

The wind blew the dust faster than he drove. Gusts would kick up and tumbleweeds darted across the road in front of him. *What the hell is going on? Three people dead in a week. Unbelievable. And sure as hell no coincidence.*

About two miles from the ranch house the road came to a clearing of buffalo grass. The sagebrush grew in small clumps and at the end stood a pole corral and a branding chute. A black shadow lay in the middle of the clearing. Bailey almost missed it except he thought he heard a painful yelp and howl. The pickup's tires left furrows in the dirt when Bailey slammed the brakes on.

"Barney!" he yelled, leaving the truck running and trotting toward the dog.

Another long drawn out howl sent a chill down Bailey's back. The dog sounded like he was mourning the deaths of his masters. Barney tried to stand but couldn't get his back legs to work. His front paws dug into the dirt and pushed and pulled himself forward. He howled again.

Bailey dropped to his knees by the side of the dog. He could see where a bullet had entered one hip. A scratched out path disappearing into the sagebrush behind them showed Bailey how far Barney had dragged himself.

"I don't want to do this, but I've got to pick you up." He tore a length of material from the bottom of his shirt and tied it around the dog's muzzle. "Easy now." As gently as he could, he slid his hands under the dog's body and lifted. Barney thrashed and let out a high pitched squeal. "It's okay, it's okay boy," Bailey said, clamping his jaw shut to keep him from yelling out threats to whoever had done this.

Bailey placed him on the passenger side of the front seat. *I meet Jordan at the ranch now or take you to the vet. If I don't get you to town, you'll die. I'll be breaking the law if I'm not at the scene when the cops show.* To him, there wasn't a choice. He turned around and drove as fast as he could toward the ranch.

He couldn't see any cars coming and ran the stop sign at the highway entrance. The government truck's speedometer almost touched ninety and held there as he flew down the hill outside of Lamont. A Highway Patrol car, its red and blue lights flashing shot past him headed the opposite direction. In the rearview mirror, Bailey saw the brake lights of the patrol car come on as the car made a sliding U-turn and white smoke flared up from the tires. It accelerated and came up alongside him. Ricconi motioned Bailey to pull over. They both came to a stop on the shoulder of the highway, Ricconi behind the pickup. Bailey jumped out of his truck and ran back to the patrol car as the brawny patrolman clambered out.

"Frank, I've got to get to town, now."

"I got a radio call there's been a murder at the Woods' place. You're supposed to be there waiting. What the hell's going on?" Riconni's hand stayed by his pistol.

"Both Albert and Jean were killed. Their dog's been shot and he's still alive. I've got to get him to the vet," he pleaded.

Ricconi wiped his face and said, "Put him in my car, I'll take him. You get back to the Woods' before Jordan gets there."

"You sure?"

"Yeah, I'm sure. Besides, the piece of shit you're driving won't go as fast as I can."

The dog didn't yelp or move when Bailey picked him up and moved him to the patrol car. "You've got to hurry."

Ricconi climbed into the car faster than he'd climbed out of it. "Take it easy. It's just a dog. Don't worry, and get your ass back out there and wait for the deputies."

The patrol car's tires smoked as it accelerated onto the highway, emergency lights still flashing. Bailey watched it disappear down the blacktop. He got in his pickup, turned around, and headed back to the Woods' ranch.

135

* * *

Two outfits from the sheriff's office and the coroner's Suburban all stopped in front of the ranch house. Five deputies and Jordan got out of the vehicles and entered the house. Bailey sat in his truck with his front door open and took a deep breath when the Undersheriff came out of the house fifteen minutes later with his hat in his hand. He looked to the mountain and walked over to Bailey's truck.

"You didn't see nobody?" Jordan asked.

"No, there wasn't anyone around. The coroner say how long he thinks they've been dead?"

"Quick guess, eight to twelve hours. We'll know for sure after the autopsy. Hey, I know they were friends of yours. I'm sorry."

"Thanks. What do you think happened?"

"Probably some doped up punks trying to score some cash. The place was trashed. They had to be looking for money." Jordan dipped some chew into his lower lip. "Believe me, dope's ruining this country."

"You don't think it odd their hands were tied and the two were pretty much executed?" Bailey saw Jordan's eyes narrow. It made him look like a short-ear slaughtering hog.

"Calhoun, these old eyes have seen a lot. Trust me, there's no conspiracy. A screwed up burglary that ended in murder. We'll find them, don't you worry."

"I having a tough time understanding something here," Bailey said. His voice took on an edge. "I find an archaeologist dead last week with an Indian artifact in his hand. Now, two people are tied up and murdered in their home after Albert found an extraordinary artifact last week. I didn't see it in the house either. Don't you think it's stretching it a little to call it a coincidence?" He couldn't believe Jordan didn't see the same things like he did.

"You know what was in the guy's hand, huh? I think you want to try to make a name for yourself again," Jordan shot back. "I'll tell you what, Mr. Hotshot. I'm gonna give you everything we have on the first dead body you found. Let's see what you do with it. And I think I know who gave you the information on him...I'll take care of him later." Jordan sounded menacing. He put his hat on and pulled it down low on his forehead. "Seems like a lot of people are turning up dead and you just happen to find them." He pointed a finger at Bailey. "Let me have your pistol."

"Are you serious?"

"Yup. I'm gonna run a nitrate test on you too. Now give me the gun." Jordan held his hand out, palm cupped, waiting for the pistol.

Bailey pulled the Glock out using his fingers to hold the butt. "If they'd been shot with a .40 caliber, it would have blown the back of their heads off."

"Maybe, maybe not. Depends on the load. Follow me." They walked over to one of the sheriff's vehicles. Jordan brought a yellow canvas bag out and laid it on the hood. "Hold your hands out," he ordered. "I need to swab your hands." He held four large cotton swabs. Bailey held his hands out and Jordan ran them over each hand and wrist, then put each swab in a different paper sack. He whistled an off-key song under his breath while he tagged and secured the bags. The pistol went into another paper sack.

"You come in this afternoon and make a statement. You understand?"

"Yeah, I got it. You're barking up the wrong tree. But, I've got to admit, you're doing it right, Jordan," Bailey said grudgingly. The coroner pushed a gurney out the front door with a black body bag strapped to it as Bailey climbed into his pickup. He pulled out then stopped on the side of the road and watched through his rear view mirror as the coroner shoved the gurney into the back of the Suburban.

He drove to the east, away from the ranch, until he came to the spot where he found the dog. Squatting on his heels, he saw the furrows in the dirt and followed them back into the sagebrush. A blotch of blood stained the desert floor. *This is where someone shot him.* He could see where the ground was torn up from Barney thrashing and his claw marks after dragging himself with his front legs.

Went about a hundred yards before I found him. God knows how long it took him. Bailey walked to the road and scanned the area, holding his hand over his eyes to keep the sun out. A reflection of metal. He took his pen out, stuck the end into a shell casing and picked it up. It came from a 9mm. So brazen, whoever shot the dog didn't think they needed to pick up the spent cartridge. Probably shot him while sitting inside a vehicle. *Bastards.*

Ricconi's patrol car was still parked at the vet's office when Bailey arrived. The patrolman stood at the counter talking with an attractive woman in a lab coat.

"Dr. Previs, how's the dog doing?" Out of the corner of his eye Bailey noticed several other people holding pets.

"Hi, Mr. Calhoun. The bullet did some damage but not nearly as much as it could have. It didn't hit any organs or shatter the bones. His name must be Lucky," the woman said.

"Is he going to be okay?"

"I'm sure he will be. Ask me again in a couple of days. He'll have to stay here, of course. We'll have to watch him and make sure there's no infection or complications with his hip. Ah…who's going to be responsible for the bill?" Her smile left and a look of business came over her face.

I don't believe this. I'll take care of it. You want me to pay now?"

The smile returned. "No, a deposit will be fine and we can wait until you pick the dog up before you pay the balance."

He took a credit card out of his wallet and hoped he wasn't over the limit. "Will a hundred be okay?" He held the card out to her and tried keeping the sarcasm out of his voice.

"Perfect. You can pay over at the window. Thank you, and have a nice day," she said in a now cheery voice.

Ricconi walked with Bailey out of the vet clinic. "Goddamn, I can't believe how money hungry everybody is anymore." Bailey fumed. "What if I wouldn't have had a credit card? I'd had to bounce a check or something. Maybe rob the bitch and pay her with her own money."

"I can't believe you're so damn concerned over a dog. Hey, wake up! Two of your friends were murdered. What the hell is a matter with you?"

"I don't know. Maybe some kind of screwy reaction because Jordan's not letting me in the loop. Barney seems to be the only thing I can focus on right now." Bailey looked withdrawn.

A big arm went around his shoulder. "I understand, I think. So settle down, the dog would have been treated. Dana used to say you cared more for animals than you did people." Ricconi squeezed and let him go.

"When did she tell you that?" Bailey stopped by his truck.

"I don't know. I visited her in the hospital once or twice. Probably then."

"Funny, I don't remember her telling me you ever saw her there." He shook his head. "Hell, I'm lucky I remember to flush the toilet anymore. Thanks, Frank. Let's get together soon."

Ricconi climbed into the patrol car. "We will. Maybe I'll come in next week. Drink some beers and barbecue. Your place."

"You're on... anytime." Bailey replied.

"I'm off Tuesday and Wednesday, so Tuesday night? Then I'll have a day to recoup before I have to go to work again. Around six?"

"Yeah. See you then." Bailey backed the truck out and followed the patrol car until it turned and headed north on the highway.

Four hours later, Jordan interviewed Bailey and took his statement. "All right, Calhoun, you can go. Kelly will give you your gun and the folder."

"Believe it or not, I'm not gonna bitch. Hard to say who'll kill someone these days," Bailey said. "Look, they were friends of mine. Will you keep me in the loop on the investigation?"

Jordan looked across the table at him. "I've never really liked you, Calhoun. You always seemed to act like you were better than me and then you turned into a drunk. How you've kept your job, I'll never know. But, yeah, I'll let you know how it's going. If I don't, I'm sure somebody else here will."

"I never thought I was better than you," Bailey replied. "To be honest, you just pissed me off with your attitude."

"I'm not gonna change the way I do things," Jordan said. "I got a job to do and I'm gonna get it done."

"Fair enough. Me too." Bailey nodded his head and left Jordan's office.

At the booking in counter, Kelly had a sack and a file folder. "Goddammit, Bailey. Did you tell Jordan I told you about this?" He thumped the folder on the counter top for emphasis.

"I just told him I knew the guy was an archaeologist and had an artifact in his hand. No names and he didn't ask for one."

Kelly looked in the direction of Jordan's office. "I'm screwed. Thanks, you prick."

"If he accuses you, let me know, I'll talk to him," Bailey said. "I'll explain it without giving you up."

"Sign for the return of the pistol and the folder," Kelly muttered. "Then get the hell out of here. I'm getting pretty tired of you right now."

"Larry…" Bailey said to the retreating back of the deputy. "Shit." He signed the paper, took his Glock out of the bag and stuck it in his holster, and left through the front door.

Chapter Twenty

The new cell phone made him a little happier, and when the clerk ran his credit card through and it didn't scream out he had gone over his measly limit, his mood lifted a little higher. Now he had the little flip phone on his belt, just like the shakers and movers.

Wild Horse Lookout sat on top of Green Mountain, forty miles north of Rawlins. Bailey could see the glow of lights from Rock Springs, to the west about ninety miles, reflecting off the storm clouds and the tiny beads of headlights from cars running down the highway, ten miles east, their glow smeared from the rain starting again. An unusual summer rain every damn night for the past week... a lot of rain. So much for the drought everyone talked about.

God, he loved it up there. It was like being on top of the world. Every day he wanted to be in the country more and more. And, heaven forbid, it seemed like he had a propensity toward pro-environmental issues. Maybe a good thing he was seeing a shrink.

An unopened six pack of beer sat on the floor of the pickup. He turned on the interior light and took a card out of his wallet. Twice, his fingers stumbled over the numbers on the cell phone keypad until he got it right.

"Dr. Radcliffe," the voice said. It sounded like he answered from inside a metal drum.

"This is Bailey Calhoun, Dr. Radcliffe. I need to ask you something."

"Are you drinking? I told you I don't want any calls from a drunk."

"Not a drop, in fact, right now, I don't have any desire for one either. I've got a question on confidentiality, you know, doctor-patient. Hypothetical, of course."

"Of course. Ask," Radcliffe said, a bit of disbelief in his voice.

"If a guy committed a crime, at least considered a crime by the state, but not to him, and he told you about it, could you tell the authorities?"

"No. Only if he told me he was *going* to commit a crime. Then I would." Radcliffe's voice came over the air gentler. "What'd you do, Bailey?"

"I had two friends die today. It seems like people I like die on me all the time."

"Starting with Dana?"

"No, with buddies back in Nam. Dana…she wanted me to help her."

"Help her do what?" Radcliffe asked.

"Cancer is a shitty disease. My friends were murdered and I found their bodies. Some son-of-a-bitch tied them up and blew their brains out."

"Good Lord! We need to…"

"I'm sorry I called you. I'll try to keep my Friday appointment. See ya, Doc." Bailey flipped the phone cover, cutting off Radcliffe's protests.

The image of the four-wheelers coming out of the timber last week played over in his mind. Tomorrow, he thought. Tomorrow will be a good day to spend finding out where the hell they'd been riding. For the moment, coincidences didn't exist so he thought he might bring the pump shotgun along. Loaded with double ought buck. The moon disappeared behind a wall of clouds behind him and the rain fell with more intensity.

* * *

Black clouds covered the western horizon and spread east. Bailey figured he had a couple of hours before the storm front moved in. Already the temperature had dropped eight degrees. It was fifty-two degrees not counting the wind-chill factor. The wind blew ahead of the storm, leading the way and warning men and animals a mean one was coming, get the hell out of the way. He knew he shouldn't go up until the weather cleared. The worst thing he could do would be to get caught up in the mountains in a flash flood or rockslide. If it rained so hard to loosen the shale and the precariously perched boulders on the ravines and canyon walls, it could get dangerous without a flood.

Dawn began two hours before, and as he headed north out of town the sun ricocheted blinding rays off the hood and into his eyes.

After talking to Radcliffe, he'd driven home and read through the file on Millhouse. The guy had been a professor of archaeology at a small college back east. Apparently it didn't pay enough because he got involved with excavating and selling artifacts to the type of people who didn't care if they had to keep them hidden away forever. He served four years in a penitentiary with no probation. Apparently, he didn't want to roll over on his cohorts if he had any. Nothing on the rap sheet after he got out. Ended up face down in a shallow grave on the edge of a sand dune with a bullet in his head. The autopsy showed the bullet was recovered. A nine-millimeter hollow point. The same caliber as the casing he found where the dog had been shot.

Bailey thought a phone call to the law enforcement department involved in prosecuting Millhouse might be fruitful. It couldn't hurt and it didn't look like anyone from the county sheriff's office had contacted them. First thing Monday.

The limestone faces of the mountains were almost obscured by a mist that hung low and layered the slopes like a blanket. When he left the highway and drove up the dirt road to the no access cuts, a threatening rumble of thunder came from the sky, now dark with pregnant storm clouds.

Bailey parked in the turnaround and put his slicker on. The shotgun, with a new leather sling, hung securely over his shoulder with a condom over the barrel to keep any rain out of it. The Glock was holstered snuggly to his left side.

Leaning into the wind, he climbed over the barrier at the end of the cut and headed in the direction he'd seen the four-wheelers come barreling down the previous week.

A nearly extinct rutted trail angled away from him on top of the second cut and disappeared around a huge granite boulder and stand of aspen trees. The mountainside was covered with rocks, trees and prickly brush that standing twice as high as Bailey's six foot-three inch frame.

The forest floor was dark and shielded from the sun if it would have been out, by a canopy of treetops. He compared the sound of the wind blowing through the aspen leaves to a man's callused hand running up the back of his lover. The leaves shimmered as they quaked and reflected the dim light straining to reach them.

Bailey maneuvered through the trees and rocks for an hour. There was definitely a trail made and used. Long slabs of granite had scuffmarks on them from tires spinning to get traction. Whoever drove over them tried keeping off the grass and sagebrush so they wouldn't mat it down. They were pretty good but Bailey could track them. *They've stayed on rocks most of the time. Damn near like a highway.*

Rather than late morning, it looked to be dusk from the storm front blocking most of the daylight out. *I ought to go back,* he thought, grabbing a branch and pulling himself up to an out-thrust of splintered rock. Intermittent raindrops fell with the promise of more to come. Bailey knew when the storm hit it could last for an hour or a day. But he'd be damned if he'd give up following the trail.

He'd hiked for several hours and climbed a steep slope of slippery rock when the rain quit teasing and came down in a torrent, pelting him with hard raindrops that stung when they hit him. The wind picked up and blew with a strength Bailey hadn't seen for years. He was also surprised he hadn't had a heart attack yet as it was beating hard and fast.

He couldn't see anything; when he stepped on the chunk of sagebrush and his feet shot out from under him, his stomach lurched as he went airborne. He came down hard on a pile of rocks and dead tree branches. A gasp blew out of him when something sharp jammed into his side. Pain, like an electric shock, radiated from his hip and ribs. The shotgun dug into his back and neck underneath him. He partially sat in a cleft that narrowed back to a rock shelf, his legs higher than his chest.

"Oh man!" he grunted, trying to get up. Every move sent bolts of pain flying up his body. His hat was somewhere down the slope from him, lost when he fell. The rain matted his hair and oozed cold water down the back of his slicker and shirt, making him shiver. *What the hell am I going to do now?* A bolt of lightning lit up the sky and a deep blast of thunder went off sounding like a howitzer. More rain fell, harder than before and harder than he ever remembered.

Water gathered in basins and ravines high above the tree line as it had been doing for the entire week. Lower on the mountain, trees blown down by past winds and fallen from disease formed natural dams that filled from the rain channeled into small streams. Every passing minute the water levels rose until the tree trunks started to move slightly from the pressure. The Indians called them *God's Tears*. To everyone else they were flash floods.

Bailey heard the snap of timbers above him. Fear grabbed the insides of his guts and he cried out in frustration and pain as he shoved against the sides of the fissure with his hands. He pushed with his left foot and turned, feeling his flesh tear. He glimpsed a bloody point of a branch when he rolled onto the shelf. The snaps turned to drawn-out cracks of breaking wood. He clinched the wound on his side with his hand and ran with a stumbling gait toward a dark notch he saw in an outcrop of limestone, the barrel of the shotgun hitting him in the back of the head with every running step.

It sounded like a waterfall above him. Bailey knew a flash flood was crashing down the mountain and he had a fleeting thought he might die. Swept away, his body hurled into the trees and mountainside, smashed beyond recognition. What seemed like slow motion, he saw a high wall of water filled with debris rushing toward him.

The black notch in the limestone looked more like an opening to a cave with a rock face below it. He threw himself in and crawled toward the back as the flood obliterated the light and deafened him. With his arms over his head he brought his knees up and tried to block out the sound. Water deflected from the rock face into the cave and ran under him, soaking his pants and shirt. He couldn't worm any farther into the depths and he had to fight back the panic of drowning in a hole. He took a deep breath and held it as a wave of dirty water washed over him and filled the cavern.

Chapter Twenty-One

"Quite the downpour we're having," Sanderson shouted, pulling his collar up as he walked rapidly from a small cement building to his house. Reese walked alongside him without commenting.

"I didn't know a cloudburst could be this powerful. Interesting country. Too bad we can't stay much longer."

"How much longer you think?" Reese asked. He turned toward the mountain, a rumble booming down from the cloud-shrouded mountain. "Hear that?"

"My God. What is it?"

"Either a landslide or flash flood," Reese replied. "Sounds like it could be up around the site. I oughta go check it."

"I think you better wait. It might be dangerous, and it's raining harder now," Sanderson said. They stood under the roof of the front porch. The pelting rain sounded like a drum beat on the roof. Pools of water formed in the road and yard. "Let's go in and have a drink."

Sanderson opened the bar and filled two glasses with bourbon and water. Reese lit the kindling and flames soon burned the logs and warmed the room. They sat down in leather chairs located in front of the fireplace.

"We fenced off the west side and put no trespassing signs up. I'm going to ride the line to keep anyone out," Reese said.

"Let's hope the BLM ranger doesn't check up on it. That's all we'd need is to have him snooping around." Sanderson went over to his desk and opened a drawer. He took a metal box out and carried it back to the chair and sat down.

"A few more of these and we'll have more money than we thought possible." He reached into the box and gently brought a leather wrapped bundle out. "Yes, my little friend," Sanderson said to the wrinkled, aged head he cradled in his hands. "We just have to dig out the rest of your brethren." He cocked his head as if hearing something. "How many more of these do you think there are?"

Reese got out of the chair and went to Sanderson's side and looked at the head. A smile appeared. "I'm thinking we've found the tribal tomb, so a hell-of-a-lot more. We just have to be more careful digging 'em out; we're breaking a lot of the bodies. I don't know if your customers would want pieces of pygmy mummies or not. Probably more money in complete ones, don't you think, Gavin?"

"Dammit! Don't call me Gavin! Only Ed, Ed Sanderson. Is his name so hard to remember?" Gavin thundered.

"Actually it is, to tell you the truth. It's not like you've been Sanderson that long. You've been Gavin to me for five years in a six by ten cell. What the hell you expect?" Reese said defensively.

Gavin put the head back and shut the lid to the box. "I'm sorry. Over reaction. We're just so close to making such a gigantic score, one little mistake like a name could ruin it for all of us." He grabbed one of Reese's biceps and squeezed. "You're my main man in this, partner, but you can't screw up like that."

"All right. All right. I won't do it again." Reese took a swallow of his drink and sat back down in the chair. "Partners, yeah. Equal partners."

One of Gavin's eyebrows lifted immeasurably. "Sure, *equal* partners.

"How long can we get away with this?" Reese asked.

"Hard to say. No one out here knows the dearly departed Sanderson by sight. If nothing digs him and his son up, we're safe until his lawyer comes out to inspect the ranch in a month or so."

"Too bad we had to get rid of Millhouse," Reese said. "We're probably going to ruin more stuff than we can salvage."

"Who cares? Now Ike knows what will happen to him if he tries stealing from us. A good lesson, don't you think?"

"It should be." Reese replied.

"I can't believe he tried sneaking out with a mummy," Gavin said. "He either lost it or hid it. The son-of-a-bitch. I should have killed him myself. He could have screwed things up for us when the old man found the head." He frowned, then said, "I wonder where the body is?"

"Hard to say. Maybe a coyote ate it or something. I couldn't find it anywhere." Reese stood up and put his empty glass on an end table. "I don't want to set the dynamite with the weather being so shitty. You'll have to let me know a couple days in advance before we leave."

"I've been thinking about that." Gavin poured himself another drink. "Do you think we need to blow it up?"

"Getting soft in your old age, *Ed?* Yeah, we gotta do it."

"I thought so. I guess I just needed confirmation," Gavin replied. "After all, we're talking some unique history here."

"So? We won't see it again. Get over it."

"I am already. It's just business."

"You got that right. Just business," Reese said.

The hollow sound of Reese's footsteps echoing down the hallway as he left the office made Gavin pause and think about the future. *He's a tough boy. I don't think I want to cross him.*

He sat at the desk and turned a Rolodex. The number he dialed was answered after two rings.

"Hello, Mr. Stemple?" Gavin said into the mouthpiece. "This is Humphrey's Reproductions."

"Yes, I've been expecting your call," the voice said cheerfully. "What do you have for me?"

"We've just finished glazing the antique doll's head. It should be ready to ship by the middle of the week."

"Wonderful! Payment as usual?" Stemple asked.

"Yes, by our usual method will be fine. One thing though. Because the mold is so limited, we've had to add a twenty percent surcharge. I'm sure you understand," Sanderson said smoothly.

"Twenty percent seems a little high, Mr. Humphrey."

"I understand completely if you would like to decline the order...?"

"No, no. Send it. After all, it's not like they grow on trees now, is it?" Stemple tried laughing but to Sanderson, it sounded more like a strangled rasp. "Ah... Mr. Humphrey, any chance you can find me a complete doll? I still want this one, of course; but if you could arrange for me to receive a full-bodied doll, I would pay a premium price."

"This is your lucky day. It's possible we could have one in the next week."

"I've got to have it, Mr. Humphrey, and the surcharge is quite acceptable," Stemple said.

"Excellent. My delivery person will contact you with this current item through the normal channels. Goodnight, sir." Gavin hung the phone up with a satisfied grin on his face. He turned to the computer that sat on a small table to the side of the desk. The cursor clicked on a file icon and asked for a password. *Nimerigar* was typed in and a spreadsheet appeared. Under a column with a heading of Stemple, he typed in: *$85,000-head*. There were six names, including Stemple's, across the top of the sheet. He made three more phone calls and afterwards typed figures in under three more names. A low whistle came out of his mouth when he tallied the figures. *Yes sir,* he thought. *There's gold in them thar hills.*

Chapter Twenty-Two

The water rushed in and filled the cave. Bailey held his breath and shoved his elbows into the dirt floor trying to push himself out of the rock coffin before he drowned. The shotgun caught on the cave ceiling and he twisted around to throw it off him. Like an opened dam, the water violently backed out, dragging him along with it. One of his boots was yanked off and disappeared. Dirt and rocks suspended in the water hit him in the head and face, torn away from the cave's end.

His body was partially outside the cave. Rain continued to come down in a heavy drizzle but seemed to have lost most of its fury. Bailey lifted his head off the ground and felt his heart hammering inside his chest. Small rivulets of water still flowed down the side of the mountain and ran against his legs.

Exhausted and bruised, he reached for his shotgun and used it as a crutch to push himself up from the ground. A sharp, jolt of pain shot up his side where the branch had punctured him, and his right hand bled from a cut alongside the meaty part of his palm. A worked piece of stone was embedded in the gash. He pulled it out and held it on end between his thumb and forefinger. *Can you believe this? A Goddamn arrowhead. Can't ever find them when you look for 'em.* It was several inches long, with the ears that rawhide string would attach to the arrow shaft, apparently broken off. It went into his jeans pocket.

The sky lightened, and to the south, sunlight streamed down through a widening break in the clouds and lit up a section of far prairie. Along with one of his boots, his hat probably lay in Natrona County. If they weren't, Bailey couldn't see them anywhere. He silently cursed himself for going into the mountains when a storm was brewing. He knew better than that. If this was some kind of mid-life crisis where he craved adventure, it was going to kill him. The climb up from his truck had been around a quarter of a mile, and he'd hiked more than a mile along the side of the mountainside. The best way for him to safely get back to his truck would be to work his way down far enough that when he headed west traversing the side, he would eventually run into the pass road.

Bailey ejected the round out of the shotgun and put the butt on the ground for support. He took his pocketknife and cut half of his pants leg off, and wrapped it around his bootless foot. A strip of denim tied around the cloth, bandage style, held it in place. Somehow, his cell phone had stayed clipped to the side of his belt. When he flipped it open, "no service" showed on the screen. Being surrounded by limestone outcroppings might be blocking the signal, he thought. A couple hundred yards and he should be in the open.

Every step seemed like a shard of rock or piece of dead brush pierced the sole of his foot through the makeshift shoe. Twice his feet slid out from under him on a talus slope of crumbled limestone and shale. He nearly sobbed with relief when he came out of the rocky formation into a small clearing. The phone showed service! His right hand had swelled and hurt when he held the phone. A shiver ran up his back while he counted the rings.

"Wyoming Game and Fish, Ropper speaking."

"Jesus, Cat. I'm glad you're home." Were his teeth chattering?

"Bailey. Where're you calling from? What's the matter?" she asked, concern sounded in her voice that made Bailey smile.

"On the north side of the Ferris. I got caught in a flash flood and..."

"Are you all right? Are you hurt? You sound hurt." She ran the sentences together and when she paused for a breath, Bailey interrupted.

"Hold on. Let me tell you, for Christ's sake."

With the way his luck had been running, he figured the battery would go down before he told her what he wanted. After a quick rundown on the events, he said, "Come up the pass road until you get to my pickup. I'll be making my way over to meet the road so honk your horn a couple of times every minute. Oh, and go to my house and bring me a pair of boots and some pants, will you?"

"Boots and pants? Uh… all right. Anything else?"

"I got a pretty good cut on my hand and side, so maybe some hydrogen peroxide and an antibiotic. They should be in my medicine cabinet. Kind of hurry, will you?" He shivered again and couldn't feel the phone in his hand.

"On my way now. I'll see you in an hour. You better be okay."

Things were changing. The phone still had juice in the battery and she was home. *Lady Luck, my name's Bailey Calhoun. Nice to see you. It's been a long time.*

Putting his right hand between the buttons of his shirt to hold it up made it a little more comfortable. Numbness had spread from his hand to his elbow. He used the shotgun more to keep his balance and took each step with care. It felt like he'd been climbing and walking for hours when he tripped over a chunk of sagebrush and fell onto the flat surface of a boulder. His vision had blurred and his swollen right hand and arm were totally numb. *I'm just gonna rest for a minute.* His eyes closed and he rolled on his back. Raindrops fell on his face after being blown off the leaves of aspen trees standing nearby. He licked at them with his tongue.

The sound of a siren kept assaulting his hearing. Had he been in a car wreck? Must be, there was someone yelling also, calling his name. His vision was still blurred and he felt disoriented. The rough stone scraped against his left hand. He pushed himself to a sitting position. Yeah, a siren was going off and someone was hollering his name. He felt a little sick to his stomach. Had he been on a binge and drank too much? Trees and a granite bluff came into focus. *Nope. I'm on the mountain.*

Bailey tried to yell back, but all that came out was a croak and it hurt like hell. The Glock's butt jammed his side. He took it out and held it barrel high. He was damned grateful it was a double-action because the odds of holding it and pulling the slide back to get a shell in the chamber would have been next to impossible.

He pulled the trigger. The gunshot deafened him for an instant and the recoil almost made him drop the pistol. He gripped harder, shoved his ear against his shoulder and pulled the trigger four more times.

Chapter Twenty-Three

"Did you hear that?" Reese asked Bodine while they walked toward the barn.

"Yeah, a siren and some gunshots."

"We better ride up there and see what the hell is going on," Reese said. "Why would a siren be going off?"

Bodine shrugged his shoulders.

They opened the barn door, pulled some slickers on hanging from the wall and climbed on two Honda four-wheelers, each one with a scabbard attached and the butt of a crossbow sticking out the end.

When they were out the barn, they accelerated down a dirt two-track road that disappeared into the high crags of the Ferris rising up in front of them. The exhaust pipes were elongated and thick. The engines' exhaust, which should have been resonant and noticeable, were muted. Mud kicked up from the tires and the tracks were deep in the wet ground.

Storm clouds covered the peaks and dropped down the mountainsides, obscuring the trees until they were within twenty yards of them. Reese and Bodine entered a narrow ravine and churned up and over rocks and downed timber, scarred with tire tracks. They came to a fissure breaking through the ravine onto a wide and flat rock shelf behind a high ridge of limestone that ran perpendicular to the rise of the mountain.

"I don't like riding in this kind of weather," Bodine said when Reese stopped on a ledge. They'd turned and worked their way through the fissure. Rain drizzled and his breath could be seen. "And it's cold."

Reese didn't say anything but thought, *If I was smart, I'd have Ike ride up by himself, but I can't trust him to do it without me along.* "Quit your bitching. If the site's okay, we'll warm up and head back. You want to take a chance it was found and we didn't do anything? Somebody was shooting up there and they weren't deer hunting."

They came to a two-foot drop from the ledge to a rock shelf. Reese gave the four- wheeler the gas and the machine leaped down to the shelf and headed west at twice the speed they'd driven coming up the mountain.

The limestone ridges of the Ferris and the shelf were formed millions of years ago from the erosion of the softer rock and ground around them. At one time, the limestone would have been a facing of the mountain and not stand up like sharks' teeth. Now, it afforded seclusion and concealment from the highway and land to the north for anyone or anything behind them.

After a mile, they drove into a creek, the water flowing fast and loud. The gravel creek bed let them ride higher up the mountainside until a wall of pine and aspen trees blocked their route. They stopped.

"First time I seen water in this old creek since I been out here," Bodine said. He didn't have to speak very loud to be heard over the four-wheeler's engine.

"Yeah, I wouldn't have come up until the rain quit but I thought I heard a flash flood earlier."

"Heard? What's one sound like?" Bodine smirked. "You trying to shit me, boy?"

"Nope. You ever hear one it'll make your balls shrivel up and you'll pray you're not below it." Reese said.

"So tell me."

"You won't hear any birds first off. Even in a rain, you'll think it's getting still out. Then it sounds like a hundred wooden gates are thrown open and God's rolling train cars down the mountain."

"You been caught in one?"

"Almost. I was poaching elk horns once in the Bighorns. I'd been tracking a big bull and working my way to get into the middle of the canyon. All day it'd been raining hard and I was too stupid to think there could be a flash flood. In fact it never crossed my mind. I saw one come down a canyon next to a ridge I stood on. I know better now. Let's get going," Reese said, squeezing the throttle on the Honda.

A tunnel-like trail opened up when they drove a short distance into the trees. The dense stand of pine trees and storm clouds made it seem more like nighttime rather than mid-afternoon. The trail ended a half-mile later when Reese stopped before a huge outcrop of granite, looking like a rock sentinel with scrub oak and brush growing out of long ragged cracks. He shut the engine off and pulled the crossbow from its scabbard. Hand signals to Bodine instructed him to follow with his crossbow ready.

The actions made Reese smile and think of his time in Iraq during Desert Storm. Good times for the three months he was there until a chicken-shit captain caught him stealing supplies and selling them on the black market. He would have liked to have stayed for a while longer. It was an exhilarating high shooting someone and seeing him flop around on the ground. Better than dope. Reese never made a quick kill; he didn't like to kill too fast. The few highs in the last couple of years came from whacking winos and hitchhikers back east. Sometimes he'd take out a business suit, just so no one felt safe.

Sanderson hired him because he'd liked the idea of having an ex-ranger for a bodyguard. It had made the old fart feel extra important. At least for a while.

He crept around the outcrop with the butt of the crossbow against his shoulder. A cutback opened into the mouth of a long, dimly lit cavern. The smell of smoke clung to the rock and several torches were jammed into cracks in the cavern wall. They crept through a busted out section of rock wall. With

Bodine behind him, Reese came out on a flat plateau on the other side of the wall and stepped over rubble on the ground left from some of the excavation.

Reese held a flashlight out to the side of him, shining the beam into the nooks and shafts that took off from the chamber. Nothing appeared disturbed. With a grunt of satisfaction he lit two torches. "We'll dry off and head back."

"Why'd you hold the light away from you? On TV, the cops always hold a flashlight next to the barrel of the gun," Bodine asked. He turned his back to a torch and stood so close, steam rose from his drenched clothes.

"If you were hiding and gonna take a shot at me in the dark, what would you shoot at?" Reese asked. He moved the flashlight from side to side.

"The light, hell, that'd be all I could see," he said. When it dawned on him the point Reese made, his voice lifted. "Sure, if I shot at the light and you were holding it away from you, I'd miss. Damn, you're good."

"Remember that, Ike. I'm damn good." Reese didn't smile.

"If I was you, I'd be a mercenary. Live the exciting life, huh?"

"I'm going take the money I get from this gig and live in Belize."

"Where the hell is that?"

"It's on the east coast of Central America. They speak English and there's a lot of Americans, so I won't stick out. Mountains, ocean-- close to enough countries if I get bored, I can do some work for a couple of guys I knew in the Rangers who live there."

"Maybe I could go with you?" Bodine asked. "Nothing for me here, I could use a change."

"Yeah, man. We'll talk about it later," Reese said. *Unfortunately Ike, I can't take a corpse on an airplane.*

Chapter Twenty-Four

"Look at his hand," the voice said. It sounded familiar. A younger man's.

"Should we call an ambulance for him?" A woman's voice this time.

"No, we can get him to the truck. It's not that far."

Bailey stood up with the help of four hands and moved with them off the boulder. The numbing had left his hand and pain made it throb with every beat of his heart. He shook his head to try and clear the muddy images he saw. "Travis? Cat?"

"We're getting you to the truck, just help us a little," Travis said.

Cat and Travis each had one of his arms around their necks as they eased him through the rocks and timber. "My goddamn hand feels the size of a balloon."

"I think you might have blood poisoning. Your veins are black going up your wrist," Cat said. "Just about there." Her breath came in gasps.

Travis and Cat settled him in the front seat of a pickup and clipped the safety belt. The motion of the truck when they left the mountain made him doze; when he woke up, two men in white orderly uniforms were laying him on a gurney and pushed him into the emergency room of Memorial Hospital.

A doctor examined Bailey's right hand and arm, then felt under his armpit where the orange-sized swollen gland was tender to the touch. "What did you get into, Mr. Calhoun?" The doctor inserted an IV into the top of his wrist. "A nasty case of blood poisoning. I'm going to give you a mega dose of antibiotics." He spoke softly to the nurse. "Let's clean up that cut and see if we can find anything in there."

"In my pocket," Bailey mumbled as the nurse turned his hand and gently ran a swab over the wound.

"Then we'll stitch it."

"I don't see anything, doctor," she said, pulling the sides a few millimeters apart.

"I said, it's in my pocket."

"What's that, Mr. Calhoun?" the doctor asked. He took Bailey's hand from the nurse and carefully examined the gash.

"A stone arrowhead or something. It cut the crap out of me and I pulled it out and stuck it in my pants pocket. Left side."

A hand went into his pocket and rummaged around. "Don't get cute, Doc," Bailey said with a weak grin.

"Here it is." The doctor held it up in his rubber-gloved hand like a prize. "There's something besides Mr. Calhoun's humorous blood on it. Have the lab run a toxicology on it." He handed the worked stone to one of the orderlies.

"We're going to keep you the night for observation," the doctor said. "We have to watch that gland under your arm and you're suffering from exhaustion."

Bailey watched another hypodermic go into his IV. He had no intention of bitching because all he wanted to do was shut his eyes and sleep. "Cat, could you get the neighbors to feed Callie?"

"I'll take care of her," she said. Cat bent over and kissed him on the cheek. "You rest and I'll be up in the morning to see you." Bailey nodded his head. His eyes fought to stay open.

"Travis, thanks. I owe you big time." He couldn't hold them open any longer and as he drifted away from the bright lights and low humming sounds of the machinery, he thought he heard someone say, "The lab says it's got some kind of toxic substance on it."

Bailey woke up once when he felt a sharp pinprick of a needle being inserted into his armpit.

"It's all right, Mr. Calhoun. We're draining the gland. This will help," an unseen voice said.

160

He drifted back to a drug induced sleep.

Later, he woke up and saw a heart monitor attached to him. A steady pulse of seventy beats.

* * *

Bailey had watched Dana's monitor as it showed sixty-five beats, then sixty… fifty… forty-five… he hadn't been able to take his eyes off it. She didn't move, in fact, she looked more peaceful than she had in the past six months. He pulled the syringe he'd used to inject the liquid morphine out of the IV and held it in his hand. Forty… thirty-five. The low pulse alarm went off and he pushed the silence button. Her breaths came in spurts. A quick sudden inhale, then nothing for nearly a minute. Quick breath, pause. Her pulse dropped to twenty-six and he put his arms around her. "I love you, Dana. I don't know what I'm going to do without you." Tears ran down his face and fell on her nightgown. Her chest didn't move and the heart monitor flat-lined, the pulse sank to zero. "Goodbye." He choked on his sobs and turned the machine off. The IV was still in her arm but he couldn't bring himself to remove it. At three-thirty in the morning he called the doctor and told him she'd died. The syringe went into the kitchen garbage can.

"I'm sorry, Bailey. I'll be right over," the doctor said.

Bailey was sitting in a chair by the bed holding Dana's hand when the doctor tapped on the door and entered the room. "Someone from Franklin's will be here to pick her up pretty soon," Dr. Tower said. He took the IV out of her arm and wrapped it around the stand. "At least she passed away at her home. That's what she wanted. Are you okay, Bailey?"

* * *

"Are you okay, Bailey?"

He opened his eyes and squinted against the invading sun that came into the room. A grunt came out as he sat up in the bed. "Hey, Cat," he said softly. "You saved my fanny. I don't know how I can ever pay you back." He held his bandaged hand out in front of him. The swelling was down and the lump under his armpit was gone, though there seemed to be a bit of a burning sensation.

"I'll think of something. You're looking a hundred percent better than yesterday. Thank God Travis came with me. Hell, thank God you fired your pistol. I don't know if we'd have found you in time if you hadn't." She sat on the bed and ran her hand over his cheek. "What were you doing up there?"

"Could you get me some water?" Cat poured a glass full and handed it to him with a plastic straw hanging over the edge. He sucked it empty and asked for more.

"Even with an IV, I feel dehydrated." Bailey thought how good she looked and the concern in her eyes made him feel wanted. A tinge of guilt with the image of Dana started to emerge from his mind, but with an effort, it was pushed back into his subconscious. He dropped the straw on the bedside table and drank more water. "I was looking for some four-wheeler signs." He told her about the two that had almost run him over the past week. "It had been a tough day with the Woods getting killed and I went up on top of Wild Horse Lookout feeling like my head was going to blow apart from all this shit. Lots going on in my mind, kid. I decided to check out where the four-wheelers had come from and nothing was going to stop me. I got a feeling it wasn't a coincidence…them being up there."

"Sounds like you're stretching trying to fit a couple of ATV's in. Anyway, if I'd gone with you, this might not have happened," she said, frowning.

"True, but the flood might have got you too…and I couldn't have taken that." He averted his eyes from her. "Don't get the wrong impression," he said brusquely.

"Quit trying to be so goddamn stoic." She made a fist and held it before his face. "Maybe a smack in the head might make you a little less tight-assed. Have you seen the doctor today?"

"Not yet, but I'm feeling better so hopefully they'll check me out this afternoon. Come over tonight and we'll have dinner," he said.

"All right. Six okay?" Bailey nodded and she stood up.

"Call me if they keep you overnight again." She kissed him and walked out of the room with Bailey admiring, for what had to be the thousandth time, the way she filled her pants.

An hour later, the doctor pronounced him reasonably fit and signed the release papers. He told Bailey the lab still had the arrowhead and he could pick it up there on his way out. "You're lucky. The lab said the toxic substance on the stone is some kind of venom and still could have killed you under the right circumstances."

Bailey agreed and thanked him. At the lab, they gave him the arrowhead enclosed in a plastic bag.

"We neutralized it with some bleach," the lab attendant said. "We had to keep a sample in case it's needed." He spoke defensively, like he thought Bailey would throw a bitch.

"That's fine. Thanks." He stuck the bag in his pocket and walked to the parking lot door when he realized he didn't have his truck. Hell, it would still be on the mountain. Bailey went to the front desk and used their phone to call Travis, who, luckily for Bailey, was at the BLM office.

A short time later Travis pulled into the parking lot and stopped by the rear door to the hospital. Bailey climbed in and buckled his safety belt. "I need a favor. I got to get my truck."

"It's at your house," Travis said. "I got one of the summer guys and we brought it back this morning."

"You're getting to be a good hand," Bailey said. He looked at him out of the corner of his eye. "I'm not kidding you."

"Jeeze, all I did was get your ratty pickup. It's not like I saved the world."

"Damn close. I didn't thank you for coming up with Cat and getting me. I owe you."

"Can I tell you something without pissing you off?" Travis asked.

"Fire away."

"You're not being the Bailey I've come to know and love. Go back to being a semi-asshole. Gruff and rough, not melancholy. Know what I mean?" Travis looked at him out of the corner of his eye.

They rode in silence for a few minutes until Bailey said, "Guess I've been feeling a little sorry for myself. Kind of like a dog wanting everybody to pet me and tell me what a great guy I've been. You know, pity praise. Anyway, you haven't been yourself either. Too cheerful and I see a haunted look lurking in your eyes. The windows to your soul, my man. What's up?" Bailey turned to him. Something you want to talk about?"

Travis kept quiet until he pulled into Bailey's driveway and shut the engine off. He stared at the floor and said, "Last year, we were responsible for three men dying."

"And your dad committing suicide," Bailey said gently.

"Yeah, that too. Do you think about it still?" Travis lifted his head and turned to Bailey. His eyes brimmed with tears and his voice cracked. "I shot and killed a man and I think about it every day, damn near every minute. I still see the bullet hole in his forehead, black with blood oozing out. It takes him forever to fall and he's staring at me the whole time. Mother of God!" Tears streaked his cheeks as he wept and turned his head away.

How do you do this? Tell a kid it doesn't bother you because they deserved it and you don't waste a second thinking about it. "It was them or us, and thankfully, it ended up being them. Travis…"

Travis lifted his head and wiped his face with a handkerchief he'd taken out of his back pocket.

"We really only killed two guys. Streck was trampled by the horses, remember?" Bailey grinned and Travis shook his head.

"If I had been a second later, my friend would be dead," Bailey continued. "The mutt was ready to cut his heart out. If you hadn't shot Lynch, he'd have shot me. How can you feel guilty about shooting a murderer? And don't forget, they were the ones who were putting the squeeze on your father."

"Isn't one of the reasons you've been drinking so much because of the deaths of those men?" Travis asked.

"Hell no. It doesn't bother me a bit. Good riddance. They were scumbags and deserved to die."

"Just Dana, then?"

Goosebumps rose on Bailey's skin. "What do you mean?"

"Her passing is what's made you such a lush? Sorry." He blushed.

"There's a little more than what meets the eye, but yeah. She wasn't a killer either, Travis. You have to put things into perspective if you're going to compare Dana's death with those slime buckets."

"I didn't mean it that way and I wasn't comparing," he stammered. "This is the first time I've talked about it and I'm rambling."

"You ought to see someone, like the psychologist who talks to the local cops. I'll bet he could help." His bandaged hand hit the armrest of the door and he grimaced from a shot of pain.

"I might do that. You need to get some rest. You want me to stick around?" Travis asked.

"No need, I'm going to lay down for a bit." He nodded approval when he noticed his pickup parked in front of them. "Tell Peter I'll be in tomorrow, will you?" Bailey opened the door and climbed out. "Getting back to work talk, there's more to these killings than Jordan acknowledges. He still thinks it was kids on dope or some crap like that."

Travis started to say something but Bailey held his hand up. "I know, it's not my job… it's the sheriff's office. Without doing anything illegal, I'm gonna make it my job too. My friends were murdered and somehow, the mummy's head from the Ferris plays into it."

"What mummy's head?"

"I'll tell you the whole story when I get back from Ft. Collins, Friday. I need to talk to an old fella again." Bailey took the sack out of his pocket that had the arrowhead in it. "I need to ask him about this." He shook the bag.

"You sure you're all right?"

"Yup. See, I'm taking your advice and reverting back. Thanks for the ride." He slammed the door and went into the house.

* * *

The neighbor eyed him suspiciously when she opened the door to his knocking.

"What do you need, Bailey?" she asked.

"A friend of mine was supposed to get Callie. She's not home so I thought I'd check to see if you were still watching her, Elizabeth."

"No one came for her so we thought she needed fed. What happened to you, anyway? You look beat up."

Bailey told her most of the story of the flood and being in the hospital. "A game warden was going to get her for me. Guess she got busy," he said lamely.

"I'm sorry you were hurt. Look, Bailey, why don't you take a couple of boards off the fence, then she can come over anytime. Jamie's starting to claim Callie as his own."

"I might be getting another dog, one—"

"You don't take care of one, let alone two. Why on earth would you get another one?" Frustration sounded in her voice.

166

"I do take care of her, I've just been extremely busy with work. This other dog was shot and left to die. He's a good dog. I'll introduce you when I get him from the vet, and if you still want me to open the fence up, I will." He held his hand out and a cracked grin spread on his face. "Still friends?"

"Yeah. You know me, opening my mouth when I ought to keep it closed," she said, taking his outstretched hand and giving it a quick, firm shake.

Barking came from the house and Callie bounded out and jumped on Bailey. "Hey, girl. Let's go home, supper's on. Thanks, Elizabeth, see you later, Jamie," he said to the boy who followed Callie out of the house."

"Bailey, take the boards off, okay?"

"Sure, I'll do it now." He walked to the middle of the fence that separated the two houses and popped two of the fence boards off. "Looks big enough, don't you think?"

A tired smile appeared on her face. "I think that's just fine." She put her arm around her son and went back into the house.

In the house, Bailey finished talking and put the phone down. "The vet says a couple of days and we can bring him home." He gave Callie a piece of beef jerky. "The bullet didn't do as much damage as she'd thought and…" He looked at the dog as she lay on the floor eating the treat. "How long have I been talking to you and expecting an answer?" His shoulders shrugged. "Doesn't mean I'm nuts, does it."

The sight of the beer in the fridge caused a twinge of craving he tried to ignore. Cat called and told him she'd bring dinner and help him relax. "Sounds great, but no pizza, okay?" he'd said. She had tried to sound angry but laughed and said he was in for a surprise.

"I'm actually cooking something," she'd said.

"I picked Callie up from the neighbor's." He paused and waited. Nothing. "You said you'd get her for me."

"Oh, damn. That's right. Completely slipped my mind," she said. "No big deal, right? I mean, they were taking care of the dog anyway."

"Yeah. No problem. Just wondering."

He opened the door when the bell rang a few hours later. Cat handed him a covered pan that gave off a mouth-watering aroma. She told him to put it on the stove and went to her truck to get a bottle of wine. Bailey set the table and lifted the tinfoil from the pan's top. Baby back ribs, and steamed vegetables surrounded by homemade French fries filled the pan to the top. He felt his mouth watering. "God, that smells good. I thought you said you couldn't cook."

"I lied," she said, handing the wine to him. "If a girl tells all of her secrets, what's left?"

He took the bottle and held it in his hand, scrutinizing the label. "You have a fine eye for wine. This is six months old. Aged just right." Bailey opened a kitchen drawer and rummaged through it until he brandished a cork opener. "I haven't had wine without a cap on the top of it for years." He stuck the end in the cork and twisted it out.

"It looks better," she said, coming over to him and lifting the bandaged hand up.

"Yeah, it is. The swelling's almost gone. Hell of a thing." Bailey took both of her hands and pulled her in close. "I'm thinking about you all the time," he said into her ear and kissed it, pushing images of Dana to the back of his mind.

"Good, because I'm doing the same thing," she said, her voice low. Her lips kissed each cheek then his lips. Long and drawn out. Her breath came in short gasps and she pushed him back. "No, goddammit."

"What? What's the matter?"

"The last time we didn't eat. I don't want to waste this dinner. Let's eat then we'll fool around, okay? I'm hungry." She saw his look. "For food."

He laughed out loud and poured her glass full. Club soda went into his glass. "Here's to you, Cat," he said, handing her a glass and raising his in a toast.

"No... here's to us." She clinked her glass against his then took a deep swallow from the glass. "You going tee-totaler on me?"

"Yeah, I gotta knock the booze off before it kills me."

"Pity, I don't think you have a problem." She finished her glass and held it out for a refill.

Bailey poured her some more. "That just shows you don't know me as well as you think."

The sun had set an hour ago. Dishes were stacked in the kitchen sink, the wine bottle, empty, lay on the table. Bailey and Cat were naked on top of the bed, arms around each other. Sweat glistened off both of their bodies and the room smelled of sex. Bailey's eyes were closed and he felt... *comfortable. Yeah, comfortable and even a little excited. It's been a long year,* he thought.

Her fingers danced lightly over his chest and sides raising goose bumps on his skin. No doubt his life was changing, he was coming out from a dark, self-destructive state of mind that covered him like a death mask. The credit, or most of it, had to go to Cat. *Do I want something more with her? If we keep this up, she's going to kill me.* He smiled in the dark at the thought and let himself drift off to sleep.

Sometime during the night he felt the bed move with Cat getting up. After the toilet flushed, he heard her dressing next to him. "Stay," he mumbled, his foot sliding over the empty spot in the bed where she'd laid.

"Can't. I've got to go to work early this morning." The sound of her pants zipper being pulled up matched her tone... subject closed.

"Ahhh, you're killing me."

There was a rustle of clothing then something hit the bed. "Here's a quarter, call someone and bitch." She bent over and kissed him.

"Are you going to work today?" Cat asked.

"Yeah, I've got some things to do. I'll try to call you later. I might run down to Ft. Collins today."

"Oh? What for?"

"Business." Bailey ran his hand over her rump. "Business for the United States Government that doesn't include the state. Sorry, kid."

"Seriously," she asked. "Does it have something to do with the murders?" Cat sat down on the edge of the bed, her features undistinguishable in the dark. "That's the sheriff's office business. I wish you'd leave it to them and stay out of it."

"I can't." He sat up and leaned against the headboard. "It turned personal when my friends were killed."

"Has the sheriff's office come up with any suspects or anything?"

"Nothing that I've heard, but as you know, I've been out of touch for a couple of days," he said sarcastically. "I'll get a hold of them today." His hand brushed the coin on the bed. He took it between his thumb and index finger and rubbed it.

"Well, I still think you shouldn't get involved in it. It's not a BLM case. You don't have any jurisdiction in a murder case." Cat's voice was steady and low. "You might get hurt."

"Guess that's a chance I'm going to have to take."

"Goddammit, you're stubborn."

"That's a trait of mine. It seems to piss a lot of people off. But here..." he took her hand and placed the quarter in her palm. "Call someone and bitch."

"Screw you, Calhoun." She stood up and dropped the quarter on his chest. "You better be careful. There's enough people around that couldn't care less if they kill a deer or a person, and they've already killed some people."

"I promise I'll be careful. I really don't want to die at my young age." He held his hands up in surrender. "But, whoever murdered the Woods better realize with me, justice takes precedence over the law."

"This is funny," Cat chuckled without humor.

"What."

"I get the impression you cross over the line sometimes… law wise, I mean. Yet, I think you're an honorable person. What do they call that, an oxymoron?" She grabbed his head and kissed him hard on the mouth. "I've got to go, talk to you later."

After the sound of her pickup faded in the night, Bailey closed his eyes and wondered if he could find the killers or was he being a modern *Don Quixote?* He found the quarter and put it on the headboard. He needed to check out the cave again to see if it was his fear and imagination, or if he really had seen something like a jumble of bones when the water receded and broke through the back wall. *I can't believe how this thing's mushrooming out of control.* A new feeling of foreboding seemed to have taken root in the pit of his stomach. One that sent a chill up his back and he didn't like it.

Chapter Twenty-Five

One advantage of Bailey's job was the ability to be gone without checking in at the office every morning. That's probably how he got away with the hard drinking for so long, he thought, leaving town toward Ft. Collins. He hoped Chandler would be coherent enough to answer some questions.

The stitched wound on his bandaged hand still tingled once in a while. On the seat beside him, in a plastic bag, was the arrowhead. It would be interesting to see what the doctor thought about that.

The past two nights had been about the only nights that he hadn't had a drink since Dana died. The hospital stay didn't count. Bailey wasn't naïve enough to think he was around the corner on the boozing. Even now, at seven in the morning, he could feel the craving and pictured a cold glass of wine with a beer chaser for a way to end the evening when he got back to Rawlins. *No way.* Maybe if he could get Cat to come over and stay awhile he wouldn't be thinking about drinking.

Cat stayed in his thoughts a lot, but the thoughts were all sexual. Something about her gave him the impression that underneath the persona everyone saw, there was a mean, tough woman out for herself. So there weren't any daydreams of sharing his life with her, the house with the picket fence, and all that. He wouldn't tell Cat, but to be honest, Dana still flourished in his mind, though he day dreamed about the game warden, good old carnal knowledge type daydreams. Strong legs squeezing his back and the thrust of her nice round fanny against him. Full breasts that reached for his lips and the little guttural sighs whispering out of her mouth. He'd look down and see the glazed look in her eyes along with the way her upper lip puckered over her front teeth and he'd have to strain to stay with her. Yeah, he'd call her when he got back to town.

Traffic in Ft. Collins filled the streets like before, but this time, he turned off of South College and took side streets to get to the nursing home. The parking lot had several cars in the visitors' parking area. He pulled his pickup next to a new hybrid Toyota. Bailey knew it was hybrid because it said so on the bumper. Gas and electric. Probably some kid's car with thoughts of saving the environment.

He'd tried calling Annie when he got into town but no one answered her phone. Maybe she was with her father.

It felt like another warm day. They could use the rain that seemed to fall every night in Rawlins. He left the windows cracked open, locked the door and went into the main building.

A nurse's aide manned the reception station. He showed her his identification and told her he'd visited Dr. Chandler last week. She frowned and muttered something about everyone coming at once and motioned him away with her hand. "Do you know where his room is?" she asked, not looking at him. A pocket novel lay open on the counter in front of her.

"Yeah, I do." He leaned over the counter. "You reading *Death by Unnatural Causes*?"

The aide nodded her head.

"He wasn't murdered, he killed himself." Bailey turned and walked down the hall, a small grin on his face.

"Prick," he heard her hiss.

Bailey entered the room and saw Annie, again sitting in a chair next to the bed. She was dressed in a running suit and had a sweatband on her forehead.

"Excuse me, am I interrupting?" he stopped by the door. Dr. Chandler saw him and waved.

"No, no. Come in, young man. This is my daughter, Ann Duncan. Annie, this is, uhh..., you'll have to introduce yourself, I'm afraid I've forgotten your name."

"I met your daughter last week when I visited you, Dr. Chandler. I'm Bailey Calhoun." He winked at Ann. "I'd like to ask him some more questions, if he feels up to it."

"Of course I do," Chandler said. "I don't have too many more days left to enjoy a good conversation."

"Now, Dad," Ann began.

"Let's not kid ourselves, Annie. And let's not talk about it, I want to hear Mr. Calhoun's questions."

"Only if you call me Bailey."

"It will be my pleasure, Bailey. Ask away."

He opened the sack and took the baggy with the arrowhead in it out. "I got caught in a storm and burrowed into a small cave. This cut my hand and made me sicker than hell. Do you recognize what tribe would have used this kind of arrowhead?"

Chandler reached for it.

"Careful, it has a toxin on it, according to the lab at the hospital," Bailey said. He snatched some quick glances at Chandler's daughter. She sat straight in the chair and took the baggy from Bailey and gave it to her father. He already had his reading glasses on.

"Annie," Chandler said. "Take it out of the bag for me and be very careful with it. Just grab it by the back on the flat sides." She did as he asked and held it in front of his face.

"I wish I had my papers. Maybe you can bring them next time you come." He cleared his throat. "Very interesting. The Nimerigar covered the blades of their weapons with the venom from a mountain toad. Venom so strong, one bite would kill a man in a matter of several minutes. The Nimerigar used the toad's venom on their knives and arrowheads. What you have here is a knife, Bailey, not an arrowhead. Go ahead and put it back, Annie."

"A knife? Everyone said it was an arrowhead. Funny, I've been with the BLM for over twenty years and I've never heard of a poisonous mountain toad that could kill someone."

"For good reason, they've been extinct for a hundred years. And you have to remember; the knife is small because the Nimerigar were small. Luckily time must have lessened the strength of the venom or you'd probably be dead now."

"Hello again." Bailey said under his breath.

"You have to remember they were a vicious tribe. It's not surprising they were known as the 'little people eaters' since they supposedly ate the children of their enemies. A strange view on death since according to the death shroud of Onatah, the elders were mummified and buried in a tomb with glory and their most valuable possessions."

"Why's that so odd?"

"Because if an elder was sick or injured, they were killed by having their skulls bashed in." Chandler dropped his head to the pillow. "I'm sorry, Bailey, I need to rest for a bit. Can you come back in a few hours?" His eyes closed.

Bailey looked at Ann and she nodded. "Of course. I'll go have breakfast and come back later," he said.

Annie patted the old man's hand and kissed his forehead. "We'll be back, Dad."

They walked out the room and down the hallway. "Join me?" Bailey asked. "We really didn't get a chance to visit before."

"I think I will, thank you. It's been hard lately, he's failing fast." They walked past the reception desk where the aide cast him a dark look. "It's been suggested he go to a hospice, but I've told them to wait another week."

"I'm sorry, it must be tough as hell for you."

"Yeah, it is, Bailey. But enough of the dreary talk, I'm hungry," Annie said.

"If you know a good café or restaurant, lead the way, I'll follow."

"Would you like to ride with me?" she asked. "My car's right over here."

Bailey almost choked when she opened the door to the hybrid Toyota.

"You didn't have this last week. Nice car," he said as they drove down the street. She had sunglasses on and held the wheel at the ten o'clock – four o'clock position.

"I had a loaner, this was getting a check-up. I like to feel I'm doing a small part for our grandchildren's grandchildren."

"You have grandchildren? You don't look old enough."

Her laugh made him feel comfortable. It was an honest, sincere laugh. Not too loud, not the kind to draw attention. A nice, pleasant sound. "Two. Both boys who I don't see nearly enough. My daughter and son in-law live in Italy. Visits are far and few between."

"I assume you're married, or am I being too nosy?"

"You're not. Divorced. Eight years ago. He ran off with a woman a few years older than our daughter." Her face seemed to darken. "Is there a Mrs. Calhoun?"

"There was, but she died last year from Cancer."

"I'm sorry."

"I think we need to change the subject," Bailey said. "Your dad has been very helpful."

"He's thrilled you came to Ft. Collins to ask him questions. It really perked him up. Dad insisted I find his files on the Nimerigar for you. I'm going through his boxes trying to find them. Oops, here we are." She shoved down on the brakes and screeched the tires turning into a restaurant called The Egg and I.

Bailey sipped his coffee after breakfast and looked at her over the rim of his cup. She wasn't pretty, she was handsome. Crow's feet were around the sides of green eyes that shined with warmth and intelligence. Her face looked smooth and makeup free with only a few wrinkles by her mouth. Light brown hair streaked with gray fell to her shoulders. He guessed her age around the late forties.

"Do you work?" he asked.

"I'm a mildly successful artist. I paint. Canvas, not houses." she said and laughed.

"Really, what of?"

"Landscapes, mostly. Some portraits. You said you've been with the Bureau of Land Management for over twenty years. What do you do?"

"Law enforcement, preserving antiquities, livestock count on leases. For a while I was involved in a wild horse refuge."

"Wild horses. That sounds fascinating."

"It's a difficult situation. They're over populated and the ranchers would just as soon not have them around."

"Why?"

"Because they drink the water and eat the grass used for cattle and sheep. Personally, I'm partial to the mustangs. I've been accused quite a bit of having more feelings for animals than humans."

She put her chin on her hand and asked, "Do you? I mean, feel more for the horses?"

He grinned. "All depends on who the people are."

On the way back to the nursing home, Bailey told her he'd like to come back and visit her father that coming Friday. He'd be in Cheyenne and it was a quick drive over. He might also have some more questions for him.

"I'm sure Dad would like that."

"Not to rush things, but if I make it over, would you care to go out for dinner? I enjoy your company." He looked out the car window at the buildings passing by. "You can turn me down... we just met last week. I'll understand." *Come on, keep me lucky.*

"Dinner would be nice."

"Hello again," he whispered.

"You said that at the hospital. Why?" Annie asked.

"My luck has finally started to change. It's been crap for quite a while but lately she seems to have taken a liking to me. I'm just telling her hello when she pops up." He thought he felt himself blush. Usually, personal information had to be pried out of him. Annie made him want to tell her his life story.

She parked by his pickup and wrote her address down on a piece of paper she'd taken from the glove box. "Call me if you can't make it. I'm home most of the time if I'm not here." Annie held her hand out. "It's been my pleasure to know you a little better, Bailey."

"Mine too. I'm looking forward to Friday. You pick the place." He shook her hand and opened the door. "Are you coming in?"

"No, tell him I'll be back later this afternoon. Drive careful."

He watched her leave and didn't go into the nursing home until she was out of sight.

* * *

Chandler sat up in bed, eating Jell-O from a small carton with a plastic spoon. "Come in, come in," he said, putting the carton down on the bed table.

"You have a nice daughter."

"Yes I do. She's been a rock for me since Mildred died and I came here." He craned his neck. "Where is she?"

"She asked me to tell you she'd be back this afternoon. We went to breakfast in her new car."

"Oh yes. Annie is an environmentalist of sorts. Not really a tree hugger, but concerned with the land being abused along with the ozone layer and the greenhouse effect. She also donates to the *Save the Whales* foundation. My little girl is very strong willed, so be careful if you debate her on the issues."

Bailey saw the pride in Chandler's face when he talked about her. "I wouldn't try. She'd probably eat me alive."

"Your knife is on the table there," Chandler pointed. "Have you met my daughter?"

"Ah... yes. You've forgotten, but I have, right here in your room."

"Oh. Good. What can I do for you?" Chandler's eyes seemed to shrink back inside his skull.

"How could poison still be active if these Indians have been extinct for, say a hundred years?" Bailey sat down in the chair. The doctor's voice grew fainter and Bailey figured he didn't have too much longer until the old fella went to sleep or spaced out.

"That is perplexing. I don't know. I also don't know how the mummies are suddenly appearing unless someone found the tomb and they're looting it. Oh my, oh my, oh my." Chandler's eyes closed. He pawed the air with one hand. "I'm afraid I've worn myself out, out, out."

Bailey stood up and leaned next to the white haired head. "When do you think the Nimerigar died out? How many years ago?"

"Oh, oh me, oh my. Two hundred. Yes, yes. Two hundred years ago." His eyes fluttered then opened wide. "Looting! Looting the Nimerigar tomb. I have to go to sleep now, sir. Goodnight." He pulled the top sheet up to his chin and squeezed his eyes shut.

"Dr. Chandler, how valuable would a mummy be?"

There was no answer. The soft, raspy snore came out of his open mouth. His face was relaxed and the skin almost translucent.

Not too much time left. Bailey patted the old man's hand. "Goodnight to you, sir. This has been quite the day, in more ways than one."

Chapter Twenty-Six

He took his time driving back to Rawlins. The day had been interesting and Annie continued to stay on the surface of his consciousness. He bought some club soda at a small liquor store six miles from town.

Something Chandler said kept playing over in his mind, like auto-replay on a tape. *Looting the tomb.* If the tomb has been found and Albert stumbled on it and found the mummy head, maybe the tomb robbers killed him to keep him quiet. Bailey would get Travis and they'd try to check out the south Ferris, above the Woods' place. He'd try to get someone to fly him over the area tomorrow to see if he could spot anything…though he had no idea what a tomb entrance would look like.

The trip back seemed to fly and when he entered his house and closed the front door, he opened a bottle of club soda and drank it empty in three swallows. Cold and wet. Bailey drank two more hoping the craving would ease. The light blinked on the answering machine. The message was from the vet: Barney could be picked up the next day and please remember payment is expected at time of pickup.

Bailey settled down in the recliner with the cordless phone in his hand. Should he call Cat and go for a wild night in the bedroom? Surprisingly, the urge from his thoughts about her that morning were replaced by reminiscing about the breakfast and conversation with Annie. *I can't believe I'm thinking about two women and lookout, here comes the guilt from the third.* With an effort, he shoved the image of Dana out of his conscious mind.

180

The telephone rang, making him jerk. After all the inner discussion, did he answer it and if it was Cat, invite her over? If it is her, say he's tired and needs rest. *Boy, my hand still hurts. I'm gonna hit the rack early.* The ringing continued until finally silence replaced the obtrusive sound. His breath came out in a faint whistle. He didn't realize he'd been holding it. Was he afraid to talk to her? No...he just didn't want to contend with questions or have her come over uninvited. She'd been doing that a couple times... showing up without being asked. Kind of bugged him.

Bailey shook his head and poked some numbers into the phone. "Hey Cat, you try calling me just now? Yeah, I walked in the door on the last ring. I thought it might be you. I'd like to, but my hand's killing me. I popped some pain pills and they're putting me to sleep. I'm hitting the rack early. *Damn, almost word for word,* he thought wryly.

He called another number, Frank Ricconi. "Why don't you come over tomorrow night and we'll eat some steaks and have some drinks and bullshit?"

"That'd work. I might have to crash at your place if I get loaded. A highway patrolman can't be picked up for DWUI, as you well know. They'd love to get my ass. Speaking of ass, you gonna have any honeys over?"

Bailey thought Frank sounded half drunk on the phone. "I'll see if I can find a couple but I'm not promising anything."

"Don't you have any neighbors?" Frank asked, with definitely a bit of a slur.

"Yeah, but they're married."

"The best kind. No strings attached and most like a quick little fling, know what I mean?"

When Frank said that, Bailey's heart picked up speed and his mouth went dry. "Good point, I'll see what I can do. Make it around six, okay?"

"You bet, I'll even bring some libation for us. I believe there's a bottle or two of Wild Turkey laying around here."

Bailey hung up after telling Frank what time to show up again. *What did they call it when understanding suddenly comes to someone? An epiphany?*

The box of the previous year's bills was stacked in the unfinished basement. A single light tacked to a ceiling joist barely drove the darkness back. He found the folder for the telephone statements and thumbed through the sheets of paper until he found the month he'd been looking for.

Bailey's eyes narrowed and his back teeth clenched. The statement went back into the box and it was left in the middle of the cement floor. His footsteps echoed off the basement's walls as he climbed the wooden steps, each one an effort.

* * *

"Peter, could I take a couple days off for vacation?" Bailey sat in the district supervisor's office. He blushed. "I need to take care of some personal things before my appointment with Dr. Radcliffe, Friday."

"How are you doing, Bailey?" Wales asked, leaning over his desk. "You've had a hell of a week."

"No kidding, but I'm coming along. I'm working on some leads having to do with illegal excavation of artifacts. I think it might tie into the Woods' murders."

"What do you have?"

"I'd rather wait until I get a little more concrete evidence. The sheriff's office gave me their blessing."

"That's what I wanted to hear. Bring me into the loop when you're ready." Wales said.

"About the time off…"

"Of course. You don't need to take it as vacation. I'm sure you'll be doing something relating to the BLM. Let me know if you need more time."

* * *

Lucky for Barney, the government had deposited Bailey's paycheck into his account the day before. "Goddamn, do you think you're worth $300?" he asked the dog.

They drove to Bailey's house from the vet's clinic. Barney's injuries weren't quite as bad as first suspected. True, he'd been shot in the hip, but the tissue that had been damaged was sewn together and the bone hadn't shattered. A nice neat hole. The white cast on the dog's leg and hip contrasted with the black and brown spotted coat. The recovered bullet was in Bailey's pocket.

Bailey thought the dog felt or knew things were different and he was going home with his new master because he glommed onto Bailey. Side touching side, a paw on Bailey's leg, Barney hung his head and looked at the man with sorrowful eyes.

"Hey, perk up. Callie's waiting for you and you've got two families, to be exact."

After they parked in the driveway, Bailey helped the dog get out of the pickup and opened the gate to the backyard. Callie raced in from the opening in the back fence and began the sniffing of personal parts. Barney froze, tail held low under his legs.

"Hi, Bailey." The young boy said from the hole the missing boards made in the fence. "Whacha doing?"

"I brought a friend for you and Callie, Jamie." He pushed Callie off and motioned the boy to come over. He ran with stubby legs and knelt down pointing to the cast.

"What happened to him?"

"He was shot, by bad people. I need you and your mom to help me take care of him, if you want to."

"Yeah, we do. I'll go ask Mom." He bounded up and ran full speed through the hole and to his house.

A few minutes later, Jamie's mother, Elizabeth, opened the gate and came up to Bailey and the dogs, wiping her hands on a dishcloth. She cocked her head and said, "Funny looking in a cute way, isn't he?" Her hand went down and stroked Barney's head.

"Would you watch them for a while? I'm getting more involved in a case and might not be around for a couple days. He won't be any trouble and I've got plenty of dog food in the shed."

Elizabeth smiled. "Hey, I'm a sucker for a hard luck dog story. Jamie really likes Callie, so what's one more, right?"

"You're great, thanks."

"Are you going to leave the fence the way it is, so they can run back and forth?" She asked.

"If you don't mind."

"I'm glad you don't have any kids, Bailey." She laughed and went back through the gate.

"Me too. These guys will be enough."

* * *

The next day began clear and hot. The courthouse bustled with activity when Bailey entered the main door and went into the sheriff's office. Kelly still acted pissed at him and talked in grunts and short phrases. Nothing new in the murders yet and did Bailey know of any relatives of the Woods?

"They never mentioned anyone to me. I know they didn't have any kids.

What happens to the ranch if you don't find any family?" Bailey asked. He stood at the counter separating the offices from the public. It looked like Kelly wasn't going to ask him back for coffee.

"That's something you'll have to ask the court. I'm busy... anything else?" Kelly picked the file up and strummed his fingers on the counter top.

"Yeah, see if this bullet matches the ones from Millhouse and the Woods." It was held between Bailey's fingers and he turned it back and forth.

"Where'd you get this?" Kelly took the bullet and held it in the palm of one of his hands.

"From Woods' dog that I found that day. He'd been shot."

"Why didn't you tell us? You could be in some deep trouble. Withholding evidence."

"Larry, get your head out of your ass. How can I be withholding if you have it in your hand?" He waited for an answer and didn't get one. "I found the dog after you guys investigated the murders and had left. I took the back way to come to town and saw him off in the brush. He was still alive so I hustled him to the vet."

"And you're telling us just now."

Bailey held his bandaged hand up. "I got hurt the next day and spent the night in the hospital. You guys aren't the only ones busy. And don't forget, Jordan gave the go-ahead to let me in on the case." He bent over the counter. "I know you're still pissed at me, but don't let it keep us from helping each other on this. I want find out who killed the Woods as much as you do. Probably more because they were my friends. Give me a call if you get anything on the bullet, okay?"

Kelly had a hurt look in his eyes. "You really screwed me over, Bailey. I trusted you and you shit on me."

"I know, and I can't tell you how sorry I am, but I didn't have any alternative. Believe me, Larry. I've apologized so much for crap I've done, it won't do any good to do it again."

Kelly held his hand out. "All right, but to be honest, it'll take some time to trust you again."

"I don't blame you. And thanks." Bailey gripped the outstretched hand.

Chapter Twenty-Seven

Carl Freel met him at the airport. The crusty old pilot could still fly a plane better than anyone else in the county. An old coyote hunter for the Cattleman's Association, Carl had flown him into a canyon the year before that was so small, Bailey was sure they'd splat against the walls trying to fly out.

The Piper Super Cub sat with its wheels chocked outside a small hanger. Anytime someone offered to pay for the fuel and throw in a few bucks for wear and tear on the plane, Carl was ready to take them up to spot elk, look for lost hunters…find a tomb.

"What's your plan, Calhoun?" Freel spoke in a rough growl caused from a lifetime of smoking roll-your-own cigarettes.

"Fly low over the south face of the Ferris. I'm looking for something that might look like a tomb."

"Tomb? What the hell is a tomb gonna look like?"

"I have no idea, maybe like a mine shaft or man-made cavern. Hell Carl, I've never seen a tomb in the mountains so your guess is as good as mine."

Freel had the flaps down and the nose lifted, flying a few miles an hour over the stall speed of the aircraft, as they skirted the side of the mountain. He'd drop so low into a canyon, Bailey had sweat pop out on his forehead and he cinched his safety belt as tight as he could stand it. His stomach protested by threatening to heave everything out that it held.

Once, a glint was seen on the side of the rock, above the tree line. Freel told him it was an old wreckage from the fifties. "A woman and her husband lived in a cave for twenty some odd days until they were found. I never heard 'em say it was anything more than a cave, though. I sure as hell would have remembered if they'd said it was a tomb."

The plane banked to the right and made a lazy circle until they were flying west, parallel to the bare peaks of the mountain. "We'll fly a grid. Maybe we'll see something," Freel said without much conviction.

After an hour of tight turns and criss-crossing the south face, Freel pulled the flaps up and gained altitude. "Nothing but some elk, Bailey. How about you?"

He was surprised how disappointed he felt. Bailey had a feeling he'd see something. "Me either, but I might check that cave out later. Let's take a quick spin over the Steamboat Lake Ranch. There's a new owner and he leased some land. Be interesting to see if we can spot his cattle."

Freel banked the plane again and flew over the eastern side of the mountain. They could see the ranch house and outbuildings. "You want me to get lower?" Freel asked.

"No, this is fine. I don't see any beef though, do you?" Bailey looked out both sides of the aircraft down to the open fields. "Take us over the breaks."

Freel banked again and flew parallel to the mountain.

"What's that?" Bailey pointed to his side.

"An old saw mill," Freel said. "It cut a lot of the timber used to build the ranch buildings around here. I think Cattle Kate's husband might have built it."

"Really, first time I've heard of it." *Okay, where's the goddamn cattle?*

"I don't see nothing, Bailey. You ready to get home?"

"Cruise above the saw mill, up by those outcroppings of limestone."

"I can't see nothing. Too many trees. Shiiit, I can't even see the ground anywhere. I need to get back or I'm gonna piss my pants. Okay?" Freel moaned for effect.

"Yeah. Guess the only thing we got out of this was a history lesson," Bailey said.

They flew back to Rawlins in silence other than a hacking cough from Freel.

* * *

Bailey called Travis after they'd landed and asked him if he'd like to do some mountain climbing. The answer was an enthusiastic yes. Bailey would pick him up the next morning. "I'm not coming back to the office. If Wales asks, you think I'm still in the country."

"No problem. What do you have going on?"

"Something personal. Nothing to worry about," Bailey said. He hung up and drove to a liquor store fifteen miles away at Fort Steele, located on the Platte River next to a state rest area.

He had driven his Explorer to the airport and took his uniform shirt off when he took the Fort Steele exit. The store had a drive-up. Bailey didn't recognize the face of the woman who waited on him and she seemed to look through him with washed out gray eyes, rather than at him. It was the look of someone tired of fighting the winters and loneliness.

The cost of the bottle of whiskey and twelve pack of beer went on his credit card.

I could use a couple of these before tonight.

* * *

There was a stirring of apprehension in his gut when the ten- year old Lincoln Town car pulled into the driveway and stopped. Ricconi climbed out carrying a brown grocery sack.

Bailey took a quick swig of olive oil. He was lucky it didn't come back up. The oil would coat his stomach and allow him to drink a fair amount without getting drunk. It seemed like a waste of good booze, but he had to stay sober and he needed

Ricconi to get drunk without wondering why Bailey wasn't drinking.

Ricconi was greeted with a slap on the back and led out to the patio. The sack had an opened bottle of whiskey in it. Callie and Barney ran up and sniffed his legs, tails wagging.

"Leave him alone, you two. They're glad to see company," Bailey said.

Ricconi patted them on their heads. One pat for each. "Yeah, cute dogs. I'm in the mood to tie one on. If I get too wasted, you gotta put me up for the night." Ricconi said, taking a tall glass of whiskey and water from Bailey. He smacked his lips after the first swallow. "Just the way I like it, strong enough to pucker your mouth."

By mutual consent, they decided food would be a deterrent to the drinking; so the grill stayed off and the two men slouched in lawn chairs making small talk as the sun dropped behind the hills.

"Tell me, Bailey, is she a good piece of ass?" Ricconi finished his drink and poured himself another. The bottles and beer sat in a cooler next to them.

"You always get this shit faced?" Bailey replied.

"Yeah, I'm half Indian."

"Sure you are. What kind of name's Ricconi, Apache?"

"Italian. My old man was Italian and my mom was full-blooded Arapaho. When you pale faces call me, 'Bear,' that's from my Indian name of 'Great Bear.' I still got family on the reservation in Riverton."

"No shit! I had no idea."

"Most don't. And I don't tell too many people, you're one of the few I've told."

"Did Dana know?"

Ricconi squinted his eyes. "Umm, no, I don't think so. Why?"

189

"She liked you, she thought you were a nice guy. Here, let me fill that glass up." Bailey poured more whiskey into the glass with a touch of water.

"Yeah, that Dana was sweet. We got along real good." He took a long swallow. "Whoa, this is strong." His sentences were slurred and a big hand wiped his face several times. "You're lucky I didn't take her away from you. You were a real shit-head then."

"When's that, Frank?"

"Last year, around the time you were spending all your time with those wild horses and she left your sorry ass. Becky had dumped me a couple weeks before and we were both lonesome."

"You and Dana?" *Maybe I oughta have him shut up. Do I want him to tell me? Yeah, dammit. I gotta hear it.*

Ricconi nodded his head and drank some more. Bailey held the bottle up and Frank held his glass out. The liquid splashing into the glass sounded loud in the room.

Bailey looked Ricconi in the eye. "She told me, Frank. About you and her having a quick little fling."

"You're shitting me. She actually told you?" He stood up and smiled. "And you're not pissed she slept with me? I'll be a son-of-a-bitch."

"Yeah, you are." Bailey lunged to his feet and swung a hard left fist at Ricconi's jaw, connecting with a solid *splat*. The force of the blow knocked Ricconi back against the couch where he sank to a sitting position.

Callie and Barney, lying on the floor, bounced up, looked at the two men and dashed out the dog door in the kitchen, Barney holding his cast off the ground.

Ricconi put a hand to the side of his jaw and winced when he smiled. "So, she didn't tell you. Go ahead, beat the shit out of me. I'm not gonna fight you." His smile disappeared and he swayed getting back up. "It wasn't like picking someone up at a bar and wham, bam, thank you, ma'am. We were both hurting.

I stopped her when she ran a stop sign. I don't know what went on with you two, but she was crying, pissed and sad at the same time. Upset and needing someone."

Bailey unclenched his fists. He wasn't sure what he was feeling. Relief that Dana wasn't perfect so he could take her off the pedestal? For some reason, the knot in his gut, the one that had been tight for a year, loosened.

Ricconi continued. "I really liked her, Bailey, I always have, but we were both human. I think we reached out to each other and it helped us through the tough times. Other than that one night, the only thing we did was tell each other our problems on the phone once in a while. We quit calling after you guys got back together. That's it, man."

"I'm not proud of myself for sucker punching you, but if it's any consolation, it helped." Bailey said. He took a swallow out of the bottle. "You can give one back to me, if you want." He braced his legs and stuck his jaw out.

Ricconi took the bottle and drank from it. "Nope. We Native Americans don't go for revenge like you pale faces. Seriously, I still want to be friends with you, if you can accept that." He held his hand out.

"Me too, Frank." Bailey shook his hand. "Stay the night. I'm going to go see someone." He stopped at the front door, opened it, and turned back to Ricconi. "Listen, it's easy talk to say I'm not going to think about it when I see you, but I'm not mad. To be honest, I'm not quite sure how I feel right now. If you can believe it, I almost feel relieved." He walked out, closing the door behind him. He didn't see the puzzled look on Ricconi's face.

Chapter Twenty-Eight

"Bailey, I thought you were busy tonight." Cat said, opening the front door. Bailey had rang the doorbell and hoped she was home.

"It finished early. How about going out to dinner with me?"

"We could send out for a pizza." She ran her hand up his arm.

"That's the best offer I've had today."

An hour later, Bailey untangled himself from Cat's arms. He dressed and kissed her on the cheek. "I've got to go, I'll talk to you later."

"Time for me to get up too. Do you want some coffee?"

"No thanks, I put some on and already had a couple cups."

"What do you have going on this early?" Cat asked as she climbed out of the bed. "After some artifact stealers?" She chuckled at the nasty look Bailey gave her.

"Possibly, young lady. Possibly." She stared at him as the door closed when he left.

He'd called his house earlier from Cat's place and no one answered the telephone. Either Ricconi was sleeping it off, or he had left early. Bailey hoped for the latter.

* * *

Travis waited in Bailey's office for him while he changed into some hiking boots kept in his closet. They were on their way out of town before any of the other BLM employees came into the building to start work.

They took the gravel road that went past the turn off to the Wood's ranch. Yellow crime scene tape still wove around the entrance gate. Several miles farther down, the road forked, with one turning into a two-track at an abandoned natural gas compressor station and heading north. The other remained gravel and continued to the east, where a man could end up practically anywhere he wanted, eventually.

"There's been some use on this," Travis said.

"Yeah, more than normal. Hell, the sagebrush is worn down."

They drove up to the mountain and stopped at the beginning of a steep draw, smothered with trees and broken rocks.

Bailey pointed high up, past the tree line. "See that reflection? We're going up there."

"Holy smokes, can you make it, old fella?"

"You bet your ass, kid. Let's grab our stuff and go," Bailey shot back. Packs with food, rope, binoculars and flashlights went on their backs. They each strapped a canteen of water on their belts and started up a dry creek bed that ran down the center of the draw and disappeared behind a jut of limestone outcropping.

Sweat drenched Bailey's shirt and face after the first two hundred yards of climbing. He cursed every time his feet slipped out from under him on a covering of loose shale and gravel sized rock. "Hold up, I got to have some water."

"At the rate we're going," Travis said, pulling his canteen out of its case and unscrewing the lid, "it's going to take us all day to get up there."

Bailey was glad to see the younger man panting and dripping sweat too. "I didn't think it'd be so damn rough." He went past Travis to a blow-down of trees and began urinating. "Hey, come here and look at this," he yelled.

"What're you doing, turning into a pervert?"

"No, not yet. It looks like there's a trail over here."

Travis pulled himself forward grabbing tree branches until he was next to Bailey, though uphill.

"See? Over by that tangle of brush."

"Yeah, I do. How'd we miss it?" Travis asked. He wiped his face with a bandana. "If this goes up most of the way, we'll have it made. Man, I'm glad you saw this."

Bailey kneeled down and brushed the dirt. "This isn't a game trail, there's signs of footprints. Several of them."

"Can you tell how big of a shoe, or how many people?" Travis knelt down also.

Bailey shook his head. "No, they're pretty much obliterated except for some heel outlines and a couple of toe indentations. No sole tread marks. You got better eyes, tell me if I missed any."

Travis moved up and down the trail on his hands and knees, his head low to the ground. "I can't tell anything, the ground's too rocky." He got back up on his feet. "Maybe we'll find some more if it gets softer."

The rest of the way up the trail Bailey and Travis scoured the ground trying to find complete footprints, but the only thing they saw were scuff marks and partial indentations.

They came out of the tree line onto a slope of hard rock, cracked with fissures, and lost the trail on solid rock. Lying on a shelf of granite another hundred yards up was a rusted, crushed fuselage of an airplane that had crashed over fifty years ago. No engines, wings, or interior left. Only an empty shell deteriorating bit by bit every year, settled below the summit of the mountain like a subtle warning.

Sheer walls of granite cliffs loomed behind the plane and seemed to reach to the gods. The mouth of a cave could be seen above the wreckage. "That's where they stayed for twenty-three days. Let's check it out," Bailey said as he led off, taking his pack off his back and opening the cover as he walked. He had his flashlight, some rope and a stick of white chalk in his hand when he reached the cave's entrance. Travis pulled his light out and looked quizzically at the chalk.

"To mark our route, so we won't get lost if it branches off in there," Bailey said. They had to turn their flashlights on after passing a low overhang of rock. A room opened up and abruptly ended. Bailey shined his light's beam over the walls. "Nothing more in here. Dammit, I hoped we'd find something."

"Like what?"

"I'm not sure. Albert told me he found the mummy head around here. The old director of the state's archaeology lab thinks someone might be looting an ancient Indian tomb and since I found the body pretty much due south in the dune, I figured there might be something up here." He stomped out, with Travis following.

"A hell of a walk for nothing." Bailey sat on a rock and took a swallow from his canteen.

"Why don't we see if we can pick the trail up farther east?" Travis asked. "Jeeze, you give up fast."

"I don't need your smart mouth," Bailey shot back. After pausing, he said grudgingly, "But you got a good idea. Why don't you drop down a little and fan out. I'll try to stay level with the plane. We'll head east and see what we can find." He slung the pack over his back.

Bailey's back protested from his walking so far bent over by cramping. "Oh, shit!" He stood up and tried stretching. Other than an occasional sound of brush snapping and a foot slipping in loose rock, he couldn't see Travis.

"Hey Bailey, over here," Travis yelled, his voice echoing off the rocks. "I think I found the trail. They're pretty crafty."

"Where you at?" Bailey still didn't see him until Travis poked his head over a mass of boulders lying on each other like fallen dominos.

"Scuff marks. It looks like someone slipped or slid down this chute using their heels to slow them down." He pointed to flat slabs of rock forming three sides and ending at the base of the cliff.

They had to climb up using their hands and feet, scrabbling for traction as the chute angled steeper. When they reached the end, Bailey's heart hammered so hard he thought it might pound a hole in his chest. He bent over, put his hands on his knees and panted, trying to catch his wind. Travis sucked in deep breaths of air.

"I never knew being up this high could wear a man down so fast," Travis said, trying to fill his lungs with oxygen.

"Well, I didn't have a heart attack yet, so I must not be in too bad of shape," Bailey wheezed. He lay down and rolled on his back. "Give me a minute to catch my breath."

Travis rinsed his mouth with water and spit it out. He leaned against an edge of a fissure jutting out from the cliff.

Bailey got up from the ground and swayed when he took a step. "Whoa, got up too fast."

Travis dropped his canteen and grabbed Bailey's arm. "Are you okay?'

"Yeah, I'm just getting too old for this mountaineering." He breathed through his nose for a minute.

"Maybe you ought to give it a rest, I can climb up there, you don't need to," Travis said.

"I don't quit, Travis. Now let's get a-looking."

Cracks and fractures ravaged a portion of the base of the cliff. Bailey told Travis he'd read where this part of Wyoming had a hell of a lot of earthquakes and movement of the earth's crust and formed what was called uplifts. He said Rawlins was built in the hollow of one and the uplifts were the reasons for the unique rock and mountain formations.

He began to say how he should have been a geologist when a fluttering of material on the sharp edge of a fissure caught his eye. It was a torn piece of cloth, with a design of small, blue checks. The fissure was the entrance of a cave. Bailey pulled it from the snag and held it between his fingers, turning it.

"Is this like the shirt the dead guy had on?" Travis asked.

"I don't remember. Could be." Bailey stuck it in his pants pocket. Kneeling down to look into the entrance he said, "This cave looks like it goes back a long ways." He took the pack off and laid it on the ground, taking his flashlight and chalk out of the pack. A compass went over his neck before he stooped over to get into the entrance. Once inside, the cavern allowed him to stand up straight. Travis's light shined on the floor as he brought up the rear.

Their footsteps echoed down the natural formed tunnel that opened up wide and high. Stalactites and stalagmites began appearing the further they walked into the mountain. Bailey came to a fork and scraped the chalk against the rock wall. One went deeper where the only thing they could see was blackness. The other fork headed north, grew smaller and descended a few degrees. A ghostly light came through a partially collapsed wall. Water lay in small pools.

A ribcage and small pile of bones could be seen near the wall. "Hey, I think this is the end of the cave I dove into when the flash flood hit." Bailey said excitedly. The passage ceiling and walls diminished until he had to get on his hands and knees for the last several yards. The beam of the flashlight wavered as he shined it on the pile of bones.

"What is it?" Travis asked.

"Shit. Just a damn deer skeleton." Several small arrowheads were embedded in the bones. Bailey backed up until he could stand up. "I thought it might be more. But that's the cave I was in. When the last wave came in and damned near sucked me out, the wall had crumbled and I thought I'd seen bones." He turned down the other fork. "Guess I figured they were human bones. Indians killed it though. There's arrowheads still stuck in the skeleton, but I'm not gonna touch 'em. They still might be poisonous."

"I think this was an entrance, look at that," Travis said. His light illuminated a notch in the rock, halfway up the side,

197

holding a smooth length of wood with a blackened end. "That's a torch unless I'm all screwed up."

"You're right. How'd I miss it?" Bailey inspected the artifact without touching it. "Let's go down the other tunnel."

"Why don't you bring it? We can get the guys at the office to try and date it." Travis suggested.

"I don't want to disturb anything now. Maybe later, on our way back."

They discovered three more side entrances, each becoming narrower as they approached the end of the passages. Two opened on the south side of the mountain and another opened on the north. Brush and overhanging rocks obscured their being seen by the outside world. Now their attention and lights also centered on the middle of the walls, and they located more torches stuck into cracks and notches of rock. Water flowing could be heard in the far darkness.

"Travis, do you realize what we're seeing?" Bailey asked in an awed voice.

"Yeah, an ancient Indian passageway inside a mountain. Unbelievable."

"It's more than that. This has to be where the Nimerigar lived on the inside of this cavern. Even after talking to Chandler and seeing the mummy head, I don't think I really believed in them. But man, I do now. I wouldn't be surprised if this doesn't run the length of damn near half the mountain top."

"All right!" Travis whooped. "High five." He held his hand up and Bailey slapped it with his.

The tunnel turned a corner and a cavern opened up in front of them. The floor smoothed out as if years of a people living and growing wore the rough stone down to a granite tile. Broken jugs and shards of pottery littered the floor. A fire pit surrounded by blackened rocks sat in the middle of the room.

Bailey and Travis circled the chamber trying to contain their excitement with each artifact they found.

"We're going into the history books," Travis said. "Let the big boys excavate this place and me and you will sit back and reap the rewards."

Bailey didn't say anything for a minute. "Keep it quiet for now, nobody needs to know what we've found yet. There's still some murders that connect to this." His light faded. "We better get back, my batteries are getting low."

"Mine too." They took another look and started back in the direction they'd come.

Bailey walked with his hand sliding along the side of the passage. It seemed endless in the fading light. "Whoa," he said, stumbling.

"What's the matter?"

"There's a break in the wall here, made me almost fall on my ass." Their lights grew fainter. "I can feel some air. Give me a second to check it out." He slipped between a slab of rock offset from the wall.

"Hurry it up," Travis said behind him. "My light's about gone."

Bailey tripped and went down on his knees. "Goddammit," he said, putting his hand down to push himself up. His light shined down a hole in the rock. A skull grinned back at him. A dump of adrenaline hit him the same time he reared back. His breath came in gasps. The light shimmered on two human skeletons lying side by side, the tops of their skulls broken and crushed. Bits of clothing remained on the bones and both skeletons had tattered, leather boots on their feet. Around the neck bone of one, a chain with a small circular band reflected the light back at him. The other, smaller skeleton had a fractured leg bone.

Bailey lay on his stomach and tried to reach the chain but it was too far away. He'd have to try to climb down and have Travis give him a hand back up.

His flashlight flickered and went off. Bailey violently shook it and a dull beam struggled to keep glowing.

"Travis, how's your flashlight doing?' he yelled.

"Getting low. We need to get out while we still got some light. Why didn't we bring more batteries?"

"Shut up," Bailey said. He hurried as fast as he could to the main passageway. "Turn your light off until mine quits. The hell with it. See if you can get one of those torches going, they should be dry."

"You got any matches? I don't."

"For Christ's sake. I don't believe this," Bailey groaned. "No, I don't."

They walked as fast as they could toward the entrance they'd come in. When Bailey's light went from a feeble glow to out, the darkness smothered them.

Travis cursed under his breath. "Crap, my light won't come on any more.

"Feel that?" Bailey asked. "There's some air moving. I think we're close to the other south opening. Grab my belt and we'll try to find it."

Like blind men moving with their hands out in front and to the side of them, they moved down the passageway.

"Here it is, I think. Watch your head," Bailey said, feeling the wall recede into the tunnel. His hand felt the ceiling lower and he bent down with Travis following and a death grip on his belt.

The sunlight blinded them when they stuck their heads through the brush covered opening of the side tunnel.

"I'm gonna tell you, I was getting spooked in there without a light," Bailey said. "Next time we come up, we bring extra batteries and some matches."

Chapter Twenty-Nine

Reese held his hand up to his mouth. "Shhh. I heard some yelling.'

Bodine craned his neck. They moved to the tunnel at the end of the tomb and put their heads inside. Faint echoes of voices floated to them.

"Goddamn, someone's in here. Let's go find 'em." Reese grabbed his crossbow and tossed Bodine his. They each picked up a flashlight and headed down the passage.

Reese put his mouth close to Bodine's ear. "We don't want them to hear us coming, so walk careful," he whispered. Bodine nodded.

Some areas they were able to pick up their pace and others they had to stoop over and almost get to their hands and knees. When they entered the great room, Reese had them stop to listen. Sounds came from the blackness. "Go," he said.

Adrenaline from the hope of a chase sped his heart up. *This is living,* he thought, lengthening his stride. He could hear Bodine falling behind, blowing hard. An out of shape, worthless piece of shit. Reese decided to leave him if he couldn't keep up. He didn't need or want any help on a hunt anyway.

* * *

Bailey and Travis sat on the gravel slope below the opening. It dropped sixty feet and kept an angle where it would have been impossible to climb back up without a rope.

"We're east of where we started. I think if we go straight down, at least to the tree line, it'll be easier than trying to traverse the mountain side, don't you think?" Bailey asked.

"Yeah, it'll be hard to keep your balance in this loose stuff. I wouldn't want to try to come back up this way either, too damn steep and slippery."

"We better get going, we've spent more time in there than I thought." Bailey stayed on his butt and stuck his feet out in front of him. He pushed off and began sliding down the slope using his feet as brakes. Travis followed.

They started a small rockslide, with small, knuckle-sized rocks tumbling with them and a cloud of dust formed from their boots digging in.

Bailey heard a yelp behind him and turned in time to see Travis go head over heels, falling out of control. He dug his feet in and stopped his descent then turned and braced himself as Travis came down, arms outstretched, legs wide, now almost rock surfing on his stomach. His hat passed Bailey.

"Dig in!" Bailey yelled. He leaned into the hill and put one knee on the slope and the other straight out, toes burrowing in for a brace.

Bailey put his shoulder into Travis's chest and stayed low when they collided, like a linebacker hitting a running back full speed. His head went under and through Travis's arm as he wrapped his arms around Travis's back. He shoved down with all his strength, straightening his back. A grunt came out of Travis when he hit Bailey.

Bailey thought his ankle would break from the pressure, but it held. They dug their hands into the rock, shredding skin from their fingers and palms.

"I thought I was going to go all the way to the trees. You saved my ass, Bailey. If I'd hit a tree, it would have been all over for me."

Bailey rubbed his calf and the small of his back. "I know. You owe me big time. And don't worry, I won't let you forget."

He looked around. "It feels like something's watching us. See anything?"

Travis craned his neck back up the slope. "Nope. Probably a deer or an elk wondering what the hell we're doing."

"Maybe. You feel up to getting down from here?" The tree line started twenty yards below them with a few struggling pines; half dead and leaning away from the direction the wind usually blew. The farther down the slope, the thicker the pines. Aspen sprouted up in a tangle of massive growths.

Travis nodded and started down. Bailey followed. The tree line came closer.

* * *

Reese ran hunched over leaving Bodine behind. He'd come from the tomb to the south entrance they used to transport the artifacts to the pickup point. From somewhere in the darkness, the panting and clomping of Bodine could be heard.

The crossbow was cocked with an arrow in it when he flattened himself against the wall of the entrance. There would be a minute or two before Bodine showed up. Reese stuck his head out the fissure and saw the backpacks lying below him. He listened and dropped down, crossbow ready. Below and to the east of him a cloud of dust hung in the air. There! Two men sitting on that gravel slope. Reese moved behind a boulder and watched as the men began sliding down the slope until they got to the trees. The bigger one looked familiar, but he couldn't place him. Indistinct voices floated up from a conversation the two were having.

Bodine arrived at the mouth of the entrance, sweat shining on his face and gasping for breath. Reese motioned for him to stop and get back.

He decided there might be a chance the two would climb back up and retrieve their packs. He dropped down and crept to them. His toe lifted the flap of one and he saw food, rope and binoculars inside. Reese left the packs where they lay and climbed back to the entrance. "There were two guys. They went down the slope over there," he said, pointing to the east. You go ahead and go back to the ranch. I'm gonna wait and see if they come back."

"Why would they come back if they're down now?" Bodine asked. Relief showed on his face.

"They left their backpacks. Give me your crossbow and I'll wait up here for a while. Go on," he said abruptly.

"Sure, sure. You bet. Here you go." Bodine handed his crossbow to Reese. "No need getting pissed."

"That's right. No need for me to get pissed. Adios." Reese turned his back to Bodine and set both crossbows by his feet. He sat down Indian style and leaned against the cavern wall. A damn good position to be in if the two came back. *Where the hell have I seen that guy?*

* * *

Bailey and Travis crossed side hill in the trees until they came to the trail well below the rock chute. They stopped and sat on a downed tree trunk catching their breath.

"Our backpacks are still up there, you know," Travis said.

"Yeah, but to be honest, if I try to climb back up to get them, you might as well bury me there," Bailey said, taking deep breaths. "Maybe we can come back tomorrow and get 'em."

"Sounds good to me. You still feel like someone's watching us?"

"Hard to say, now. I'm so damn petered out all I want to do is get off the mountain and get home."

"You want to tell the archaeologists at the office what we found?" Travis asked.

"Not yet. I want to get a better look and see where it ends. If the good doctor is right, then somewhere there's a tomb that's being looted. And one thing we don't need is a bunch of college boys getting in the way." Bailey stood up and gave Travis a hand up. "That work with you?"

"You're calling the shots, Boss. For what it's worth, I agree," Travis said.

Bailey dropped Travis off at his house an hour before sunset. After such a grueling physical day, a few beers would help him to relax and recoup but he fought the urge. *Is it getting easier?*

The two dogs greeted him when he came through the door by Callie jumping on him and Barney trying to work his way between Callie and Bailey. He saw their bowls had food in them and the water bowl was full. *Thank the Lord for good neighbors,* he thought.

They followed him as he took off his clothes and dropped them on the bedroom floor. He took a club soda with him into the shower and drank it while the needle spray bit into his back with water so hot it turned his skin bright red. When the water turned cold, he reluctantly got out of the shower and toweled off. Another soda went down while he dried his hair and combed it.

With the towel around him, he flopped down in the recliner. He decided he needed to drink something else besides the soda, something with a kick but no alcohol. Maybe the new stuff that was chalk full of caffeine. He thought he'd ask Radcliffe what he recommended for a substitute.

The barking woke him up. He saw Barney's tail as he shot through the kitchen doggie door on his way outside. Cat opened the front door and shoved Callie off her.

"Hey, where you been?" she asked. In her hands was a barrel of KFC. "I thought you might like to have some dinner with me."

Bailey moaned, held the towel and got out of the chair. "Yeah, I got the beer you can drink. Food will do me some good." He shambled toward the bedroom. "Let me get some clothes on."

"Oh, don't. You're fine the way you are," Cat said. Her eyes locked on the towel. She pulled a half-pint of bourbon, not quite full, out of her back pocket, unscrewed the lid and took a long swallow. "Yeah, you're just fine the way you are."

Bailey grinned and went to the kitchen. He plopped down in a chair at the table after putting down two paper plates. "Maybe you'd be more comfortable in a towel? He leered.

"Good idea," she said, unbuttoning her shirt.

He heard the water going in the bathroom. The dogs hadn't come back in and he decided he should find out where they were. The same time he stood up she came out with a towel tied around her. It barely covered her breasts and rode high up her legs.

"You used all the hot water," she said, shivering. "Let's eat the food first."

* * *

The ringing of the telephone woke him. The digital clock read 9:22 P.M. Two thoughts entered his mind at the same time. One: he hoped the top of his head didn't blow off, each ring of the phone coincided with a dull thud in his brain, and two: he hadn't thought of Dana when he and Cat thrashed around on the bed. A step forward. How he stayed off the beer when she was there had to be the big question. No booze and he felt like he had a hangover. Too much sex and chicken in the same night?

"Calhoun," he rasped into the phone. Cat buried her head under a pillow.

"Bailey? This is Ann Duncan," she said, her voice sounding unsure.

"Oh sure, sure. Sorry, I was asleep. What can I do for you, Ann?"

"I wanted to tell you Dad died tonight, about an hour ago."

He wiped his face with a hand. "Aw, man. I'm sorry. I wish I could have known him better...I liked him."

"He enjoyed your visits. I have his files for you. You can get them next time you're down or I'll send them to you."

"When's the funeral? I'd like to come," Bailey said. He'd slung his feet over the side of the bed and sat hunched over, his hand pushing on his throbbing temple.

"Dad requested to be cremated. I'm going to...to," Her voice cracked and he heard her cry softly. She coughed and cleared her throat. "I'm sorry. Even when you know he could go anytime, it's still a shock when it happens. There's so much you wish you'd have told him."

"Yeah, I know exactly what you're feeling. I went through the same thing last year."

"Who'szat you talk'in to?" Cat mumbled, rolling onto her side away from Bailey.

Bailey ignored her and moved down the bed farther. "I'm on a few days off, can I come down and help you with anything?"

"Actually—" Her voice broke again. "I should have all kinds of friends to call on, but I don't. My kids are overseas... I need to go through his files for you. I'm so damn upset and I don't know why. My God, he was in his nineties... he had a good, long life. I shouldn't be crying on your shoulder, I hardly know you, but I like what I do know and Dad did too."

"Listen, I'll be in Ft. Collins before lunch today. I'll call when I get in and you can give me directions to your house. Okay?" A pause. "Okay, Annie?" he asked softly.

"Okay. Thanks, Bailey. I feel better already."

After hanging up the phone, Bailey pushed himself out of bed and went into the kitchen. He took four Excedrin and drank three glasses of water. He felt like crap and stumbled back to the bedroom. When he opened the shades, moonlight came in the window and bathed the room in a pale, silver light. Barney was lying down in the grass, looking at the window. *Now why the hell hasn't he come in? I hope the guy isn't going strange on me now.*

Cat lay on her side snoring gently, the sheet pulled above her legs. A tangle of sweat-formed curls circled her face and a false eyelash hung precariously from one of her upper eyelids. She stirred and a fart squeaked out from under the sheet.

Bailey watched her for a moment and looked at her strong legs that had been locked around his sides not long ago. Strange, he didn't feel anything for her at that moment. He wondered if this was the finish for them; his hand reached toward her shoulder - he had an urge to wake her up and tell her to leave. *Maybe it's just this damn headache but she's not looking too appealing right now. Hell, I'm sure I'm not either. The son-of-a-bitch in me is coming out because I'm tired and feel like I have one hell of a hangover. Better sleep on it.* He hoped his life wouldn't begin to have more complications.

Cat woke him up later when she left the bed and asked who was on the phone. He told her the daughter of a friend, informing him her father had died. Unfortunately, he found his feelings from the previous night hadn't changed.

After she left, Barney came back into the house and wouldn't let Bailey out of his sight.

*   *   *

"Take a break today, we'll go get the packs tomorrow," Bailey told Travis on his cell phone as he drove past Walcott Junction on his way to Ft. Collins, two hours later. He explained to Travis why he was going and said the files he would get could shed more light on the past inhabitants of the cavern.

"I might run up and get our backpacks. You gotta remember I'm not as old as you are. A goodnight's sleep charged me back up."

"If you do, don't go in the cave," Bailey ordered. "I'll be back either late tonight or in the morning. In fact, wait until I'm back and we'll both go. There's been three murders in the south Ferris area. No use taking any unnecessary chances."

He heard a sigh. "All right. Guess I can go out to the refuge and check on the horses," Travis said. "Hey, maybe I'll see if Cat wants to go with me. Would you mind?"

Bailey almost laughed out loud. "I don't have her in my sights... have at her."

"I thought you two were an item."

"No... I'd call it a fling instead, I think."

"All right, I'll see you tomorrow," Travis said, and hung up.

Bailey dropped his cell phone on the seat and put his sun glasses on. *I wish you would get something going with her, that'd help me out.*

Chapter Thirty

The headlights of the four-wheeler reflected off the metal building when Reese drove into the ranch. He parked at the main house and walked in going to the office. Gavin sat at the desk, a ledger in front of him.

"Where you been?" Gavin asked, closing the ledger. "Ike said you saw some guys up around the caverns and were waiting for them."

"Close. I think they were in the cave. Not the tomb, but the chamber down from it. I heard them shouting and tried catching up but they went out a side tunnel and slid down the slope. I didn't know the damn thing was there."

"Did they know you were after them?"

"I don't think so. When I saw them, they were bullshitting. I think I've seen one of them before. A big guy, with a bit of a gut and looked older than us."

Gavin closed his eyes and steepled his fingers in front of him. "You remember that BLM character? The one who brought the lease out and had a couple of beers? He was big and older. Had a little gut on him too, if I remember right."

"That could be him. I didn't get a close look at his face, but it could be. I think we better shut down for a few days and see what happens."

Gavin slammed his hand down on the desk. "Why'd that goddamn Millhouse have to try and rip us off? It was bad enough he took a mummy, but losing it and that old man finding it was the worst luck we could have had."

"Not really," Reese poured a drink and sat down. "One thing, we got the head back, the second thing is nobody will suspect us, hell, we're on the other side of the mountain. The paper says the cops don't have any leads on the old folks and it didn't say nothing about connecting them with Millhouse. Anyway, we didn't kill him; our little friend capped them. It's a good thing we got rid of the thieving bastard before he took a lot more."

"Reese, for such a smart man, you can act pretty dumb at times. If that BLM guy, I think his name is Calhoun, finds the tomb, he'll find the entrance, which is on the *north* side of the mountain." Gavin got a glass and poured a drink. "But you're right. We'll close the operation down for a few days and see what happens."

"How much time would you need to make one more big haul? Big enough we can get out of here," Reese asked.

"With what we have stashed here and say…half a dozen more of the mummies… a week. Of course, if we didn't have to include Ike in the split, three to four days if I make some calls tonight," Gavin said thoughtfully. "We wouldn't need as much without him."

"Ike can be taken care of fairly easy. I think we ought to pack it in. I can set some charges and seal the tomb with Ike in it. Tie up all the loose ends. By the time anyone finds out, we'll be long gone to Mexico," Reese said.

"How's this sound? We shut down for a few days and you keep an eye out to see if anyone comes back to the south entrance. I'll start getting things in place for one last big haul."

Reese nodded his head. "I like it. Show me what we have here ready to go."

Gavin stood up and took a key out of his pants pocket. He walked over to a built-in bookcase that was four feet wide and six feet high. The fingers on one hand pushed a button recessed in the upper corner. There was a click and the bookcase popped open several inches revealing a metal door with a locking handle. Gavin stabbed the key in and turned it, then shoved the handle down and pulled the door open. Inside, concrete walls with shelves on the three sides held several wooden boxes and one large black satchel.

"Take a gander," Gavin said, opening the satchel.

Reese gave out a low whistle. He stuck his hands in and pulled out thin ribbons of gold and small bands made from copper and silver etched with gold. "I didn't realize we'd found this much. What do you think it's worth?" he asked quietly.

"I'm thinking close to a million- that's the jewelry and the mummies." Gavin saw Reese's eyes brighten. "I've been negotiating with someone who's collecting things like this for his private use. We talked at Sanderson's last year and he'll be the one who'll buy all of the rest, I think."

"You're not worried he might tell the cops?"

Gavin laughed and said, "Hell no. He's a capo in the mob. No one crosses this guy. I'll call him and see if he'll take delivery of what we have now. I'm gonna have him pay all the money up front first, though."

Reese gently lowered the gold and bands back into the satchel. "Why?"

"I don't know if I trust him enough to let him pay C.O.D. He might try ripping us off if we're there when we swap for the cash. That old saying of honor among thieves is bullshit. We'll give him half of the artifacts for the full amount and then the other half when we have the money in our hot little hands."

"You don't trust him, yet you think he'll trust you?" Reese shook his head. "Man, that's thinking big time."

"Look, he knows we won't screw him because he can find us and have us whacked. Even you, tough as you are. You can't hide from the Mafia. I think he'll go along with it. Besides, we're not the errand boys, so that's a good point in our favor."

"You got balls, Gavin, I'll say that," Reese said.

"Yeah, I know, I just don't like to tell too many people." He smirked. "Because if I do, then they expect more out of me."

The metal door shut with a heavy thud. After locking it, Gavin closed the bookcase. "I'll get busy trying to make this deal. You going to keep an eye on the south entrance tomorrow?"

Reese nodded. "What if someone comes up?" He drew a finger across his neck. "Take care of them?"

"We need some warning. If a bunch of cops climb up there, I'd say no, get back here. If it's the same two guys from today... I don't know." Gavin snapped his fingers. "Take some of the dynamite Bodine stole and rig it up so you can seal off the passage near the chamber if you think someone's following you. They wouldn't know there's a north entrance, at least for a while. It'd give us some more time to get away."

"Okay, I'll go ahead and rig it up to blow the tomb to shit also. Kill two birds with one stick of dynamite, as they say." He chuckled at his own humor. "You get the passports for us yet?"

"A month ago. Cost me some big bucks but we'll have everything we need. You're Thomas Benson and I'm Harrison Colby. Pretty different names. You know why, don't you?"

Reese furrowed his brow and shook his head. "No, tell me."

"Most people who take an alias use their old initials or middle names, something familiar to them. These two names aren't even close to ours."

"You're sharp, Gavin. Where are they?"

"In the safe room. When we get the artifacts we'll take them, do our business with Ike and fade away into the night."

"I guess tomorrow will tell whether we're in the shit or not," Reese said.

"You like this, don't you? I mean, the chase and the kill and all," Gavin said. He screwed the lid on the bottle and put it away in his desk.

"Yeah, it makes my blood run. There's nothing like it. I've been called a psycho, especially after Desert Storm, but... goddamn, I love it." Reese had a dreamy look on his face, as if he were running someone down and killing them in his mind.

After Reese left, Gavin opened a drawer on the desk and took out a .38 caliber Smith and Wesson snub nose pistol. It couldn't hit a barn wall if you were more than six feet away, but it was a good close-up gun. He tied an ankle holster on, stuck the gun in it, and sat down to do some dealing over the telephone.

Chapter Thirty-One

Bailey called Annie on his cell phone when he turned onto U.S. 287, after bypassing the small community of LaPorte. He was six miles from Ft. Collins. She gave him directions to her house and twenty minutes later he pulled into the driveway of a well-kept ranch, with towering weeping willow trees surrounding what appeared to be a fair-sized, landscaped lot.

She greeted him at the front door before he rang the bell, dressed in jeans and a sleeveless western shirt.

"Bailey, thanks for coming," she said, taking his hand and holding it with both of hers.

He saw a living room filled with art. Pictures on the wall, sculptures in some of the corners and a bookcase filled with more books than he'd ever seen in a private home.

"I've gone through his files and have them in the kitchen. If you like, we can have some coffee and look to see what you want." She sounded nervous and almost raced to the kitchen.

Two stacks of folders reached midway between the floor and the countertop. Bailey sat down at the table and sipped from the cup of coffee she placed in front of him. "These are sixty years of files?" he asked, disbelieving.

"Lord, no. Let me show you something," she said getting up and opening a door that went to the basement. Annie flicked a light on and Bailey followed her down the steps.

Against one wall, eight-drawer file cabinets were lined up from corner to corner. Twenty more cabinets stood along the adjacent wall.

"That's more what I had in mind," Bailey said. "What're you going to do with all these?"

She shut the light off and the two went back to the table. "After you get what you want, I'm going to contact the state and let them have what they want for their archives."

"Lots of luck if you have to talk to the same joker I did. He's a bit of a pompous ass, if you ask me. He's the first one I contacted trying to find out about the Nimerigar, wouldn't have a thing to do with me. He said it was all a hoax. If the secretary hadn't worked for your father and told me where I could find him, I don't know where I'd be."

"And just where are you now? I mean, are you close to finding anything?"

"I already have. Yesterday another ranger and I found an entrance into a mountain that led to a huge chamber with so many artifacts there you'd think they still lived in it. Are you aware of what your father had to do with the Nimerigar?"

"Sure, I wasn't born when he was given the mummy, of course, but he told me all about it. I think he was still bitter to the end that those gold miners took it back."

"I found the skeletons of them," Bailey stated, almost smugly.

"Who?"

"The gold miners… in a side tunnel off the main passageway in the mountain. Their skulls were crushed and both skeletons had small arrowheads embedded in their bones."

"How do you know it was the ones that had found the mummy? After all it happened sixty years ago," Annie said. She stood up and washed her coffee cup out in the sink.

"Because one had a chain with a metal band around its neck. One like your father described to me last week. I— Goddamn!" His eyes widened and he stood up.

Annie jerked back, her hands held up for protection. "What's the matter?"

He paced around the room, head down and his fist thumping on his leg.

"You're scaring me, Bailey, maybe you should leave," she said, backing away from the kitchen sink.

"No, no. I'm sorry. Look, the Nimerigar were supposed to have died out hundreds of years ago, right?" He could feel his temples pulsating and his excitement rose to another level.

"Yes, so long ago they were a legend or a myth rather than a known fact. What's your point?" Annie quit backing up and came closer. She looked around as if making sure she had an escape route should he go crazy.

"The miners found the mummy in 1932 or so, right?" Bailey asked. Annie nodded her head. "After they took the mummy back from your father, they were never heard from or seen again until I found them."

"Like I said, what's your point?"

"*The miners were killed by the Nimerigar!* Skulls crushed, small arrowheads in them." He held his bandaged hand in the air. "This was from an Indian stone knife that had a poison on it and damned near killed me. Poison couldn't stay toxic for a hundred years, particularly exposed to the environment."

"You're saying the Nimerigar still live?"

"No, but I'd say they didn't disappear a couple of hundred years ago like everybody thought. I wish your dad were alive, it would be damn interesting to hear what he'd have said about this," Bailey said, sitting back down. "Can I go through the files?"

"Yes, that's why I brought them up. They aren't all about the Indians. I didn't want to go through them so I brought up all the files he'd made from 1932 through 1945." She dabbed her eyes with a Kleenex.

"Hey, I'm being rude," Bailey said softly. "Can I help with the arrangements or something? I know it's tough to clean out personal belongings, but maybe I can do that for you?"

She laid a hand on his arm. "Thanks, I appreciate the offer but there's nothing to do, really. When he went to the home I gave away most of his clothes and things. He's being cremated, so later I'll have a memorial service. Probably the end of the month. You're welcome to attend. He liked you, you know. Which is odd, considering he didn't know you more than a few hours, weeks apart."

"It seems I either piss people off or they like me when I meet them. Hopefully, you're in the latter part rather than the former." He smiled at her, hoping to make her more at ease with him.

A thought came into his mind that surprised him. *I can see myself with this woman someday.* He shook his head.

"Are you okay?" she asked.

"Yeah, just a wild thought rattling around inside my skull." He picked a handful of files off the closest stack and began looking through them.

"Can I help?"

"Sure, I'm looking for anything concerning the Nimerigar or the two miners, I think their names were, ah…yeah, Meggert and Davison."

Annie took a pile of files off the stack and set in down in front of her. "I'll separate these," she said.

Together, they sat at the kitchen table going through the cardboard folders. Annie made coffee, and later, sandwiches, which Bailey wolfed down.

The sounds of increased traffic from one street over made Bailey notice the time. "Whoa, we've been at it all afternoon. Jeeze, it's four o'clock all ready." The stack against the counter was gone, moved to an area by the basement door. There were five thick folders on the floor next to Bailey's leg. "Finished. Can I take you to dinner?"

"You don't owe me anything, Bailey," she replied.

"That's debatable, but I'd like to take you out. Look at it as a date."

She chewed her lip and stared at a spot over his shoulder.

"Are you unavailable? If you aren't, instead of putting you on a spot in case you just don't want to go out with me, I'll retract the offer." He tried to act nonchalant and picked the folders up from the floor.

"I haven't gone out with a man for over a year," she began. "The men I went out with were academicians from the college and artists. Either total bores or so self-centered I decided I could do without for a while. You're down to earth, real. I can see why Dad liked you. It would be my pleasure if you'll retract the retraction."

"Six o'clock work for you? I'll go find me a motel and clean up." He paused to see if she'd offer him a place to stay. "Okay, I'll see you then."

When she spoke, he had the front door open. "Bailey..."

He turned back and smiled.

"The Comfort Suites is a great place to stay," she said. "On Harmony, down by the shopping center."

*   *   *

They ate in a small Italian restaurant that was hidden behind a bank.

"Are you going back to Rawlins tomorrow?" Annie asked. She held her wineglass with both hands in front of her.

"After a quick trip to Cheyenne in the morning. I have an early appointment." *Was that a look of disappointment on her face?* He hoped so.

"I've never seen the Ferris Mountains. After hearing you and Dad talking about them, they sound magnificent," she said.

Bailey felt himself loosen up and relaxed. "Beautiful and unique, and even more unique knowing there's a series of caverns and passageways apparently through-out the eastern summit. You ought to see it, the edge of the Red Desert's like an ocean tide, lapping up on the south side of the foothills. Sand dunes, canyons, creeks, a quiet desolation where you could go for miles without seeing anyone." His face turned dark. "At least it used to be that way. Three people have been murdered out there now. Unbelievable."

"If it's so solitary and barren, the murderers should be found, shouldn't they? Someone should have seen something, I'd think."

"Like I said, it's a big country, Annie, and the law enforcement's barking up the wrong tree, in my opinion."

"Dad always said use patience and analyze the evidence from the back to the front first, then go over it again from the front to the back."

"I'll keep that in mind," Bailey said dryly.

The night stayed hot and humid even with a slight breeze blowing out of the west. After finishing dinner they took a back road past the brewery and made a loop ending with Bailey parking in Annie's driveway.

He walked her to the house and held the screen door open while she unlocked and opened the front door.

"Can I call you? Maybe come down and take you out again?" he asked.

"I'd like that. Sometime I hope you'll take me to see the mountain." She kissed him lightly on the cheek and said, "Goodnight, Bailey, I appreciate your coming down." She went in the house.

Bailey turned and walked to his truck, a grin spreading across his face. *I want to show you the mountain.*

Chapter Thirty-Two

"Sit down, Bailey. After your phone call last week, I didn't think you'd show up," Dr. Radcliffe said, offering coffee.

"I damn near didn't, I'm really pressed for time, but Peter made me promise, so here I am." He took the cup and sipped the coffee.

"Your word's pretty important to you, is it?"

"At one time it didn't seem to be. Now it is again," Bailey replied, feeling his face get hot.

"Caused by your drinking?" Radcliffe asked. He held a hand up. "You asked me about confidentiality last time. We also talked about your wife. You've shown the tendencies of feeling guilt, either from an action or inaction. Want to talk about it?"

Bailey chewed his lip and wished he had a beer. It was so much easier to talk from the gut when a guy's had two or three drinks under his belt. Should he or shouldn't he talk about it?

"I killed her." He waited for a response from Radcliffe.

Other than an eyebrow lifting, the doctor sat silently in his chair.

"Dana was in pain all the time...from the cancer. She begged me every time I was with her. *Please, Bailey, you've got to help me.* The oncologist had given her less than three months to live and she was on the third month." He stood up and walked to the window. "I don't think she weighted eighty pounds. Couldn't eat anything, took everything by IV. Finally, I—" Bailey stared out the window, not speaking.

"You what? Get it off your chest, Bailey," Radcliffe encouraged "You've kept it bottled up too damn long,"

"I overdosed her with liquid morphine. Put it in her IV and watched her heartbeat drop to nothing while I held her." He shook his head and his voice turned raspy as his eyes turned glassy. "For almost a year all I've done is remember her begging me to help her and seeing her die in my arms."

"And you've only remembered the good, never the bad. You put her on a pedestal and began dwelling on her request for help, transforming an act of mercy to… your words…'I killed her.'"

"That's exactly right, until a couple of days ago," Bailey said, still facing the window.

"And what was that?"

"I found out that when we were having problems last year and she left me, she had an affair with someone I know."

Radcliffe sat up straighter in chair. "You're certain?"

"Yeah, I got him drunk and he told me. Said they both needed someone and when Dana and I got back together, it ended." He smiled wryly. "I knocked him on his ass after he told me and then felt guilty as hell."

"And what do you think about that?"

"Betrayed. I can't accept her sleeping with someone. We were still married, just living apart to work our problems out." Bailey turned from the window and faced Radcliffe. "And she never told me, even when we knew she was going to die."

"You mean confessed her sins to you? Radcliffe asked. "I don't think a reasonable man could expect a death bed confession for what sounds like a one-time emotional mistake."

"I don't know that I ever said I was a reasonable man. After I knocked the guy on his ass, I apologized, shook his hand. And I did feel… what, relief maybe? Is that reasonable? I've been working things out in my own mind."

Radcliffe straightened up in his chair. "I think—"

"I killed a man last summer when he tried murdering a friend of mine," Bailey interrupted. "That's not what I did to Dana. I feel in my heart it wasn't wrong, she was in so much pain. I also know she loved me and we were human. Not perfect, just a man and woman who took a wrong step once or twice." His vision blurred. "I can put her to rest now, I think. I'll always love her, but I can get on with my life... I hope."

"You might have resolved it. I'm impressed, but let me warn you," Radcliffe said, placing his fingers together on his lips. "I think you might have recognized some of your problems, but you aren't out of the woods yet." He motioned for Bailey to sit down.

"There's going to be times this will hit you like a sledgehammer. All the pain and guilt will be back, but probably ten-fold. I can help you so you won't get drunk to escape from your memories."

"I've got things to do. I'd rather try to handle it myself right now. If I can't, I'll come and see you. Okay?"

Radcliffe saw the desperation in his patient's eyes. He took his pen and scribbled on a sheet of paper, not saying anything.

"What do you say?"

The pen clicked and went in his shirt pocket. "Come back in a month." He held his hand up. "That's the best I can do, Bailey."

"I'm not arguing. You'll let Wales know?"

"I'll call him," Radcliffe said. "Don't let me down."

"Do you think I need some tranquilizers, in case I start getting stressed out?"

Radcliffe pulled his pen back out of his shirt pocket and wrote a prescription for a thirty-day supply of Valium. "No more than one a day, and only if you need it, understand?" He handed the prescription across the desk. "I don't want an alcoholic turning into a drug addict."

"I swear, you don't have to worry about that. Thanks, I'll see you next month." He stood up, clutching the prescription in his hand. "Can I get this filled here?"

"Across the street. Bailey—"

"Yeah?"

"Don't drink and take the Valium, you might have some complications."

"Like what?"

"Cramps, sick, hallucinate. It's hard to say which one, but booze also diminishes the efficiency of drugs. So don't do it." Radcliff warned.

Chapter Thirty-Three

Bailey had to wait until he crossed the summit on Sherman Pass and headed down toward Laramie before he had service on his cell phone. He tried calling Travis first. Dora said he was out in the field and not expected back that day. Bailey left him a voice mail telling him he'd be back the next morning and they'd go get their packs.

The second call was to Frank Ricconi.

"What do you want, Bailey?" he asked warily.

"Is your grandfather on the Split Rock reservation?"

"Yeah, why?"

"I'd like to… ask him to tell me about an Indian legend," Bailey said. Static crackled over the phone. "Tonight if he could."

"So, it's let bygones be bygones now that you need something from me, right?"

"Frank, I thought we were straight on this. You want to smack me to get even, fine, you can do it later. Now, how about seeing your grandfather?"

Ricconi told him he'd check and got Bailey's cell number.

The windmills that lined the high ridge at Arlington were in Bailey's rearview mirror when the cell rang. Ricconi's grandfather would see him an hour after the sun set.

"Pick me up at my house and I'll ride with you," Ricconi said.

* * *

Bailey stopped in Rawlins and fed the dogs. They'd come running through the hole in the fence when they heard him park in the driveway. He dropped his bag on the bedroom floor, gave his apologies to Elizabeth over the fence and promised he'd spend more time with the dogs after the case was closed. That seemed to mollify her and she called the dogs to her.

After gassing the truck, he headed north toward Jeffrey City, where Ricconi lived. The smell of sagebrush drifted in through the open window from the sun baking the prairie. Ugly fingers of alkali spread out from the edges of stagnant pools of water and antelope grazed while the bucks guarded the herd. He saw two bands of wild horses just past Lamont. *God, I love this country.* He felt like he was where he belonged.

He passed by the gravel road that led to the Stone Gulch Ranch and saw a Game and Fish pickup driving toward the highway from the east, dust billowing up behind it. *Must be Cat.* He honked his horn and waved. *I need to figure out how I feel about her.* He smiled. *That Annie, now there's a woman. What the hell's a matter with you? Thinking about two women at one time, you got problems, my man.*

Clouds in the sky were streaked with red and yellow from a sun easing its way behind the Wind River Mountains to the west of Jeffrey City. It was a town born from the uranium boom of years past and only a few hundred hardy souls kept the town alive.

Ricconi's patrol car was backed in the driveway of the state-furnished house on Western Nuclear Avenue. Half of the houses on both sides were empty. Bailey parked by the side of the patrol car. Ricconi opened the front door of the house, holding a beer. He waved for Bailey to come inside.

Feeling some apprehension on his way to the house, Bailey wondered if Ricconi would hold a grudge. *Screw it, I'll find out, maybe the hard way.*

He was greeted with an ice-cold bottle of beer being shoved into his hand.

226

"Drink up, Kemosabe," Ricconi raised his bottle in a mock toast and chugged it down. The side of his jaw had a slight bluish tinge. A smile showed his teeth.

Bailey raised his bottle, stuck his tongue in the end and acted like he was taking a long swallow. "I'm glad we're—"

His head rocked to the side and he flew back into the wall. He put his hand to the side of his mouth and dabbed at the blood running down. "So that's the way it's going to be," he said, pushing off from the wall, fists clenched. The bottle of beer laid on the floor in a pool of foam. The first pump of adrenaline gave him tunnel vision with the end of it being Ricconi.

"We're even," Ricconi said, turning away.

Bailey stumbled to a stop, his chest heaving. "You hit me when I wasn't expecting it."

"Kind of like *déjà vu*, isn't it? Now what do you want to do, fight or have a beer and go see my grandfather?" He took another two bottles out of an ice chest sitting on the floor.

"Guess I'm a bit of a hypocrite, aren't I?" Bailey asked, taking the beer.

"Yeah, but so am I. Let's go, it's getting late. My grandfather goes to bed early."

*　*　*

"What's up with wanting to speak to my grandfather?" Ricconi asked. He had his arm out the window as they drove down a dirt road in Bailey's truck, dust and gravel kicking up behind them.

"I've heard of a legend, or myth, about a tribe of pygmy Indians living in the mountains. Travis Knight and I found this cavern in the Ferris two days ago with a lot of artifacts and remnants of Indians. I think the Indians had a tomb and it's being looted, and the Wood's murders and the dead guy I found have something to do with it."

"Fine, what's that have to do with seeing my grandfather?" Ricconi asked again.

Bailey slammed on the brakes and came to a stop. He threw the gearshift into neutral and turned to face Ricconi. "This is all coming to a conclusion. I heard about the Nimerigar from an old state archaeologist living in a rest home. I've seen a mummified head Albert found and it disappeared after he was murdered. Millhouse, the dead guy I found, had a headband in his hand, or at least I was told it was a headband." He opened a small bottle and shook a green pill into his hand. It went in his mouth and he swallowed it dry.

"What's the pill?"

"Something to settle me down. I feel as nervous as a whore in church right now. A lot of excitement and stuff lately," Bailey said. "That's why I want to get this done now."

"So finish the story, Bailey."

"Yeah. I've got all this information based on one old man that died the night before last and some evidence to support what he told me. I want to hear a real Indian tell me about the Nimerigar - to collaborate the whole works. If your grandfather never heard about them, if they aren't a legend, maybe Jean and Albert *were* killed by some transits. Maybe I didn't really see the mummy and their murders aren't connected to Millhouse. Hell, I might have been going in the wrong direction the whole time."

He pulled the pickup into gear and stomped on the gas. The backend fishtailed as they accelerated down the road, spraying fine bits of gravel up behind them again.

Ricconi leaned against the back of the seat and looked at him. "Settle down, man. You sound a little close to going off the deep end."

The Split Rock Indian Reservation began behind the barren Rattlesnake Mountains and spread out to encompass 15,000 acres of parched, nearly useless land. Islands of stunted scrub oak dotted from rock crevices and the only flowing water came from a branch of the Sweetwater River that seemed to slither through the reservation in as short of journey possible. Single-wide trailer houses and corrugated roofed shanties lined a gravel street where a general store stood at one end and a distribution building at the other. Several of the homes had corrals with horses and a cow or two chewing cud.

A tipi with paintings of animals on the sides and smoke drifting out its top sat across the street surrounded by a dozen other tipis. The entrance flap was tied partially open. The tipis surrounded a fire pit where sparks flickered and lifted in the breeze.

Ricconi pointed and said, "Park to the side." He sounded apologetic. "They've tried to maintain the old ways but it's hard to do with so little money. The young Indians don't want to stay. In a couple of years this will be gone, I think, because the Bureau of Indian Affairs wants to move them to the reservation at Riverton. They say there's not enough Indians to warrant the cost of keeping the land as a reservation."

Bailey was led inside and introduced to Hantaki, an ancient looking Indian, sitting cross-legged around a small fire. His hair was long and white, and sunken eyes showed honor and pride. A sense of strength enveloped Bailey when he clasped the old man's arm.

Several elderly Indian men came into the tipi and listened as Bailey asked Hantaki to tell him about the legend of the Nimerigar.

Smokey haze filled the tipi when the old man began his story. He was old he said, and his father's grandfather, Kohanbu, lived in the high mountains as a child. Kohanbu's mother spirited him to safety before a battle began with the Nimerigar. There had been many stories told of other battles with the "tiny people eaters."

Bailey sat and thought the smell from the fire was familiar. Almost like they were burning marijuana.

Yeah, it smelled just like a gigantic joint. The plant grew naturally in some parts of Wyoming, and apparently, Bailey laughed inwardly, the government didn't know it grew around here. Shadows grew and danced on the walls of the tipi. The old man's voice cracked and faltered at times, and Bailey picked out Frank intermittently translating an Indian word to English.

* * *

Arapaho warriors, their bows notched with arrows, peered into the darkness and strained to hear the approaching invaders. Fear of an enemy armed with poison arrows and more vicious than the dreaded Lakota Kangi-Yuha warriors showed in the braves' s eyes. Quiet questions asked among the younger Indian braves preparing to die drifted on the wind. "How can this be? To battle a legend."

In the center of the camp most of the women huddled in a tipi with their arms encircling the children protectively. Each squaw held a knife at the ready, no child would be taken while they lived. Too many stories of the dreaded Nimerigar eating children alive had been passed down over the ages. One woman sneaked from the camp with her child.

A war cry echoed down from a granite bluff above them, penetrating the heart of every Arapaho, like a lance thrust hard into their chest. The medicine man began a chant for victory from their gods when an arrow sank deep in his back. He crumpled to the ground without a sound, dead. The battle began. Shadows the size of badgers swarmed over the rocks and through the crevices, lunging at the throats of the Arapaho then dragging them to the ground and hacking at their bodies with knives and axes. Warriors fought back with a ferocity born out of desperation. The bigger Nimerigar swung war clubs and crushed the skulls of the braves who still fought to protect the women and children. Flames lit the sky and danced over the camp like a canopy of fire.

The first light from the quarter moon, as the clouds passed, fell on the smoldering ruins of the center tipi. The once proud Arapaho summer camp was littered with the bodies of men, women and children – children whose throats were cut with sharp knives. The Nimerigar hadn't gotten them...at least alive.

Kohanbu and his mother hid in the brush and watched the attack. Hours later, they fled to another Arapaho camp. They told the story to the warriors who immediately jumped on their horses and raced to the battle site. No Nimerigar was found No sign, no tracks.

As time passed, other similar stories of the Nimerigar killing and mutilating their enemies surfaced and spread among the tribes of Crow, Sioux, Cheyenne and Arapaho.

* * *

Bailey saw the images of death play like a movie in his mind. Whatever he was breathing must be making him hallucinate, he thought.

"Our people feared only one tribe," the old Indian's voice droned on. "It is said even today the Nimerigar live. They wander from the bowels of high mountains leaving their dead after honoring them."

A hand shook his shoulder and abruptly brought him back to awareness of being in the tipi. "C'mon, Bailey, we gotta get home," Frank said, heaving Bailey to his feet.

The tipi stood empty, the fire burned down to embers. "Did they get me stoned?" Bailey asked. He took a deep breath and sucked in clean, night air.

"Probably," Frank said, a huge grin across his face. "Man, you're almost a brother now."

No lights shined from the windows of the houses or through the closed flaps of the other tipis, but Bailey felt the presence of the Indians watching him in the darkness.

On the way back to Jeffrey City, Frank asked if Bailey got what he wanted.

"Yeah, it's exactly what I needed to hear. Old Doctor Chandler was right. I didn't imagine the mummy's head. The Nimerigar were a real tribe of mean, people-eating pygmies." Bailey paused for a moment. "It also made me feel sorry as hell for your grandfather. It's a shame they might lose their way of life just because there's not enough money to either fight the government or quit being dependent on the BIA."

"You probably saw the last camp on the reservation. I'll bet in a year or so, it'll be gone. Bulldozed over and in place of the tipis and houses, some ranchettes for sale." Frank spit out the open window. "Pisses me off, but nothing I can do about it."

Bailey turned down a beer for the road after they arrived at Frank's house. He left for Rawlins anxious to read the files of Dr. Chandler's, lying on the back floorboard of his pickup. He thought it would be interesting to see what information matched from the tale he'd heard and the history on the death shroud the good doctor had translated and written down.

The dogs ran through the fence and greeted him when he came into the back yard after parking in the driveway. They jumped and lunged at him, almost knocking him down. "Settle down, you two, it's late." He had the files in his hands and his pistol belt over his shoulder.

They went in the back door and Bailey turned a light on in the kitchen. He dropped the files on the floor, pulled the Glock out of its holster and crouched next to the counter. The end table next to the recliner was lying on its side, the shade smashed. An upside down pizza box with pieces of pizza on the carpet, and a six pack of beer, bottles scattered littered the living room floor. The front door stood cracked open and a bloody smear was on the door jam.

232

"What the hell went on here?" He stayed low and went down the hallway, checking both bedrooms. Empty.

He called Cat on the phone.

"Game and Fish," the voice said brusquely.

"Cat, this is Bailey. Were you at my house tonight?"

"Yeah, and your goddamn dogs attacked me. That black mongrel took me pretty good. They better have had their shots, Calhoun."

"I don't know what to say. Callie hasn't ever gone after anyone, and I'd never seen Barney be aggressive at the Wood's."

"Woods? The black dog is the one from the ranch? The one that got shot?" She still sounded angry.

"That's right. I got him a few days ago, he was here when you came over the last time," Bailey said. "How'd you know he got shot?"

"You told me. Well, I never saw him at your house. You better get rid of the mutt, he's dangerous."

Bailey frowned. "He's all right. What were you doing coming in my house? Sounds like the dogs were just defending it."

"Screw you, Calhoun. I thought you might like something to eat and relax with a beer or two." Her voice raised.

"Listen," he said into a dead line after she'd slammed the phone down. "Man, what a temper."

Bailey redialed her number. It rang once, then....

"What?"

"I didn't get to ask you, are you hurt? I saw some blood by the door."

"Nice of you to ask. Yeah, my arm's got a bite on it bad enough it bled, but it's okay now."

"You should put some antiseptic on it."

"I know how to take care of it. So, does the dog have his shots up to date?"

"Yeah, all of them. You won't get rabies." Bailey replied.

233

"I could come over and show you the wound, have you comfort me."

"Ah, I'd like to, but I'm really tired, Cat. A lot of traveling today." *Something's changed all right,* he thought, *because I have no desire to take her to bed.*

"Me too," she said. "How about tomorrow night, you want to get together?"

"Let me see what I've got going on, and I'll call you."

"Sure," she said suspiciously. "By the way, Travis asked me out."

"Are you going to go out with him?"

"No, I told him I was involved." She paused. "Am I?"

"I think we need to talk," Bailey said.

"Yeah, it sounds like it. I'm gonna be gone tomorrow so I'll give me you a call when I get back. Should be the day after." Again, she hung up, but with less force this time.

He held the phone in his hand. *God, this feels like an infected boil being lanced. Why don't I want anything to do with her all of a sudden? It's not Dana. No, I feel like Cat used me like I used her. A trade off and now we're even. She did help me. Am I gonna miss those strong legs and raw sex? Probably. Hell, maybe I'm jumping off the ship too quick. I ought to wait and give it a little time. No, I don't think so.*

Whether it was the Valium or the lack of sleep, he knew the files would have to wait until the next day. Without taking off his clothes he flopped on the unmade bed, and a minute later was snoring from a deep, dreamless sleep.

The sun came up the same time he put the coffee on to brew. The files lay on the table waiting for him.

Chandler had learned the language and the history of the Nimerigar from the death shroud. Bailey was amazed at how much the old man had deciphered. Their language seemed to be a mix of Sioux and Crow. Were they an anomaly from other tribes?

The shroud told of a victory celebration after a battle with Arapahos and the death of Onatah. Bailey didn't care how accurate the translations were; it was collaboration the Nimerigar tribe existed, hell, *might* exist still, in the Ferris Mountains.

Originally, Chandler had written, his theory explained the mummy found by the miners as being a deformed baby dying from lack of a complete brain and mummified by time and atmosphere of a cavern. After he studied the shroud and artifacts, and x-rayed the mummy, he became positive a new tribe of Indians had been discovered, though an extinct tribe.

If someone else had found the tomb, and there were more of the Nimerigar mummies with gold and copper artifacts, they would be worth a substantial amount of money on the black market.

Looting a tomb and murder. It made sense to him. Day after tomorrow he and Travis would go back up and see if they could find the tomb. From there, he bet they'd find a link to Millhouse and Jean and Albert.

He poured another cup of coffee, sat down and opened a second folder. In it, the description of a victory celebration and the death of a seer.

Miles away, in a deep ravine that led to a rocky cavern, the victors danced around a towering fire. The gods were with them since they suffered few casualties, with the exception of Onatah, the seer. He lay on a deerskin; eyes open, taking short, quick breaths - his chest a bloody mass where an Arapaho knife had ripped it apart. The tribal chief, Hache-hi, walked up on short, stubby legs and stood next to Onatah.

"You know what you must do," the aged seer said, wincing from the pain.

"Yes, but with a heavy heart," Hache-hi answered. He squatted down and put his face came close to Onatah's. "Do you see the trails we will walk. Not now, but a hundred winters from now?" he whispered.

Onatah closed his eyes and a hoarse rasp of air came from his mouth. The blood on his chest bubbled from air escaping his torn lungs. His eyes shot open and he tried to rise to his feet. Several hands pushed him back down. He struggled for a moment and then an expression of sorrow passed over his face.

"What do you see?" The chief asked, rising to his feet.

"The trail will be bare of footprints. No one walks it."

Hache-hi brought a war club down with a force that shattered the old man's skull like a dry, brittle piece of bark. His arms and legs twitched for a moment until death overcame him.

"Prepare him for eternity," the chief said, turning away and throwing the bloody club to the ground. He approached one of the women and handed her a copper band with gold etchings. "For Onatah's meeting with the gods."

* * *

Bailey closed the folder and sat sipping coffee wondering what the next step would be. Murder and looting. An Indian tribe thought to have been extinct for two hundred years still alive sixty years ago. Were they still living and hidden in the high peaks of the Ferris or the Pedros?

He knew he should turn the whole thing over to the sheriff's office or the U.S. Marshall's office, hell, maybe the FBI. But, with Jordan saying some transients or dopers probably committed the murders, and the only real evidence being the head band, the regional office would probably demote him to working in the warehouse for trying to make such a wild case if they didn't fire his ass first.

Why can't I have a normal life? The wild horses last year, now this. If I quit sticking my nose in where I've been told it doesn't belong, everyone would be happy. No worrying about who killed Albert and Jean, no one to give a shit about some artifacts being stolen or destroyed. It would be better for me to fade into the background. Yassir, Deputy Jordan, yassir, Mr. Wales. I'm going to go count some cows, that's all.

He rotated his neck and heard, rather than felt, a snap. Callie came into the kitchen and sat down on the floor next to his chair. The snap was from the doggie door hitting the magnet.

"Yup, I think I'll keep seeing Cat and forget about Annie… I probably never had a chance in hell with her anyway." His hand scratched between the dog's ears. Out of his peripheral vision, he saw Barney lay down and look at him, the cast now dirty and stained.

"Will you two get off my back? I'm feeling sorry for myself. Yeah, I'm tired. No, I'm not quitting. I've never quit before and Goddammit, I'm going to hand Jordan the killers on a silver platter. *Big talk, now get off your dead ass and get busy. You've got work to do.*

Chapter Thirty-Four

Just like waiting in a deer stand, Reese thought. The two backpacks were still below him. *No one is going to leave them with those binoculars inside. They looked like a big buck item.*

He told Gavin he'd spend one more day waiting at the entrance while Ike collected the last of the mummies they'd excavated out of the tomb over the past week. The delivery of those would finish the deal with the last buyer, the mob guy. They would receive the full amount of money tomorrow and the goods were the last half owed.

At the tomb, earlier, Reese set the explosives and had the plunger box ready, needing only one wire connected to complete the circuit. When he blew it, the tomb and chamber would be blown to hell, along with Ike.

Reese didn't feel any remorse over whacking an old friend. Even when he was a kid, hurting or killing things never bothered him. When he had been beaten up in junior high by two older students, he stayed in the attic of his family's house until he had a plan to get even. The old man used to give him the strap if anyone whipped him in a fight, fair or not. The leather had been well oiled and bit deep when it was used. It wasn't hard to avoid his father so he wouldn't see his bruised face until he could say he came out ahead.

Knives were his friends. His favorite was a Gerber, with a six-inch blade, sharp as a razor. He'd draw it down the back of his hand and push until a thin bead of blood formed. It tasted sweet on his tongue.

Reese followed the two older boys one summer night when they went to the banks of the Platte River, under the Rector Avenue Bridge. They had a bottle of wine and a couple of joints. An hour later, Reese walked home with his hand gripping the knife so tight his knuckles hurt. The murders made the papers across the country. They didn't even make the last page three months later when no suspects were found.

Reese first heard the young man in a gray uniform, then saw him climbing up the chute. There wasn't any attempt to be quiet. He had all the stealth of a water buffalo. Slipping, cursing out loud when he stumbled, panting and not looking at his surroundings.

What have we got here? He who waits with patience is rewarded. I can't believe it. He's not even checking things out. Just bumbling on up. Foolish man. Lucky me.

Reese pushed back into the darkness of the cavern and watched as the BLM ranger sat down by the backpacks and drank from a water bottle he'd pulled out of his pocket. It wasn't Calhoun, but the younger one who'd been with him.

Like a statue, Reese moved only his eyes and watched the man stand up, stretch, pick up the packs and start down the mountain. When the ranger was out of sight, Reese climbed down from the opening and began to hunt. *What a rush! I don't know if I wanna kill him or play with him.* There was a buzz in his ears from the adrenaline and he felt his heart beat elevate. Holding the crossbow in front of him, he picked up his pace down to the tree line.

"Hold it!" The order came behind him. The ranger crouched behind a fallen aspen, his pistol in his hand. "Drop the bow."

He froze. The crossbow clattered to the ground. "What's going on?"

"You're following me. Why?" Travis stood up and came around the tree to face Reese. "Let me see some I.D," he demanded after the silence.

Reese saw the ranger lick his lips and knew he was jittery. "I saw you going down the side and wondered where you were going, that's all. No crime. I didn't know you were the law."

Travis nodded at the crossbow lying on the ground. "You hunting?"

"Nope. It's not the season." *For deer anyway.* "I'm just hiking. Some guys carry guns when they're in the country, I carry the bow." He saw the indecision cross the eyes of the ranger.

"The I.D." Travis's hand extended and his fingers curled back and forth. He held the pistol close to his chest.

Oh man, you oughta have me put it on the ground. Reese dug his wallet out of his back pocket and held it out.

"Take the I.D. out of your wallet."

"Sure. What's your name?" Reese slipped a driver's license out of the glassine cover and again held it out toward the ranger.

"Travis Knight. I'm a Bureau of Land Management Ranger."

"So what's the BLM got to do with me hiking with a bow?"

"We're involved in an ongoing investigation." Travis took the license.

"Ranger Knight, what do you see in my eyes?" Reese inched closer.

"Back off before I—"

Reese's foot came up and kicked Travis in his chest, knocking him backward into the downed timber. His pistol clattered over some rocks and dropped into a wide crack. Reese came in fast and booted Travis twice in the ribs. He kneeled over Travis and grabbed him by his hair. "What do you see in my eyes?" His fist slammed into Travis's face like a piston on a pump. Blood sprayed when the ranger's nose broke and his lips split open from the impact of the blows.

Travis flailed back, his fists brushing off Reese's chest without any power. One hand groped over a ragged stone. He took it and hit Reese in the side of the head with a roundhouse swing.

"Oh!" Reese reeled back and put his hand to his head. "You bastard!" He put a knee over Travis's arm and hit him in the

240

forehead. Travis's head bounced off the ground. Blood ran into Reese's eye from a gash on the side of his head.

Reese got up and searched for the pistol. "Goddammit." He saw it down in the crack. Laying on the ground the crack widened enough he could put his arm in, but the pistol was four feet from his reach.

The ranger didn't move, his face hard to recognize. "You shouldn't a done that, slick," Reese said, wiping more blood from his face. He picked the cross- bow up, aimed and pulled the trigger.

* * *

When Travis didn't answer his telephone, Bailey called Dora at her home.

"Do you know where Travis is?" he asked when she answered the phone.

"I haven't heard from him since yesterday, but that's not unusual. I didn't think there was anything to worry about. Is there?" she asked. "Mr. Wales left town for the weekend, but he gave me a number where I could call him, if needed."

"I'm here and calling you because I'm worried. I can't believe you aren't."

"Bailey, it's a quarter after seven," she said, frostily. "You of all people should know he camps out at the refuge sometimes. Just like you used to."

Aw, crap. Pissed another one off. "I'm sorry, Dora. I apologize. I haven't been getting much sleep lately."

"Obviously. Anything else I can do for you?"

"No. I'm going out to the Ferris and see if he's around where we hiked the other day. If you don't hear from me by this afternoon, call the sheriff's office and tell them to come out and look for me."

"Do you think something has happened to him? Maybe I should contact Mr. Wales," she said.

"I don't want to cry wolf. Like you said, he's stayed overnight at the refuge before, or he could be broke down and can't get out with his cell phone or radio. Let me check first, okay? Plus, there's nothing that Peter can do that I can't."

"All right," she said warily. "Call me tonight and let me know what's going on. I really feel I should call him."

He sighed. "Do what you think best, Dora. I'm leaving now to go find him."

Bailey hung up after promising again to call her if he found Travis or came up empty handed. He fed the dogs and strapped his gun belt on after sliding a loaded two-clip holder next to the pistol.

The gas gauge was reading empty so he had to stop and get gas. His gut twisted with a feeling of apprehension as he filled the tank. Five minutes later he pushed the pickup to ninety mph on the highway heading north.

Nothing's wrong. The kid just broke down or he's shacking with some babe in town and forgot to check in. If that's it, I'm gonna slap the crap out of him. C'mon, God. Let him be all right.

A lingering thought nagged him. *The one that got shot?* He couldn't recall if he'd told Cat about Barney or not. He'd have to think about that.

Chapter Thirty-Five

"I killed that BLM guy this morning," Reese said without any emotion. His hand went to the ragged cut on the side of his head.

"Calhoun? He do that to you?"

"Not him, the other one. I think he said his name was Knight. The bastard hit me with a rock."

"Christ, why'd you kill him? We don't need this." Gavin felt things were going too fast, getting out of his control.

"I saw him pick the packs up and decided to follow him down the mountain for aways. He must have seen me because he hid out then drew down on me when I went past him."

"Now he's dead."

"Yeah."

Gavin paced around the office. "I'll make a call and see if the money's here. Goddammit, why the hell did you have to screw with him? Especially now?"

"I think he was on to us. Checking things out, shit like that. Too late to cry about it now," Reese said. "What about Bodine?"

"He's here. He was supposed to get the last of the artifacts this afternoon. I'll take care of him and get the stuff from the tomb. You go up and keep an eye out for Calhoun in case he's out there too. If he finds the body he'll be going for the cops so fast we won't get a half mile."

"He won't. I dragged Knight off the trail and covered him with some brush. Why not have the money delivered here? Save some time having to go through the mountain."

"You don't deviate from a plan. There's more cops toward Casper. If somehow we're being looked for, it'll be safer going over the back roads to Laramie. Trust me," Gavin said. "I'm still worried about Calhoun finding the other guy."

"I told you I hid the body. I don't want no extra trouble either. Calhoun won't find nothing if he sniffs around," Reese said.

Why do I think he's lying? The psycho wants a piece of Calhoun. Gavin didn't like what he was thinking but knew if he accosted Reese with it, it would hurt rather than help things. *Might be a silver lining if they run into each other and Calhoun kills him. Yeah, that'd be nice.*

"I hope not. Take off and I'll be coming down in an hour or so. Shit!" Gavin took a cell phone out of the desk and punched in some numbers.

"Change of plans," he announced when the phone was answered. "You can take us to Laramie when we get the money today." He noticed Reese had left and saw him walking toward the four-wheeler parked by the metal building. "Reese screwed things up. I'll explain later. How long before you can get there?" He listened and frowned. "Okay." The cover flipped down disconnecting the call and he headed outside.

"Ike!" Gavin yelled, approaching the bunkhouse. He carried the black satchel and had the Smith and Wesson tucked into the waistband of his pants.

"Yo," Bodine replied, opening the door and coming out onto the porch scratching his belly.

"Let's go get the rest of the stuff. We're finished here," Gavin said.

"Done? Good, I was getting nervous thinking we were sticking around too long."

Gavin told him to drive the Mule and he'd take the Honda. They followed in the dust of Reese's four-wheeler.

At the sawmill, Reese turned to the west while Gavin and Bodine continued up the now well-worn trail into the timber. They traveled through and over the maze of crevices and fissures in the rock shelves until they came out below the entrance to the tomb.

Bodine lit a torch when they entered. "Man, it was getting spooky in here. I swear I heard things running through the tunnels."

"Probably animals scurrying around." Gavin looked around, the torchlight flickering off the walls. "Where's the rest of the mummies?"

Bodine picked up a canvas bag from behind a boulder. He used both hands. "Got to be careful with this one. I packed it good, but it's full and we don't wanna break nothing, do we?" He made his donkey bray laugh.

"You're right. You carry it." Gavin led off, down to the end of the tomb and taking the tunnel that would lead them to the south face of the mountain.

"I gotta take a break," Bodine said, after passing through the chamber. He set the bag down and wiped the sweat off his face with the back of his hand. "How much richer is the stuff in this bag gonna make us?" His eyes had a sly look.

"Probably a couple hundred grand each. Except for you, Ike, you're getting a bonus." Gavin turned sideways to Bodine and slipped the gun out of his waistband.

"I am? Man, I ain't saying I don't deserve it, because I do. Thanks, Gavin." He stuck his hand out and moved toward him.

Bodine took three shots to his chest, his eyes wide in surprise and confusion. He sat down hard, looked at the blood coming out of him and leaned his head back against a slab of rock.

Gavin stuck the pistol back in his pants and picked the bag up using both hands. "I should have waited till we got out of here," he said to the corpse. "Goddamn bag's heavy."

Chapter Thirty-Six

Bailey took the Stone Gulch Ranch road and had to slow down when the road turned rough. He pushed his Explorer as fast as he could. *Why didn't I go with him yesterday? I didn't need to hear the old Indian last night. It could have waited.* Tire tracks through drifted sand on the road showed someone had driven through recently. The wind blew out of the south and would have covered day-old tracks.

That's a good sign. I'm getting myself worked up over nothing.

The boom of the tire blowing out came at the same time the steering wheel spun violently to the right. The rear end of the Explorer tried passing the front.

Bailey stomped the brake pedal hard and felt the chatter as the anti-skid kicked in. The vehicle climbed up the side of the dirt road and stopped.

He got out and saw the front tire. "Goddammit, I can't believe this. I haven't blown a tire in ten years. Why now?"

The Explorer bounced as he rummaged in the back for the jack and lug wrench. Then he had to figure out how to get the tire down from under the rear bumper.

When he had the spare on and the flat tire thrown in the back, an hour had passed.

Travis's BLM truck sat off the road at the mouth of the canyon they'd climbed three days ago. Bailey parked and put his hand on the hood. Warmth radiated from it but he couldn't tell if it was from engine heat or the sun. He reached under the fender and grabbed the exhaust pipe. Not cold, and a little warmer than ambient temperature. *I think Travis might have driven in this morning.*

He cupped his hands around his mouth to yell, then stopped. *You're getting half-dumb in your old age. Who knows who's up there besides Travis? There have been three murders around here and you're getting ready to yell?*

The sound of an engine reached him before he saw the green pickup coming. Dust rose from the back and it fishtailed around the corners. Cat slid to a stop by Travis's truck.

"What's going on, Bailey?" she asked, getting out of the truck.

"I'm looking for Travis. He didn't come back last night. What are you doing here?"

"We got a call on some poaching. It must have been you or Travis they saw."

"I need you to help me, Cat. Call Jordan at the sheriff's office and tell him to bring some deputies and come out. I've got a bad feeling about the kid."

"Hold on and I'll go up with you," she said, pulling the radio microphone out of the pickup.

"No, I need you to stay here and set up a command post. Don't argue, please."

"Sure, Bailey. Go, I'll take care of things here."

He headed up the mountain, using the same trail he and Travis had used before.

The going seemed a little easier. *It's gotta be from knocking off some pounds and not drinking so much lately.*

The muffled echo of gunshots came from above him. Bailey dropped to one knee and put his hand on the Glock. He was panting and tried to slow his heart down. The timber surrounded him but he felt naked and worked his way up the slope into a deeper strand of trees.

He thought he heard a rock fall to his left and took cover next to a towering aspen. In a partial clearing, Bailey saw a deer and then Travis, sprawled out on his back on the ground. An arrow stuck out of his stomach and his shirt was stained with blood.

"Travis!" *Shit, I can't tell if he's breathing. Beat up hard and gut shot with an arrow. I'll kill the son-of-a-bitch who did this.*

When the arrow hit him in the back and pinned him to the tree trunk, searing pain burned like a white-hot prod. Bailey could see some of the shaft coming out the front of his inside shoulder and disappearing into the tree. *Oh God!* He tried to reach the shaft with his left hand but when he turned his body, he yelled out in pain.

"You look like a fish flopping around like that."

Bailey couldn't see who spoke. A shadow formed to his side and he heard the man's footsteps crunching over rock. He pulled back and groaned. *Get loose, you're gonna die if you don't!*

"I killed your little buddy there. You didn't train him too good. Now I'm gonna kill you," Reese spoke in a mocking tone.

There was the sound of a ratchet being cranked. His shadow moved closer and lengthened.

"The sheriff's right behind me. They'll catch you," Bailey said through gritted teeth. *Talk to him, make some time...do something.* "I don't know what you look like, if you leave now, you'll get away."

"I'll take my chances. I'm enjoying the drama. I've been having a lot of fun out here, there's nothing like a chase. Too bad you won't see me kill you."

"Chase? You shot me in the back. You don't have the guts to face me, even now." Every breath Bailey took made more blood ooze out from between him and the tree. He tried pulling loose. "You're a goddamn coward."

"You just bought a little more time because I'm gonna skin your ass first."

I'm not gonna die like this! Bailey pulled the Glock out and twisted his hand so the barrel pointed behind him. He pulled the trigger and moved the pistol side to side as thirteen rounds fired out of the barrel. Hot shells bounced off his wrist and shirt. The continued clicking of the hammer falling on an empty chamber made him realize the Glock's clip was empty. Bailey tried hunching his back, waiting for another arrow to ram through his back. He couldn't hear anything except a loud ringing in his ears. The pistol dropped to the ground.

Sweat poured from his face and his right shoulder felt paralyzed. *I got to get loose.* He clenched his jaw and put his left hand on the tree trunk then shoved and reared back.

There was a sucking sound and a tear of flesh. He didn't hear himself cry out as he fell to the ground and rolled to his stomach. The pain gave him tunnel vision and red flashes shot across his eyes. The arrow stuck out of the tree, a muddy red.

In front of him, a big man was on his back with his knee bent and raised, swaying back and forth. Bailey pushed himself to his feet and staggered to Travis. He put a finger on his neck and felt for a pulse. He couldn't keep his concentration on his fingers. "Travis, if you can hear me, help's on the way. Hold on."

A crossbow with an arrow notched was on the ground. Bailey recognized the man when he saw the biceps and face. *The guy from the Steamboat Lake Ranch, where's the rest of them?* It looked like he had a couple of bullet holes in his chest.

He's a tough bastard; he's still alive.

The man grunted and rolled over to his side. His fingers dug gouges into the ground, trying to grab the butt of the crossbow. Bailey stepped over to him and kicked him hard in the side of the head, making a sound like a dropped melon. He nearly fell down from the force of the kick. The man's body quivered and went still. Bailey bent down and heard the death rattle escape from his lips. *That's for Travis, you bastard.*

His hand shook when he picked the Glock up with his left hand and ejected the empty clip. With a groan, he reached around him and pulled a full clip out of the holder. He had to wedge the Glock between his legs to shove the clip in and turn it over to pull the slide back putting a live round in the chamber. He could move his right arm a little, but when he did, pain bent him over. He pulled the belt out from his pants and swung it around his neck. One-handed, he buckled it and pulled it down over his chest and arm, gently cinching it tight enough to keep his arm immobile. His gun belt, still around his waist would ride up, but there wasn't anything he could do about it. With the pistol in its holster, it was the first time he ever gave thanks for being left-handed.

"Hold on, kid, I'll be right back with someone." *I'll get Cat up here. She can help him.* He turned and stumbled. Black dots flashed before his eyes. *Don't fall!* He picked the crossbow up to use to help steady him and headed down the mountain.

* * *

Gavin heard the gunshots and wanted to move faster, but the precious cargo in the canvas bag made him suppress the urge. The satchel seemed to have added ten pounds and he wasn't going to leave either of them. He knew if he fell he'd probably smash the mummies; and no goods meant his life wouldn't be worth a nickel when the Man didn't get his merchandise he already paid for. On one hand he hoped it was Reese doing the shooting, but on the other, he wished Reese might not come down the mountain, at least alive.

* * *

Bailey skirted a gorge filled with broken and dead trees and reached the limestone slab outcroppings where the path merged into a dry creek bed between two of the slabs. The incline of the slope became less severe when he passed the limestone and came out of the trees. The first thing he saw stopped him in his tracks. Two pickups and a SUV. Someone stood by one of the trucks. He touched the butt of his pistol.

250

Every step jarred his shoulder. Using the crossbow as a crutch helped but the burning sensation increased. One time when the belt loosened, he tried hugging his right arm so it wouldn't swing but it threw him off balance and he stumbled and almost fell. Sweat ran off his face stinging his eyes and his lungs felt as if they were bringing in only a thimble of air with every gasp.

I gotta rest. Just for a second. Quit whining! You sound like an old lady. Move your dead ass. Travis needs help. Hell, Cat might need help too.

He broke through the trees and saw Cat standing below another man. *Sanderson!* "Cat! Watch him!" he yelled.

She looked up and saw him then pulled her pistol.

Bailey stumbled faster down the remaining slope until he came to a stop behind and to the side of Gavin, who turned and dropped the satchel when he heard Bailey's footsteps.

"Where's my brother?" Cat demanded, her pistol leveled at Gavin's chest.

"Reese killed him," Gavin said, turning back to Cat. He gently lowered the bag with the mummies and raised his hands in front of him. "I tried to stop him, but I was too late."

"Brother? What the hell? You know this guy, Cat?" A look of puzzlement spread over Bailey's face.

"Yes I do, dear Bailey," she answered. "We're partners. Gavin here brings me the goods and I deliver them to the buyers who fly in to Laramie. I bring him back the money. It works for me" Her pistol moved from Gavin to Bailey and Cat pulled the trigger.

The bullet caught Bailey in the hip, spinning him around and dropping him to the ground. He lay on his left side, covering the Glock, secure in its holster.

Gavin ducked when Cat had fired. When he saw the ranger down he smiled and straightened up. "I've got the last of the artifacts and mummies plus our cash from the ranch. You have the money?"

"Yeah, three quarters of a million. If Reese killed Ike, then where's Reese?" She still had the pistol in front of her.

"I think Calhoun got him. I heard some shots as I was coming down the mountain." His hand inched toward the rear of his waistband. "Now there's just the two of us to split the bucks. We'll go to Mexico. What do you say?"

"What, no split on the Indian stuff?"

"That's gotta go to the buyer. If he doesn't get it, he'll track me down and bye-bye Gavin. We'll drop this off at the Laramie airport on our way out of the country. They told you they'd wait, didn't they?"

Bailey moved and tried propping himself up on an elbow. With a groan he said, "Cat, don't listen to him. Travis is up there with an arrow in him, you got to call for help. Please." Bailey pleaded as blood seeped from under his side, "Get some help."

"There's two men here wanting me to do something for them besides going to bed. What to do?" She fired the pistol twice.

Gavin had been reaching for his gun when the bullets struck him in the X zone of his chest. He fell hard and sprawled out. Cat strolled over to him and aimed the pistol. "You should have brought Ike down with you." Again the pistol fired. Gavin's head jerked when the bullet entered his forehead.

Holding the pistol by her leg, Cat turned to face Bailey and reached into her pocket. "I thought you'd bend more. But you didn't. You just had to be the hero, didn't you? Well, not quite, but almost." She tossed a quarter toward him and raised the pistol. "Guess you can call someone who—"

Bailey rolled to his right and brought the crossbow up in his left hand, pulling the trigger. The arrow shot out. He dropped the bow and clawed for his Glock. He pulled it out of the holster and stopped when he saw her pistol fall to the ground.

She looked at him, hate burning in her eyes, then sank to her knees, the arrow shaft sticking out from between her lovely breasts. Cat grimaced and smiled, then fell forward. The arrow ripped her shirt as the arrowhead was shoved through her chest and out her back.

Bailey kept the pistol pointed in her direction until he put his hand on the ground and pushed himself up. His hip and shoulder screamed out in agony. *Don't pass out, not yet.*

He staggered to Cat's pickup and opened the right side door. A gray nylon bag sat on the seat blocking him from the radio. With an effort, he threw it out the door and reached for the microphone on the dashboard. While he gave directions to the sheriff's office dispatcher for an ambulance and deputies, he noticed the bag was lying open on its side in the dirt. He stared at it in surprise: bound bills of money spilled onto the ground from the inside of the bag. He didn't know how much, but he saw packets of money with $10,000 bands on them. The dispatcher had to repeat a question when he mumbled an answer. Bailey could see at least a dozen packets and thought there must be a lot more because the bag looked full.

Chapter Thirty-Seven
Three months later

In the late fall, leaves from the aspen trees fell and scattered on the wind. The mountain looked formidable with the stark skeletons of aspen bunched together in groves and the pine and scrub oak still covering the mountainside like camouflage.

A Ford Explorer pulled to a stop and two dogs jumped out when Bailey opened the door. "Don't run off, we're not staying long."

He still limped a little from where he'd been shot in the hip, but his shoulder had mended nicely. Travis survived, barely. Another couple of hours without attention and he would have died.

All hell had broken loose when he'd radioed for help. A dead game warden alongside another body that was thought to be a wealthy rancher. A near dead BLM ranger up the mountain with an arrow in him. Artifacts in a satchel along with cash, a canvas bag containing small mummies thought to be ancient Indians, and two more men found dead up on the mountain brought a flurry of activity from the sheriff's office and the criminal division of the state attorney general.

Bailey had to admit Jordan and the A.G. agents did a fine job in getting the facts straight. The Nimerigar tomb had been looted and the artifacts sold, apparently on a black market. Bullets from the bodies of the Woods, Millhouse, and Barney matched Cat's Beretta. She didn't even use a different pistol when she murdered them. Her service issue. Who would have thought someone could have been so arrogant?

Some questions would never be answered. Why did they kill Millhouse? Did he have something to do with the head

254

Albert found? The bodies of Edward Sanderson and his son, Ronnie, were never found. The family lawyer came out and identified McQuery, Compton, and Millhouse. He told them how the elder Sanderson had befriended the three because they protected the son in prison. Too much good faith in man and the Lord, the lawyer supposed.

A sign posted on a ledge above the Explorer read, "Robert Chandler Excavation Site. Use the Steamboat Lake Ranch Entry." He thought the old doctor deserved to have the site named after him. If it wouldn't have been for him, who knew if the case would have been solved.

Bailey walked to a flat slab of shale lying against a formation of boulders. It was a thin slab he easily shoved aside. A gray bag peered out at him from a hollow in the rocks. No one alive knew about it so no one would care. *A couple things to take care of then I'm on my way to Fort Collins to see Annie.*

* * *

The sun broke over the eastern mountains at the Split Rock Indian Reservation. Hantaki opened the flap of his tipi, stepped outside and scratched his chest as he looked to the horizon. The gray bag lying in front of the entryway caught his eye. He pushed it tentatively with his toe, then bent over and unzipped it. Hantaki dragged the bag into the tipi and gently shook his wife awake. "Our prayers have been answered," he whispered.

The End

Author's note: *Nimerigar*--Indian legends of the Arapaho, Sioux, Cheyenne, and Crow, tell of "tiny people eaters" who stand 24 inches tall. Over the years the pygmy mummy has brought bad luck and omens to those who possessed it. The Indian people still warn others to beware of the "tiny people eaters" as they are rumored to still live a hidden life in the mountains and high places of Wyoming. Such a 'pygmy' was found in the Pedro Mountains, sixty-five miles northeast of Rawlins, Wyoming, by two gold miners in 1932. They burrowed into a natural pocket in the granite rock and found, on a ledge, a 20-inch mummy.

www.ingramcontent.com/pod-product-compliance
Lightning Source LLC
Chambersburg PA
CBHW072214170626
46813CB00003B/929